MATCH
MAKER

MATCH MAKER

Quill & Flame
FIREBRAND

HOPE BOLINGER

Quill & Flame
PUBLISHING HOUSE

Matchmaker

Copyright ©2025 by Hope Bolinger

Published by Quill & Flame Publishing House, an imprint of Book Bash Media, LLC.

www.quillandflame.com

Cover design by Quill & Flame Publishing House

Artwork by Angela Lynum

To the fifty guys I went on dates with before writing this...
Thanks for the inspiration, I guess?

Some Notes

A Note on the Rep

I mention a few things in this book, from PCOS to late-diagnosed autism. I have all these things, and how it is presented in this book is authentic to my own experience. With that said, neither are monoliths. Not everyone with PCOS or autism is going to look the same. It really helps to ask people to share their stories, since I'm only offering one perspective.

A Note on the Audacity

There are going to be things in the book that will make you say, "There's no way that could ever happen." To which, let me assure you, yes it can. All these dating experiences were either partaken of by yours truly, or by those very close to me who shared their insights for the book. Unfortunately, yes, it's that bad out there. But hopefully we can do something to change it. And in terms of all the Christian University stuff, this was also experienced by yours truly (down to the bugs we found in the salads). Let's also change that too, please and thank you.

Chapter One

THE COUPLE WOULD MATCH. Emerson Levi just knew it.

She peered over her laptop lid to watch as Fire Girl and Curly Boy leaned toward each other. Of course, they didn't really go by "Fire Girl" and "Curly Boy". But Em had so many students to keep track of in The Matchmaking Database, she'd started associating them by their hair color and type.

Em's own hair, stick-straight and dark black, clung to her cheeks in the humidity. At least the campus apartments this year would blast AC. The last three years in the non-coolant dorms took their toll on her wardrobe. Armpit stains still wouldn't wash out, especially in the moldy dorm washers.

You'd think with what we're paying for tuition that they'd at least keep us cool.

In The Student Center, known at Mansfield Christian College as "TSC", air conditioners *did* rumble in silver piping on the ceiling. Mansfield spared no expense when it came to keeping the buildings shipshape. After all, donors traversed the state-of-the-art science labs and TSC. No one expected them to swing by the girls' dorms.

Em trained her focus back on the couple. Fire Girl leaned in farther, cupping an ice-drink in her palms. Condensation streaked down the sides like rain droplets.

"Good, that's good." Em typed a note to herself in the spreadsheet she'd made for the couple.

Fire Girl: Leaning forward on the first date. That's a sign she's interested.

What about Curly Boy? One side of his lip cut up his cheek. Dimples surfaced. "Also good. At least the body language indicates strong potential." She thought about how her best friend Noah would laugh at her observation. As a late-diagnosed autistic, she didn't always catch onto the "hip" words to say.

Only two more dates to go, and they'll both owe me five hundred dollars.

Fire Girl smirked at the boy, and he blushed. *Good, some emotion shown too.* Em wasn't always the best at displaying emotion herself, so she knew not everyone showed the emotions they felt deep inside. It was hard to explain to other people as to why she didn't always display outwardly what she was supposed to. Another quirk when it came to how her brain worked.

Which they hopefully would do soon. The gas alone to get to campus from grocery store trips would clean Em out of a good chunk of that. For some reason, despite Indiana existing in the middle of nowhere, they charged astronomical gas prices. Plus, her car chugged the whole way on Highway 30. That would require some repairs and soon.

Fire Girl sneaked a glance back at Em. A flicker of a smile, then she turned back.

From what Em had discovered in her matchmaking sessions, the girls always wanted a spy on the first date, in case the man turned out to be a serial killer or something. Although most clients spared her the details about dates, she'd heard enough to know that men pulled some pretty shady business on some of the excursions.

Yes, even at a Christian college.

Em returned to her laptop and checked over some of the couple-hopefuls who'd filled out her survey she had posted over the summer. Although matching thirty couples in three years didn't seem like a lot, she vetted everyone. And to her surprise, men and women had filled it out equally.

Guess the need to find a spouse is equal for guys and girls.

Spotty blurs from overuse of her vision burned her eyes from staring at the computer screen too long, but she read the bios of the ones who sent in a form. If she found any matches, she'd start them on the first date. "The first three dates are free", stated her website. "After the third date, if you choose to stay together, the matchmaker will charge you each $500."

At Mansfield, three dates practically meant a marriage proposal.

Okay, girl, focus on the bios. Let's try to find one more match today.

Name: Joseph Peters

Age: 23

Tell Me a Little about Yourself: I'm a master's student in higher education. Went to Taylor University up the road for my bachelors. I love to cook, and my dog thinks I'm funny. So there's that.

What Are You Looking for in a Match: She needs to be a Christian, obviously, but I'd like some shared values. Some girls have some unrealistic expectations, so I'd like to set the record straight.

She sighed. *Well, he had me in the first half.*

It didn't surprise her that another master's student had reached out. Her most popular clients? Seniors and those pursuing a master's or doctorate. Once or twice a professor had even requested her services, but she'd figured that would be a conflict of interest. *At the very least, it's weird. Asking some twenty-two-year-old to find a fifty-nine-year-old man his "second and future wife".*

Em marked a note for herself to follow-up with Joseph and tease his meaning of "unrealistic expectations". Some men had valid reasons. She remembered one man, with dark brown eyes, who said a girl wouldn't go out with him because he didn't wear glasses.

"Can you believe that?" He'd pinched his nose. "I offered to wear fake ones, but she sighed and said, 'It wouldn't be the same.'"

But for other guys...

"Unrealistic expectations" meant expecting him to act like a decent human being.

She sipped on her straw. Watery chai from ice that had melted funneled down her throat. She'd need to get a refill on this thing. Dabbing the cinnamon off her lips, she crumpled the napkin. Then she headed to the coffee stand.

Barista Man, who'd forgotten his name tag today, bunched up a rag and rested it against his hip. "Another one?" His eyebrows shot up.

Once Barista Man had hit her up for her services but decided partway through that he wanted to pursue singleness. No shame in that. Plenty of misfires happened on the first or second date. Hence why thirty students felt like a small success to her. *And thirty thousand dollars is nothing to blush at.*

Her mom back home would often laugh that she hadn't completely paid off her loans at this point. Being a college student was expensive. With the dorm fees, groceries, taxes, and cost of books (even used ones), it all added up. Even with her academic scholarship for high marks on her high school GPA, she'd have to match ten more pairs to break even on her school payments. She did want to have zero loans to pay when she left this place, after all. She'd heard too many horror stories of students who'd spent decades whittling down those student payments.

"Extra nutmeg this time, please?" She dug into her shorts pocket for her wallet.

Barista Man threw up a hand. "This one's on the house. If you get my sister a date," he nodded at Fire Girl, "it'll be well-worth the price of an iced chai."

Em cocked her head.

She hadn't put two and two together. Probably should've paid more attention to the last names of the people who filled out the survey. Still, working a full-time job at Kohl's for the summer didn't help. It was late August now, and her Kohl's job had ended, but she still had some catchup to do with her matches.

As Barista Man swirled a boxed chai into a cup, she spotted a familiar figure in the corner of her eye. Noah Brandon hung a bright orange poster on a column in the TSC. Curly hair clung to his forehead. A little darker than Curly Boy's and with more kink to the coils. His dark skin had shaded even deeper over the summer.

She threw a wave at him as he finished tacking up the paper. He grinned, displaying all his teeth. Since his father took up the art of dentistry, he wasted no moment showing off the pearly whites.

"Long time, no see." He bent down and hugged her. She hoisted herself onto her tiptoes to take in his squeeze. As a theater boy, Noah rolled like that. Some people gave side hugs, but he believed in embracing life all the way.

They released and she scooped up her drink on the coffee shop counter. She jiggled it and the ice clacked against the container. "Good summer?" She sucked in cinnamon sweetness from the chai. Ah yes, that was the good stuff.

"Eh." Noah shrugged. "A local theater had me intern with them. Had to for practicum."

Ah yes, ever since Em and Noah met during their freshman year at a brother-and-sister floor event, he'd recruited her to help with theater projects. Not that she minded. "And how was that?"

He winced and wicked sweat off his upper lip with his knuckle. "Let's just say that as much as I love kids, I don't know if I want to see another one for about a year."

She giggled. They parked at a low-top table, near a Chick-fil-A housed on campus. Scents of chicken sandwiches and fresh cut fries busied her senses. She peeked over her shoulder. Good, she could still spot Fire Girl—in case Curly Boy decided to yank out a knife and reveal his True Crime ways.

Em jostled the idea out of her noggin with a head shake. *You need to stop listening to those podcasts on the drive to school.*

"So." She gestured at a stack of orange papers on the table. "Are you advertising something, or just trying to burn all the students' eyes out of their sockets?"

He thumbed his chin. Whiskers scratched underneath his clean fingernails. "You know, I was wondering if that paper would be too bright."

"It's fine. It's very you."

"I'm trying to decide if you just complimented me or insulted me."

She winked. "The best people can do both at the same time. Let me read it."

Noah slid her one across the table. After squinting to block out the heinous color of orange, she read.

DO GOOD: MANSFIELD THEATER CAMPUS-WIDE EVENT

The Mansfield Theater is presenting a Do Good event, to support the FREE fall performance in remembrance of theater alumna Yvonne Rinberg, who passed away in 2004.

This year, we're asking students to use their gifts and talents to "bless" another student. It could be baking them cookies, doing a car wash for them, etc. Sky's the limit. When you Do Good, hand them one of these posters. Event runs from welcome weekend until the first performance of Matchmaker *on October 3rd.*

"Hmm, nice."

She passed the paper back to him and sucked in another gulp of chai. A pair of students, in the booth next to them, chatted animatedly about beach vacations they took in the past year.

Unease niggled her gut. Her parents certainly didn't accept food stamps from the government by any means. In fact, her mom used to own a successful salon in the Raleigh area. Thanks to that shutting down, though, they'd put Em's college tuition in her own hands.

Although some students on campus worked jobs, several roved around in brand new vehicles. Not a single Instagram post scrolled by without someone posting about a new trip they'd gone on during the past three months. Good thing her matchmaking business could almost get her to keep up with them in terms of finances.

Noah jabbed a finger at Em. "You actually inspired this year's theme."

Head cock. "I did?"

"Mhmm. I see you all the time going around campus, helping people with various tasks. From copy-editing papers to staying late nights in the theater with me to paint set pieces. You, Emerson Levi, do good all the time."

Huh, she hadn't considered that all that much. In her opinion, if something needed fixing or help, why not roll up your sleeves and pitch in?

Noah placed his elbow against his chair headrest. The entire atrium echoed with chatter. Because of the extrovert nature of the campus, students could seldom find any place for peace and quiet. At least, some place that didn't feature a couple making out.

"So, Em, you wanna help out? What's your do-good thing?"

She shrugged. "Not really sure. I mean, the poster mentions gifts and talents. I don't really have those except..."

Eyes roved back to the couple. Now Fire Girl and Curly boy held hands underneath their table.

Her gaze returned, but Noah's hadn't. He'd followed her line of sight. His face fell.

Ah yes, he never approved of the matchmaking stuff. *Noah wouldn't get it, though. His parents are paying his tuition.*

"I'll try to think of something." Taking her cue for her exit, she rose from the table. "But I'm sure you'll get lots of interest in this, no doubt. You tend to have a lot of influence."

This brightened his eyes. Still, he shook his head. "No, Em, *you* are the one with influence."

An arm triangled on her hip. "That's not true. Y'all sell out your shows all the time, because of you." Noah landed leads in almost every production. His beautiful baritone voice aided a great deal to secure main roles in the musicals and operas.

"The only reason people attend half the shows is because you advertise it. You have a decently high following on social media and people listen to what you have to say. People really look up to you, Em. Remember that."

Fire smoldered in his pupils for just a moment. Guilt clenched her gut. With a throat clear, she saluted him with two fingers and moved back to her high-top table with the laptop. Thankfully, thievery didn't usually happen at this campus. Even with ten thousand students in total, it felt small. Everyone knew everyone's business.

As she marched back to her device, Fire Girl approached her, face alight. "Wow, Em, had no idea you were here!"

Yeesh, don't sign this girl up for any theater classes. Fire Girl's voice had emerged in a stilted way. Almost as if reading a script for the first time in an English class.

"Yeah, ha-ha." She gestured at her laptop. "Figured I'd get some work done before checking into the apartments."

Fire Girl waved goodbye to the Curly Boy. He dipped a nod at Em. Then Fire Girl turned back to Em. "Oh, girl, you're in the apartments too?"

"Yeah." Em scrunched her ponytail, because she could feel the hair slipping down her neck. "Couldn't stand another year in the dorms, you know?"

"Oh, I hear you. I also hear that a ton of last-minute people registered for the apartments. Got a new roommate in ours that we weren't expecting."

Em's lips sagged. *Shoot.* She and her roommate from the dorms, Laila, had waited in a line last semester at 6am, only to get an apartment placement. Memories blurred, but she recalled a vague email that went something along the lines of:

Dear Students,

If you have fewer than four apartment residents, you may be assigned one at random. Because we like to save as much money as possible.

Thanks, love ya.

The Money People at the University

Of course, the email probably sounded a little different than that, but that's how she read most communications from the university. They always operated based on the "Dear people who pay us, we've decided to mess with you again. Because we can. In Jesus' Name. Sincerely, University People Who Make More Money Than You Ever Will" formula.

The email wasn't as much as a shock as it was a bitter disappointment. The university would once again find a way to make their lives miserable.

Em shoved her laptop into its purple cloth case. "Thanks for the heads up. I'd better get over there."

Fire Girl's face sagged. "You're in Apartment 103, right? Woodhouse Hall?"

Rocks sank into her stomach. "Yeah, how did you..."

"I met one of your apartment-mates earlier." Fire Girl twirled a blazing strand of hair around her index finger. "I'm afraid to say she already hates you."

Chapter Two

Em never thought she'd praise the Lord for a grocery run. But here, in the middle of a sizzling asphalt parking lot outside of the apartments, she'd do just that.

Her roomie Laila's brown and blonde braids bounced as she bolted over to wrap Em in a hug. Sweat clung to both of them in the August heat as cicadas screamed in the distance.

"Girl." Em squeezed Laila tight. "We finally get AC. We'll actually get to sleep the first two months of school."

Despite blowing box fans in their room from August to October, the gusts of wind did little to fight the dorm heat the past three years. According to the school handbook, students could not bring any AC units to the school. Likely because it would blow out the power grid in middle-of-nowhere Indiana.

"Yeah." Laila released and rolled her eyes. Today she'd sported long eyelashes, maybe for a final Welcome Weekend hurrah. "And two new roommates."

"*Two?*"

"Get in the car." She beeped the keys to a rusty red Honda. "I'll explain everything on the way to the grocery store."

Right, the dorms had one thing going for them—toilet paper. Students in apartment housing had to provide everything from food to toiletries and everything in between. According to their RA, a maintenance man could help occasionally with clogged drains and sinks, since the latter didn't come with a garbage disposal. From what Em had heard from previous seniors, though, it could take them weeks to step in and fix something.

Em shoved herself into the passenger seat and moved her AC vent to blow in her face. Air cranked at a high level in the car, so the two had to shout on the way to Walmart.

"Did I hear you right when you said *two* roommates?" Granted, the University could allow for a max of four people per apartment unit. But that meant they'd have to share rooms, something Laila and Em hoped to avoid this year. They'd spent the whole summer making plans for movie nights and knitting parties. Since Laila snored and Em spoke in her sleep, the distance would've given them some actual snooze time this year.

Not with two strangers, though. Laila won't want to room with someone random, especially not during senior year.

"Yeah, already met the one and she's a piece of work."

Right, the one who hates me.

Perhaps Noah had spoken some truth that Em had garnered a decent amount of influence in her time at Mansfield. Influence meant haters, though.

On the way to the grocery store, Laila recounted some of the more heinous crimes of the new roommate, "Jana". One included her taking up ninety percent of the kitchen with her own utensils and pans.

Because Welcome Weekend stretched over three days, roomie number four may not appear for some time. Em couldn't fight the feeling of being like a passenger on a plane hoping someone wouldn't sit in the middle seat.

Once Laila managed to snag a spot, they bolted into the store. Parents with freshman students clogged the aisles with carts full of Pop Tarts and shelving units.

Good luck trying to make use of that dorm space, guys.

Even with their beds bunked the last three years, most fights between Laila and Em broke out due to the lack of room in their dorm.

Laila shoved a squeaky cart into the toilet paper aisle and threw several packs of rolls into the cart.

"You think we need that many?" Em cringed at the thought of the remaining money in her checking account going toward toilet paper that other girls would use.

"We're girls. This will last us maybe two weeks."

Fair.

They split up and Em zipped into the pasta aisle. Bundles of mac and cheese were cradled in her arms as she found Laila in another aisle, placing tinfoil and plastic wrap into the basket.

Laila's nose ring disappeared as her nostrils wrinkled. "Absolutely not."

Em dumped them into the cart anyway. "We're college students. We live on this stuff."

Laila plucked one of the boxes out. "Seriously? SpongeBob shapes?"

"It's a necessity, Laila."

She hmphed, but still threw it back on top of the pile of kitchen supplies. "Hey, if you want Jana to have more reasons to hate you..."

"Is she a health freak or something?"

"Or something." As they swerved into the main aisle, Laila placed a Lays bag on her clavicle. "Get it? She has a chip on her shoulder. Hey." She snapped her fingers at Em's eye roll. "I can be funny too."

"Haha. Hilarious. What do you mean by chip on her shoulder?"

Laila shrugged and dodged past a freshman boy who held up the largest container of Mountain Dew Em had ever witnessed.

Again, good luck trying to even get a mini fridge into the room, dude.

"I don't know." Laila thumbed her chin in the snack aisle. She decided, at last, to go for the Family Size box of Wheat Thins. "It's like she's really bitter about something. She's worse than Meemaw. And my Meemaw is like as bitter as kale."

Ah yes, she'd heard many a tale about Laila's grandmother. The last saga involved her pelting Laila with green grapes for some reason. "I mean, we are college students. There's a lot to be annoyed about."

"I know but." Laila sucked on her teeth. "It's different. It's like she's suffered, so everyone else has to...you know what? You'll see when we get back."

Yippee.

Tension pounded in her temples on the bumpy, narrow, pothole-ridden ride back. Something about these winding roads, shielded by trees, made the claustrophobia seep through her pores.

Why did it matter to her if Jana hated her? Plenty of people expressed a dislike of her throughout the years. One girl, in choir class back at high school, told her she thought she was a "brat" because she sang a solo well.

And the girl didn't use the word "brat".

Over time, though, Em had proved her wrong. She went out of her way to be nice to that girl and talk with the girl about similar interests.

"I learned you were actually nice," the girl finally admitted during the graduation of their senior year of high school. "People with talent or looks or whatever can often be brats."

Again, didn't use that word.

She could clear up this whole misunderstanding with Jana. If her PR/Marketing major had taught her anything, she could learn how to spin a story.

After Laila rumbled into one of the last parking spots, they exited the car. Laila's key reader beeped at the door, and they entered. Em basked in the AC for the briefest of moments until Laila dug out her keys.

I'll check in soon.

She'd just have to make things right with Jana first. Best not have tension in the apartment on the first day. Seniors from last year had advised how the simplest of things such as trash piling or undone dishes could fizzle friendships.

Once Laila swung the door open, they stepped inside. And froze.

A woman with the physique of a direct sales/exercise/marketing company executive stood on a chair. She taped paper lanterns to the ceiling, above the family room living area. In the corner of Em's eye, she watched Laila pinch the bridge of her nose.

Laila, a girl with an affinity for interior design, probably felt her intestines wither inside of herself right now. It felt like some 2010 Pinterest board had thrown up all over the apartment.

"Oh, no." Laila released a long breath. "I'm going to get set up in my room before—"

She passed Em a knowing nod.

Before she combusts, got it.

Laila padded down a narrow hallway toward the first room on the left. Meanwhile, Em hovered by the door, hands clasped in front of her. Should she say anything? Jana's blonde bangs shielded her eyes from her, and she seemed focused on the task at hand...

"Oh. My. Gosh."

Laila bolted out of her room, pink streamer in hand.

"Jana." Laila exhaled long, slow. Keeping her voice pleasant, at least, Em thought so. "Did you—pick the first room on the left for yourself?"

In fairness, Laila hadn't claimed the room or labelled it for herself. That could have gotten anyone confused.

Jana released her fingers from the tape to brush the hair out of her eyes. Her lips twitched. "Hope you don't mind." Her voice reminded Em of one of those people on social media who said "hey girl" a lot. "I just liked the feel of that room better. But I'm sure you and your roommate won't mind the other one."

Laila's teeth crashed onto her bottom lip. "That's the larger of the rooms, Jana. The one you picked."

"Oh, is it?" Jana stepped down from the chair and squinched her eyelids. "Oh, well, I'm sure it's not that much bigger. As we all know, the school certainly doesn't give much space in general. I'm sure you two"—she tossed a pointed look at Em—"will still enjoy the other room. It'll have much more space than the dorms."

Em watched Laila's nails bite into her skin. She returned to the door and clapped a hand against Em's shoulder. "I'm going to go check out the thing going on by the lake. Pretty sure it's going to get started soon."

On their drive back, bass had throbbed through the car. Inflatables and snack stations littered the lawn right by the campus lake. The students often asked where the tuition money went. The answer: to student events like the Welcome Weekend Bash.

"Have fun," Em squeaked back in the present, as Laila left the apartment.

The door slammed shut. Silence shrouded the two of them. Jana plucked a paper lantern, this one fuchsia-hued, and stood on the chair once more.

"Can you do me a favor?" Jana motioned to a roll of tape below. "Cut me one of those? There's scissors on the kitchen table."

"Sure thing." Good, they'd get off to a better start, with Em helping her with her—admittedly heinous—decorations.

Em tore a piece of tape off and handed it to Jana.

"Thanks."

Huh, weird. This girl didn't sound like she hated her. Maybe Fire Girl had met the *other* roommate, who despised Em for some reason.

Once Jana patted the ceiling, she thumped to the floor and parked in the chair. "You're Em, right?" Mirth had drained from her voice.

Em's throat dried. "Umm, yep, that's what most people call me. Apart from the occasional curse word or people who cannot pronounce 'Emerson' for some reason."

"Yeah, umm, you're not going to be doing that matchmaking thing in this apartment are you?" Jana pointed at the floor.

Em eyed the long acrylic fingernails. Could Jana poke an eye out with those things?

Em's hands cupped her elbows. She leaned against the doorframe for support and to make an exit if needed. "Is that...why you hate me?"

Jana wrinkled her nose. "Who told you that?" Something smoldered in Jana's pupils. Quite a sight with those brilliant green eyes.

A niggling feeling clenched Em's intestines. If she gave away Fire Girl's identity, would Jana somehow retaliate against her client? Em shrugged. Best to play it off nonchalant. "Well, do you?"

Jana's thinly plucked brow furrowed for a few moments. Then she dabbed the sweat of her fingertips off on her crop top and motioned Em over. "I want to show you a picture, Em."

Sucking in a breath and holding it in her gut, Em tiptoed over. Jana pulled up a social media app and tapped on her profile picture. In it, a man kissed her temple, and she grinned at the camera lens.

"Cute. How long have you two been together?" If Em learned anything about relationships, the more you got the other person talking about themselves...the more they liked you.

A flicker of a grin passed over Jana's features. "Five months. We met at the tail end of the semester last year."

"Congrats, I—"

A hand flew up from Jana, and the words silenced in Em's throat. Then Jana's fingers dropped into her lap, along with the phone. "I'm twenty-four, Em. Two years older than you, at least, from what I can tell on your social media. Joined college a little late in the game, and you wanna know what I learned over the past six years?"

She didn't wait for a response, not that Em planned to give one.

"I learned that dating sucks, Em. I have stories, *stories* I could tell of what happened before I met Chen. And let me tell you, it was horrible."

Em's brows furrowed as she backed away. Something in Jana's tone sounded threatening. Em's autism sometimes got her into trouble where she'd accidentally annoy someone. And it wasn't until someone got in her face that she'd realized she'd done something wrong. "I've heard stories from tons of people, Jana. That's why I do what I do."

Jana shook her head. "You do it for money. You charge each person five hundred dollars to match them." Her tone had a bite to it.

Yeah, after three dates. And after heavily vetting them. Em bit back the response.

"And," Jana swiveled on the chair until she faced Em, "you're not even dating someone yourself." A scoff sounded in the back of her throat. "You're another unmarried marriage counselor."

Heat pounded in Em's neck veins. She breathed in and out several times to cool it. "I get results, Jana." Em's tone turned placating. For some reasons, girls did not like her when they first met her. But hopefully she could get past that phase with Jana soon. "Most of the couples I've matched are engaged or married now, and I can bet you most couples will spend more than five hundred dollars on dates before they find the one."

Heck, most matchmakers she found online charged anything from $15,000 up to $100,000. She'd given these students a huge discount, if anything.

Jana's upper lip drew into a sneer. "Unless you go through what your couples have gone through, Em, you won't get it. You should stop taking money from people if you don't even know what it's like."

How did Jana know what she'd gone through? Had someone told her? Plenty of students before Jana had bugged her to jump into the dating pool, but she'd held off. Seen plenty of bitter exchanges between her parents to want to navigate those waters at a young age.

Maybe when I'm in my mid-twenties, she had told herself.

Em folded her arms. "Well, feel free to set that up if you really want that to happen. I'm not matchmaking for myself."

The comment appeared to sting Jana for a second. Then her lips twitched. "Actually, that's not a bad idea. I could put you through *my* matchmaking services."

"Your matchmaking services?" Em blinked.

"Yeah, I'll basically let you go through what the other students go through in the dating realm at Mansfield. So you can better understand your"—her lip curled again—"clients. I'm betting you wouldn't last a year. And since it's your senior year, you're expected to have a ring by spring. Think you can do that, sweetie?" She splayed her fingertips as if showing off an engagement ring.

Heat singed Em's neck again. "Oh yeah? You don't think I could get a ring by spring? What are you betting, exactly?"

Jana thought about it for a moment. "Twenty thousand dollars."

Holy.

Em's stomach buckled and she almost ejected her chai onto the carpet. Twenty grand could not only take her out of student debt, but get her a few months of apartment rent post-graduation. Heck, if she matched a few more couples, that could make a down payment on a small house.

"It's an inheritance from my grandma. Rest in peace, Gigi. But"—Jana lifted a finger—"if you lose and don't get a ring by spring, you have to pay back every student you matched. Deal?" Her hand shot forward.

Again...holy.

That would put her $30,000 under in student debt, not to mention this school year.

"What, girlie?" Jana blinked her eyes wide and slow, as though confused. "Are you trying to say that you—who is giving all these girls dating advice—can't find a man yourself? Are you admitting that your business model isn't super airtight?"

Em blew a short breath out of her nostrils, and then clapped her hand into Jana's. Dang, those nails *could* puncture skin. "You, Jana, have yourself a deal."

Chapter Three

Oh gosh, what did I just agree to?

Right after the handshake of doom, Em fled outdoors, operating under the excuse of needing to get her parking pass. Which she did. She dug into her wallet and pulled out a crisp forty dollars: two twenties. That would cover the fee, right? The school always seemed to hike the prices for everything. Parking passes had been twenty-five dollars her freshman year and had bumped up another fifteen since.

Sweat glistened on her upper lip. She licked off the saltiness and exhaled long, slow. *You can do this.*

She'd coached dozens of people on dates. No doubt, she could manage a few interactions, maybe get a guy to fall in love with her. Then if the engagement went south, she could cancel it, right?

I can't do that to someone though, right?

Em shook her head, hair sticking to her neck from the humidity outside. Maybe a walk would jog the ol' noggin. Bass directed her steps. A cool breeze from the lake could help to at least save her from this heat. Fists balled, she marched up the sidewalk and around the loop that surrounded campus. Sure enough, she spotted the token couple traversing the sidewalk. Men and women would round the loop whenever they wanted to have DTR—a "define the relationship" talk.

Recognition dawned. Didn't she have class with that one girl last year? The one who wore clothing that looked like it was straight out of the sixties' hippy era. Sure enough, white flowers dotted flared pants. She waved at Em with her free hand. The other one gripped a man's hand.

The girl arched a brow. Was that look haughty? Or had she squinted at the sun too long?

Some couples made a point to show themselves around Em. To prove to her that they could find love without her matchmaking services. Wasn't this girl a professional writing major? She'd helped a lot of students edit their papers, charged an arm and a leg for that too.

Em had once asked her, in class, if she got a lot of flak for that.

Editor Girl nodded over her open laptop lid, "Yeah, people just want you to give stuff for free. The teacher says that if you have a skill, that you should never do it *gratis*, though."

Em had assumed she could apply the same principle to her matchmaking business. According to Jana, though, she'd taken advantage of students' desperation.

She nodded at them with her best smile possible.

Editor Girl shielded an eye roll under sunglasses—shades she'd just donned moments ago. They passed her without saying anything. A loud laugh from the Editor Girl pierced Em's ears and halted her steps. She parked onto a bench, nearest the campus postage office, and gulped in steady breaths.

Your skills and talents are worth it, girl. Remember some of those testi monials you got a few months ago.

Last semester, she'd asked some of her clients to send her recommendations that she could post on her site. Tapping into the school's abysmal WiFi, she pulled up her site and read some of the quotes on the front page:

"Em's a lifesaver. If you think $500 is too much, think about how much you spend on a date. $20? $25? And how many dates do you go on before you finally find that one. It's well worth it."

"It's one thing for a friend to set you up on a blind date. But that's what they really are…BLIND dates. Sometimes they work, but sometimes they are just plain awful. Em vets the dates and, honestly, it's a match made in heaven. I don't know how she does it."

"I married my husband because of Em. Can you believe that? Married. I thought I couldn't find the one, and it turns out that he was in several of my gen-eds the whole time. Thank you! And I seriously recommend this service to anyone."

Light glowed in her chest. Okay, she'd helped people before with this. Certainly, she could help herself.

Lawn mowers roared in the distance. The smell of freshly cut grass drifted into her senses. Okay, Jana would probably try to sabotage her in the dating program she set up for her. So if she could find a match for herself—before Jana—then she could get the ball rolling on this thing.

Music thumped the ground, even several hundred meters away from the lake. *There.* What better way to meet someone than Welcome Weekend?

A smaller girl skittered past the bench with a map crumpled in her hands. She paused and backpedaled. "You know where the lake is?" Freckles dotted her nose.

Em nodded at Freckle Girl and bolted off the bench. "I'm actually heading there right now. I'll lead you there."

Freckle Girl's shoulders relaxed. "Thanks." She folded the map and tucked it into her bag. After a few moments of silence, she spoke. "There was a guy who was very eager to show me a tour of campus. Got a weird feeling around him, so I, uh, ditched."

Memories reeled from Em's freshman year. Most of that Welcome Week had passed in a blur, but she did remember one thing. Boys swarmed her, and other girls in her dorm, like Indiana vultures. "You a freshman?"

Freckle Girl nodded.

"Was he, uh, a senior?"

She frowned. "Umm, he didn't say. But he did talk about some of his classes, and they didn't sound like hundred-level ones, you know?"

Got it, senior indeed.

"That's called the freshman frenzy." Em rolled her eyes. Sunbeams scorched her retinas. Hopefully the trees by the lake would provide more shade. "Senior guys get excited about the—and this is their own words—'fresh meat'. My advice? Find other girls, stay in a group, and wait for the week to blow over."

By the first few weeks of classes, seniors got overwhelmed with their studies and forgot about the fresh meat.

Freckle Girl let out all the air in her lungs and clasped a hand to her chest. "Thanks. I appreciate it. People are weird."

They parted ways at a grassy hill. Strobe lights bounced from black balls, hardly visible in the late-afternoon light. Em eyed a guy nearest a punch table and beelined toward him. She reminded herself of the flirting tips she'd given to so many of her past clients. Despite being "liked" on campus, she had to admit that the autism got in the way when it came to certain social interactions. And besides, she was popular for what she could do for people. If an elephant could stick two people together for life, people wouldn't question if it was an elephant. They'd just say, "Thank you, kind elephant. I want to be your friend forever."

Her eyebrows scrunched. Why was she thinking of elephants right now? Never mind, back to the dating tips.

Tip One: Laugh a Lot

I don't know why people like to be laughed at, or really, laughed with. But there's something so comforting in knowing you're funny. So laugh at their jokes. Even if you want to cringe. And also, it never hurts to make them laugh too. Everyone puts down "has a sense of humor" on their wants list. There's something so beautiful, I suppose, about waking up next to someone who is going to make the sad world a little brighter.

Tip Two: Ask Open-Ended Questions

Nothing that's going to end in a "yes" or "no". So no, "Do you like your major?" Instead, "What do you like about your major?" Get people to talking about themselves. Of course, make sure they ask *you* questions too.

Tip Three: Confidence Is Key

No one likes a pick-me. Sorry, but we can't stand the whine and the heavy sigh, followed by, "Nice guys/girls finish last." Make eye contact and be unashamedly yourself. So many people—from what I've seen—try to hide parts of themselves until they know they've secured someone in a label or in an engagement. Of course, don't share ALL your dark secrets, but don't be afraid of who you are.

Okay, whew: laugh, questions, confidence, I can do that.

Em tugged a strand of hair behind her ear and waved at the pale boy the punch bowl. He quirked a brow and ladled bright red liquid into his cup in silence. After two throat clears from Em, he turned to her.

"Can I help you?"

Em giggled. "Oh my gosh, stop." She'd seen popular girls flirt this way. She even batted her hand as if waving away some kind of smell. *What have I become?*

Her eyes widened and she scooped the ladle into her hands. Time to salvage this with the next step—questions.

"So." She batted her eyes at him and bit back a yelp when the punch spilled onto the table and dribbled down the plastic cloth onto her open-toed shoes. Great, she'd dye her toesies red for a bit. She forced a smile, hoping his eyes didn't follow the liquid's trail. "What's your, umm, major?"

"Business."

Shoot. It wasn't a "yes" or "no" question, but it had definitely led to a one-word answer. She should've gone for "what do you like about your major" instead?

Students whooped nearby at a sand volleyball court. The boy clocked them, and he pushed himself away from the table. Yikes, she had seconds to recover.

Step three time—confidence.

"I"—she jabbed a finger at him—"am Emerson Levi. And I cannot help who I am. Take me or leave me, sir."

His eyes widened and he backed away, toward the courts. "Okayyy then, Emerson. You have fun with that." His steps grew quicker and he dashed toward the game.

As sand splashed like water off the court and into the grass, Em deflated. Why did it feel so much harder to flirt in person? On paper, it seemed simpler. Most of her clients got the hang of things after those first date jitters.

Memories reeled back to Editing Girl in their shared Gen Ed class. Em had asked her why she didn't do writing, since the professional writing major involved...well, writing.

Editing Girl chewed on a pen cap. "Well, because I'm good at editing. I can tell people how to write well. I can't write for beans. But I can show someone the way."

What if that means I can teach "the flirt" but cannot do "the flirt" myself.

Fingers clenched. No, if she went back to Jana now to rescind the bet, Jana would inform the whole school about how "her business is a scam". Even if some people didn't believe her—after all, one bad review wouldn't hurt—no one would want to get with a matchmaker who couldn't use the skills she taught.

She observed a water balloon tossing station. A man at the back of the line shoved his fingers into his cargo shorts pockets. *Well, doesn't hurt to get some practice in.*

Ignoring the sticky residue on her feet from the punch, she ambled toward the line. Just as she neared the man, another girl slid in behind him. She sported knee-high socks, cat ears, and school-girl loafers. Something about this girl felt like she was straight out of an anime. And she giggled, loudly. She doubled over, snorted, and slapped her knee—like he'd uttered the most hilarious joke ever.

The boy scrunched his eyebrows and backed away, toward the GaGa ball pit. Slaps against the ball punctured his steps. The girl rolled herself up and swiped a finger underneath her eye. She discerned Em's presence and waved, happy as ever.

"Were you?" Em winced. "Were you flirting with him?"

Did I look like that at the punch table?

The girl shrugged. "Eh, they like me. They don't like me. Who's to say? *Rawr.*" She made a cat claw with her hand. "Harmony is gonna be Harmony either way."

"Is Harmony your name?"

"Tis. Tis."

"And do you usually refer to yourself in the third-person?"

"Only when we feel like it?"

Em frowned. "Who's 'we'?"

Harmony raised a finger to her lips, shushed, and winked.

"Okayy, then, Harmony. I..." Relief flooded her. "Think I see my friend Noah over there, so I might—"

"Waaaait!" Harmony bounced up and down. The others in the line curled brows at her and turned to brightly-lit devices. Maybe to message friends about the weirdo in the queue.

"Okay, I'm, umm, waiting?"

"Good. Are you Emerson Levi perchance? I saw your picture on the social medias. The interwebs."

Em's stomach dropped. "Yeah, why?"

"Ooh, ooh, ooh." Harmony jumped up and down clapping her hands. "Okay, I'm your other apartment-mate. I didn't have a chance to check in because they were taking a lunch at the time. But I'm getting my key right after this thing."

Oh boy, this girl?

Em debated as to whether she'd prefer a Jana to a Harmony in her apartment. Sneers from other girls in the line incensed Em's skin, though. Didn't she advise everyone to be their true selves? Why couldn't she allow for Harmony to do so, despite her quirks?

"Also, your friend, Noah. Was he the one with the orange fliers?"

Harmony swiveled her backpack from her back to her stomach. Why hadn't Em noticed this before? No doubt, no one else thought to bring a book bag to a party. Zippers flew and Harmony pulled out a Do Good sheet. "Since we're apartment mates and all, I figured we might be able to Do Good together. I'm pretty good at baking. And I've been obsessed with all things Japan lately. Obviously." She gestured at her outfit. "So maybe we can do mochi. Or *dango*. And give it to the other people in the building, and—"

Em held up a hand. "Hold on, you said that you've been *recently* obsessed with Japan?"

"Yeah." Harmony snorted. "My outfits go through phases. So many phases." She whispered, "We don't talk about the onesie phase."

Someone in line snickered at this and whispered to someone else. Once again Em's skin singed. Did they view Harmony the same way that Jana saw her? Un-dateable, washed up?

We'll see about that. She'd show Jana that she *could* in fact do charity work, whilst working her gifts and talents.

Em took a good long look at Harmony. Lots to work with. Beautiful bone structure in the cheeks, enough nerdy appeal for the Star Wars guys who filled out her form—Lord knew there were plenty of those waiting for her to match them with someone else—and deep passion. So many guys complained to Em about how girls had nothing to say on dates. But someone Harmony could keep conversations going for hours.

Like Em, it would just take a little work on the flirting. And maybe coaxing Harmony out of this anime phase. Outrageous outfits had a track record of scaring away most men.

Men do scare away easy, don't they? She glared at the man from the punch table, who spiked a volleyball onto the sand. *Forget him.*

Em swiveled back to Harmony and tapped the orange paper. "Speaking of Do Good. How would you, Harmony, like to find your future husband?"

Chapter Four

"Em, I can't do it. You do it for me."

Tara Bates quaked in the middle of the Dining Commons. The plate in her hands shook. Em grabbed the plate from her and set it down on one of the non-packed circular tables. Soon, their entire wing of twenty-four girls would attempt to squish themselves around an area really meant for a maximum of ten chairs.

"Do what?" Em wiped a smear of mashed potatoes on the heel of her hand against a scratchy brown napkin. The dining commons napkins did little to absorb stains or food streaks.

At least they have napkins in here.

In the dorms, not a paper towel could be spotted in sight. Part of the campus's green initiative, they replaced all paper towel dispensers with air dryers. Never mind that the wind turbines on campus sucked more energy than they put out. Some school newspaper article a while back had put out an article about the benefits of switching back to towels. But the school would hear nothing of it. Once a college had its mind set on a budget cut, it could listen to no reason.

"The Dash Date." Tara squeaked this while pinching the bridge of her nose. A table of guffawing boys took notice of the shriek and scooted their plates a little closer to themselves. "I've already asked like ten guys."

Mansfield had a way of encouraging "the youth" to go on not-dates. Em learned early on that they could be broken into three categories:

- Girls Ask: A girl asks a boy on a not-date. Popular activities included archery, laser tag, pumpkin patch runs, and the occasional haunted maze during Halloween season.

- Boys Ask: Same concept, except the boys ask girls.

- Dash Date: Unlike a "Boys Ask" or "Girls Ask," where the asker would have weeks to approach the askee, a Dash Date was announced two hours before the actual event. Everyone on the wing would have to secure a date within that time frame.

And Em's wing had announced that date an hour and a half ago—a roller-skating-rink affair. Em, of course, had asked her bestie Noah. They'd met in a First Year Experience class and, thus, their friendship bloomed. Since neither of them liked the idea of dating during college, they would default to asking each other so they could relieve that pressure.

Tara's nose scrunched within her boxy glasses. "No luck. I hear you're good at getting girls dates. Can you help?"

True, Em did have a knack for securing dates for some of the more socially anxious girls. She clapped Tara's shoulder. "I'll see what I can do, okay?"

Tara bit her lip and nodded.

With that, Em dashed over to Noah's table. He held his fingertips up to receive a paper football from one of his wing-mates. "Noah, I need a Dash Date. Anyone on our brother floor that can help?"

Mansfield broke up the "wings" on campus into Brother Floors and Sister Floors. Each brother floor would get paired with a sister floor. Much to Em's surprise and delight, she learned early on that Noah lived on her wing's "brother floor". Most of the dates she secured for her girls hailed from there.

Noah winced and almost bumped a clear cup full of orange soda when he retrieved a wayward "football". "Sorry, Em, but I think most of the guys have been asked. If they didn't already say yes, they probably have some prior club or commitment."

True, most Mansfield students had a problem with overcommitting themselves to about five or six activities or clubs. Counseling centers on campus filled to the brim with students who didn't know how to say no to one more event.

She parked beside him and rested her fist against her chin. "It's fine but—I'm trying to find a date for a really shy girl. Our brother floor was safe, you know?"

He nodded. "If anyone can find one, it'll be you."

"Why's that?"

"You see the potential in everyone. You're really good at that. Did you know that your last 'match' is actually dating now?"

Her eyes widened. "They are?"

"Yeah. The last Girls Pick couple you found were spotted walking the loop yesterday. So I guess you could say they're getting serious."

Walking the loop on campus was how guys and girls showed they liked each other. They'd hold hands and circle the perimeter, until someone confessed their love.

Huh. She'd never considered that before. True, she did have a knack for divvying up roles in group projects. And once, in high school, she'd directed a student play. Someone informed her that she casted every part to perfection.

Of course, theater took way too much time, and she had no desire to compete against the talent of the Mansfield Theater. Hence why her thespian career ended after graduation.

She shut her eyelids and did her best to tune out the din of the cafeteria. The smell of mashed potatoes wafted nearby. One of the "safe" options in a dining commons that liked to experiment with spare ingredients too often.

Images flickered of men in her Gen Eds. She halted on one.

Maverick.

A quiet type, loved to listen. Those types of boys caused even the shyest of girls to peel open their shells. She'd noticed how Tara shrank into her shoulders whenever they'd head over to their brother floor and a loud extrovert would get overly excited about winning a ping pong match.

No, Maverick stood for everything opposite of that.

Resolution surged in her veins. She lifted herself from the table, saluted Noah, and beelined for the food queue. She spotted Maverick, cloaked in a hoodie, near the pasta line. Scooping a plate into her hands, she sidled next to him. "You doing anything tonight, Maverick?" She ladled undercooked orzo onto her green plate.

He pulled out his earphones, and she repeated the question.

Once he admitted that he was free, she pitched.

Success. A smile cut up his cheek at the name of "Tara". Could've been Em's imagination, but maybe he'd been wanting her to ask him out all this time. Perhaps the last few Boys Asks, he'd hoped to muster the courage.

Sometimes people need a little extra push to find their brave.

Half an hour later, everyone piled into rusty cars to head to a roller rink—thirty minutes away. In the middle of the Indiana cornfields, nothing lingered in close vicinity. Once at the rink, Em stuffed her feet into blocky skates and held the crook of Noah's arm as they approached the slippery floor.

She fell no less than nine times.

Disco lights whirred as a man, in a referee jersey, held up a limbo stick. Em giggled on the sidelines with Noah and watched as Tara and Maverick attempted to bend underneath the stick together. It whacked them in their midsections, and they collapsed, giggling.

After some time making rounds around the floor, Noah and Em headed to the concessions stand. They each purchased one of the pretzels rotating underneath beams of light. Salt danced on her tongue as they sat at a table.

"Appreciate you going with me, Noah." Em sipped on a tangy blue raspberry lemonade she'd also purchased. "I know you've got a lot of theater stuff going on."

"Eh." He shrugged. "Tonight they're working on the set instead of rehearsing so"—he winked—"you saved me from that."

A laugh bounced in her throat. Oh ho, she could relate. After certain productions she'd helped with in the past, she never wanted to see sawdust or bent nails ever again.

Noah brushed pretzel salt off his shorts. "Besides, we're here to rescue each other from the school's ridiculous dating culture."

"True." With the freshman frenzy being over, you'd think people would've calmed down by now. It seemed like every other conversation she had with someone on her floor involved one of the girls talking about an encounter with a boy of some sort.

Tara swept damp bangs away from her face as she rolled toward Noah and Em. She and Maverick parted ways as he trundled toward the concessions stand. How much time had passed by?

Conversations with Noah always dissolved minutes, it seemed.

"Em." Tara parked beside her and clapped a clammy hand on Em's forearm. "You're a miracle worker. I know it's only been two hours, but we've been talking nonstop the whole time. I owe you big time."

Before Em could register Tara's words, Tara yanked out a wallet. She unzipped the blue fabric and pulled out five twenties. "Least I could do."

She slapped the wad of cash onto the table and lifted herself up on her skates. It took her a few seconds to regain her balance. "Let's just say, if things keep progressing, you're invited to the wedding."

Seems a little forward.

Right before Em had a chance to even gawk or utter, "I can't take your money", Tara rolled toward the concessions stand. A high-pitched laugh followed. She must've found her man.

Blood drained from Em's face into her stomach. She shared a glance with Noah. "I can't take that money, right?"

Noah palmed his neck. Unease settled into the lines on his forehead. "I don't know, Em. I mean I guess you technically set it up, and you can't stop her from—"

A tap on Em's shoulder interrupted the speech.

She glanced behind and one of the other girls on her floor—one who she hadn't learned the name of yet, with knee-high green socks—gave a shy wave. "Hey, couldn't help but overhear, but did you just set up Tara with Maverick?"

"I—um, guess I did?"

The girl held up several twenties between her fingers. "How much for you to find *me* my future husband?"

Present Day

"Let Harmony get this straight." Harmony rubbed her hands up and down her knees as the two of them parked at a picnic table near the lake. A fire roared nearby as students crowded around the flames to crisp marshmallows. "You want to set me up with some guy?"

"For the Do Good event, yes. I usually provide matchmaking services to students, that includes coaching and vetting and such. But I'd want to do this at no charge."

It surprised Em that Harmony hadn't heard of her. Several Mansfield Mirror articles had featured her business, and many of the students followed the social media pages she had set up for her matchmaking services.

"Sorry." Harmony seized an unused marshmallow skewer nearby and started poking another student in the back with it. The student cursed at her and padded away. No wonder. That could've technically been considered assault. "But I'm a new transfer." For the first time, Harmony's voice sobered. Part of Em wondered if the weird stuff was a defense mechanism or part of some sort of act. "My small Christian college shut down, and I was on my last semester there. Most credits transferred, but..."

Got it.

According to classmates who graduated before her, most seniors didn't stand a chance at finding their "one" by the time they reached their final year. Let alone someone new to the campus.

Harmony, on their way over to the benches, had also mentioned a year or two at community college before the other small university. And she'd mentioned a gap year or two to save up money. That had to put her age at twenty-three or twenty-four. For some reason, people on campus hissed if someone breached the age of twenty-two in the dating pool.

"Anyway." Harmony flicked the skewer like a wizard wand. Students in the vicinity scooched away. Smells of burnt marshmallows permeated the air. "I have two semesters to go. Think you can help a hopeless case?"

Em shrugged. "My first technical client, Tara, used to punch guys if they flirted with her. She legit didn't know what to do when she felt anxious, so she turned to violence."

"Violence." Glints of fire lighted Harmony's pupils. "I love her already."

"Now, in order to find you a match, I need to put you in my database." Em yanked out her phone. "Let's go over some of the questions. Since this is Do Good, whoever you end up matching with won't have to pay either. We'll let that be a nice surprise for him."

Wind rippled off the lake, forming small waves as Em dug up the questionnaire form. "Okay, let's assume you make it past the first round, because that one is only about three questions long. And it's mostly to weed out the weirdos."

"The weirdos?" Harmony's nose wrinkled.

"Not you weirdo. Like *weirdo* weirdo."

"Ah." Harmony nodded and drew a snake in the dirt with her skewer. "I went out with a few of those at community college. One tracked me down to my workplace—even though I didn't tell him where I worked—and wouldn't stop singing the 'Baby Shark' song to lure me in. I was in my shark phase. Curse him."

Shock jolted Em's chest.

"I'm sorry. Did you just say he *stalked* you?"

"Eh." Harmony shrugged. "We went out a few times after that. The shark plushies were hard to say no to."

Yikes. A few girls on her wing in previous years had shared stories about creepy guys, but Em shuddered to think about a man who could find her at a workplace setting.

Two answers in, a figure surfaced in her periphery. "Hey, Em. Oh, and umm, hi. Nice cat ears."

Ah, she recognized that baritone. Noah. He pointed a finger gun at Harmony. "If we ever do a production of *Cats*, I'll make sure to hit you up first."

Lord help them the day that their college chose to have students crawling up and down the stage in fur costumes. Already, their theater had put on a production of *The Birds* by Aristophanes, and that got weird. The director had thought it "artistic" to have literally every actor in a bird costume for some reason.

Noah always defended the eccentric woman, though. "Her mind just works a little bit differently, Em. Okay, a lotta bit differently. But I think this world could use a lot of different. Who wants vanilla ice cream when you can have curry-flavored custard?"

From that day forward, Em vowed to never go to the eccentric ice cream festivals Noah's hometown apparently had.

"*Rawr.*" Harmony pawed at him, then sobered. "Your bestie is gonna find my future husband for me."

Noah tossed a glare at Em. How did he make even *glares* feel like he was throwing teddy bears at her or something? "Mhmm. Glad to see you're always on the clock, Em."

"For freeee!" Harmony pumped her fists and ran laps around the fire.

Noah's arms shielded his chest when he folded them. "Wow, how generous of you. Charity work."

"Do Good-ing." She lifted a finger. "I believe a *certain someone* told me that we're supposed to do kind acts to benefit the play he's in."

"Oh my word, Em. You literally could've done anything else for Do Good."

"And if I recall correctly, you were with me when Tara shoved her money at me for the first time. I can't *help* it if people pay for my services. Student debt's not going to pay for itself, you know."

He let out a long sigh and jabbed a thumb over his shoulder.

"Fine, go." Em shooed him away, surprised at the anger in her voice. They only fought on one thing: her matchmaking.

Without elaborating further, he headed for one of the fire pits.

Chapter Five

"I'm sorry, Em, but are you trying to chase me around the apartment with SpongeBob mac and cheese?"

"Sorry, Laila, but Harmony told me to do it."

Harmony chuckled on the family room couch whilst snuggling a unicorn plushie. At last, she'd emerged from her Japanese clothing phase. Now, Harmony bedecked herself in sparkly boots with a shimmery skirt and crop top to match.

Laila rolled her eyes, but Em didn't fail to spot the lip twitch. It'd taken her a few hours to warm up to Harmony, but after a while, she deemed her more likable than Jana. Jana evaded the apartment most hours and hit the on-campus gym during her free time.

"And why"—Laila held up a hand to block the plastic spoon full of mac and cheese—"did she tell you to do this, exactly?"

Cheesy scents permeated the small kitchen. The smoke alarm had already gone off twice that day, thanks to the older stovetop and oven.

"Says she won't finish the matchmaking survey until I convince you that *this* is a delicacy. We've been so caught up in welcome weekend activities that we haven't had a chance to sit down."

Harmony had apparently signed up as a stringer for the Mansfield Mirror. According to her, she dug up some of the juiciest leads at her previous school. One involved the college pocketing money for their president: "By the time the article rolled out, it was too late. It was our last issue. Buuut, a byline's a byline, no matter how small."

Some of the weirdness added up when Em learned Harmony's major: professional writing. Besides Editing Girl, most of the students in that major had some sort of unhinged quality about them. This ranged from them cosplaying as their favorite book characters to literally dressing up in armor for LARPing activities. All things considered, Harmony felt relatively balanced in comparison with some of them.

Laila boxed Em out, a classic basketball move to keep people away from the hoop, and rushed to the stove top to turn down a burner beneath boiling broccoli, her contribution to the evening since, "Y'all are going to die if you two won't eat vegetables with your meals."

In Em's defense, plenty of the dining commons vegetables were rotting or had literal insects in them. One of the cafeteria workers asserted, "That's how you know it's organic. When you find a dead caterpillar."

"Besides," Laila stirred the greenish water with another spoon, "you don't need her to answer those questions. Just put down the most unhinged thing possible, and it's probably accurate."

Not wrong.

Earlier, the answered questions went somewhere along the lines of:

What do you look for in a man: Someone who isn't afraid that I can stab him when I'm in a stabby mood.

Favorite movie type: Either slasher horror or a Disney musical. I'm pretty easy to please.

Ideal first date: An abandoned parking lot or a haunted mine.

When Em had begged Harmony to take the survey seriously, Harmony stated, "Well, that's how I feel at this current moment. The answers may change in a week or so. Give it time."

Em dropped the spoon into the pot and huffed a dramatic sigh. "Fine, but life's no fun if you can't chase someone around with noodles."

She often would show this funny side with people once they got to know her more. It was so strange how often people would say things like, "I had no idea you were this sweet." Or, "Since when were you this silly?"

Autism had a way of doing that. She could never show the right emotions that people wanted at the right times. Maybe that was why she could never date someone. They would never really like the true her.

Laila snorted and clicked off the burner for the broccoli. Right as she did so, keys jostled in the lock outside the door. Jana banged the door opened and jabbed a finger at Em. "You." She stepped into the apartment and reached for the towel draped around her neck. Then she dabbed her forehead. "You have a date in ten minutes. And I suggest you wear something, and I quote, 'classy'."

Em blinked several times until the words clicked. "I'm sorry, a date?"

"Yep. Ten minutes. Chop, chop."

Em glanced down at her Winnie the Pooh pajama pants, and her fingers reached up into her messy bun. "Couldn't have given me more of a heads up, Jana?"

"Blind dates sometimes work like this. Welcome to the dating experience, girlie. Now get changed."

Yeah, Em was rather sure blind dates never actually worked like that.

Despite Jana claiming that she wouldn't sabotage Em throughout the bet process, Em held her serious doubts. At the very least, Jana promised that other students would pick the dates for Em, so Jana wouldn't get tempted to put her with the worst possible candidates.

Still...

"I'm pretty sure you secured this date long before ten minutes ago," Em grumbled as she slathered lavender deodorant over her pits and hopped into the nicest dress in her closet, a fit-and-flare number. Blue, because she'd heard that was a calming color. Men sometimes got intimidated by red dresses on the first date, because red proclaimed "power". At least, a class on color theory had taught her that for a marketing requisite.

She glimpsed the mirror, underneath a buzzing light. Even though Laila had put in a work request for the maintenance man to stop by and replace the bulb, they'd heard nothing since the email went out. After she dabbed some light brown eyeshadow and circled her lips with some gloss, she forced her hair into a nicer bun. Her straight hair wouldn't hold a curl anyway, not that she had the time to do anything with it.

As soon as she looped her bag around her shoulders, she heard a knock at the front door. *That was way less than ten minutes.*

Slipping her feet into flats—some men still didn't like a woman taller than them in heels—she padded toward the front door and opened it with the best smile she could muster.

Oh no.

A three-piece suit greeted her. And from what she could tell, the man, with very pinkish skin, had slicked back his blond hair with gel. He eyed her up and down, concern donning his face. "Oh." He clasped his hands in front. "I was told that you were going to be done-up this evening."

Had he now?

She tossed a withering glare back at Jana, who perused a textbook on the couch.

"Haha." She clasped her hands in front of her. Sometimes her autism had her mirror reactions of people until she knew she was safe with them and could act like herself. "Sorry, there was quite a bit to take care of. Hopefully the dress works."

"Mm." He offered the crook of his arm to her. What was this, the 1950s? "I can smell the meal from your kitchen. I can see why you had yourself busied. It's important to feed others in your household before attending to other things."

Where did Jana find this guy? He spoke like he'd hailed from some Jane Austen novel.

"Right." She stepped into the hallway and clicked the door behind her. "Shall we get going—"

"Although, I will say, should this lend itself to a second date, I must tell you that I prefer a woman to wear pantyhose, longer dresses, and heels. After all"—he raised his hand to the crown of his head—"I am six foot, which I hear is a 'hot commodity', as they say with the ladies on campus."

Em's nose bunched as if someone had just filled her nostrils with garbage. *I can duck out of this thing, right?* Because the Lord knew she wanted to rage quit.

No, she couldn't. That would admit to Jana that she couldn't handle the Christian dating culture that every student *apparently* went through. She, at the very least, had to give this thing thirty minutes.

As thoughts buzzed in her skull, he introduced himself. She didn't remember the name, but decided on Gel Hair for this one. Ickiness surged in her fingertips as she held onto his arm, and they strolled out into the humid air. Heaven knew why he expected women to wear tights. Did anyone mandate that beyond the 1960s?

"I must ask, m'lady." His dress shoes pounded the pavement as they headed toward the campus entrance. Ah, he must be taking her to the ice cream joint one mile away. The only restaurant that a student could walk to in this cornfield city. "What are your intentions as we court each other?"

My intentions?

Didn't *he* want to go on this date?

Also "courting"? What?

"Um." She kept her eyes pressed onto the asphalt road nearest the sidewalk and prayed that few students would be circling the loop at this hour to spot her with Gel Hair. Salmon sunsets streaked the skies. "I think that anyone at this college would say that they're dating with the intention of finding their future spouse, right?"

"Mm, an excellent answer. I would have to stop this thing dead-on-sight if you were to have answered differently. It would surprise you that so many young ladies at this campus are commitment-afraid. It's the curse of modern culture, if you ask me."

Disc golf discs whizzed past as they clanged into metal nets. She prayed that the night could pass by in, as she imagined Gel Hair would say, "a jiffy."

After Gel Hair recounted for her his work that he did at a local church, they skittered along the main road that led to the ice cream shop. Gel Hair cleared his throat and held his elbow even higher—as if displaying his feat of strength for carrying her hand for so long.

"So, dearest Emerson, since we both court with the intention of pursuing a marriage with someone, I believe it is important to ask each other important questions. Although some 'dating experts'," with his one free hand, he threw up an air quote, "claim you should wait until the second or third date, I say that is nonsense. What would you say to that?"

I would say that you really need to invest in some deodorant, sir.

She smiled, nodded.

He mirrored her gaze, as if delighted at having procured such a demure prospect. "I must say that I do appreciate that you have not put on so much makeup, Emerson. Some women can be so deceitful. It's not right, and it's not biblical."

Oh, *oh* the strength it took to hold back that eye roll.

"But circling back to important questions, I must ask, have you ever thought about the future?"

"The future?"

Yes and no. So much of her life had been consumed by the matchmaking clients that she hadn't considered much about her PR/marketing degree. According to her teachers, loads of companies needed new hires in that area all the time.

"Yes, about family life and such. Are you thinking about having a family some day?"

Her nose wrinkled. "I mean, who doesn't?"

What little girl didn't play house at one point? Yes, she'd even had lists of potential names if she had boys or girls down the road. But that would be years down the road, after she'd accrued funds and balanced stay-at-home life with her future husband. If she'd learned anything from her parents, it was important to save up as much as possible in the beginning years.

"That's delightful to hear, Emerson. You would not believe the number of ladies on this campus who do not want to be mothers. Selfish, if you ask me. What's the point of marriage if you aren't creating more Christians to spread the Gospel?"

Unease clenched her gut. Yes, she admired the stay-at-home moms in her church back home. She had no idea how they did it. But what about infertile couples? Did they count as a selfish type of marriage?

At last, they reached the shop. Usually, at five or six in the evening, the line stretched out the door. But since they'd reached it closer to eight, they didn't have to wait.

Without thinking, she held open the door for him. He planted his fists on his hips. "I shall never let a lady hold open the door for me. Allow me."

He gripped the handle and beckoned her in with an arm sweep. Once inside, she scanned the wall behind the counter to peruse the one hundred something ice cream flavors the little shop boasted of. She settled on a buckeye and approached the counter. Once she'd ordered, she pulled out a five and handed it to the cashier.

After Gel Hair ordered, he seized her elbow and yanked her outside. With her heartbeat pounding her temples, she took a few seconds to register what happened. By that point, he was in her face. "I didn't want to cause a commotion in there, Emerson, but," he sighed, "I must ask you to never pay for yourself on a date again. A man's honor is at stake if a woman had to foot a bill. After all, men are expected to work, and women are expected to raise families. It's biblical."

Heat surged into her cheeks. She could duck out now, right? Well, she could, if she wasn't so scared. "I—" Her voice cracked. "You're right. Come to think of it—"

How could she spin this angle? After all, if she told him he did anything wrong, he might take it out on her in some way. He seemed like the type to raise a hand behind closed doors. After all, he'd pulled her out of the shop for *paying for ice cream*.

Someone on the loudspeaker outside—for when summer lines trailed all the way to the road—told a man named "Todd" that his order was ready.

"—I think that I am not ready to court. Today has taught me that. I believe I—" She cringed inwardly and promised she'd forgive herself later for these words. "I need to learn some more submissiveness if I'm going to be someone's wife and mother someday."

Gel Hair relaxed his grip and blinked away the moisture in his eyes. "I—" He sighed. "I was going to say something but was worried I would offend you. But I agree with you, Emerson. You have some growing to do before you are ready for that world. For your sake," he took her hands in his, "I hope that it happens soon. You are in your twenties, after all."

Mosquitos buzzed around them as they waited in awkward silence to retrieve their orders. Praline ice cream in hand, he shook her hand goodbye and trekked toward campus. She waited until he'd reached the road and shifted into the darkness, between the streetlights. Then she pulled out her phone and dialed Noah. Sticky ice cream bled onto her hands before he finally picked up.

"What's up?"

"Noah, I think I've been traumatized."

His usually playful voice sobered. "What happened?"

A hysterical laugh bubbled in her stomach. "I think I just went on the worst date in the history of dates, but I wouldn't know." Since she had technically not been on a date before, she couldn't judge. "Can you—"

She chewed on her lip. Could she ask him to do this? Classes started tomorrow and some students had already started on homework. Professors assigned readings due on the first day. That reminded her, she had to get through the first fifty pages of *Emma* by tomorrow for her Gen Ed English class. Most seniors had extra core curriculum, and many had one or two Gen Ed classes to knock out before graduation.

Resolution surged into her throat. She'd gone through it tonight and shouldn't have to go through it alone. "Can you stop by that ice cream shop on campus? I don't think I want to be alone right now."

He didn't wait even a second. "I'll be there in five."

Chapter Six

"So why did you agree to this bet?" Noah dipped a cheese stick into a cup full of marinara sauce and crunched off the top. Mozzarella strings hung off his lips.

She sighed and scooped the remaining ice cream soup out of her bowl. Why did she crunch all the buckeyes first? Those peanut butter chocolates made up the best part of the dessert. "Jana will tell the campus that I'm a fraud if I can't find a date for myself. I checked her out on social media this past weekend. She has a decent following."

It turned out that Jana *had* joined a direct sales company for exercise and weight loss products. She must've done well, because she had a "k" in her Instagram following, and her posts received hundreds of likes.

"So you're going to force yourself to marry someone after a year?"

"No, not really." She crumpled her napkin and tossed it into the bowl. A woman in the table next to hers placed her maraschino cherry on her date's ice cream "Engagements can last a long time, and you can break them off if it doesn't work. Besides..." Em rubbed her palms up and down her knees, praising God that she didn't follow Gel Hair's suggestion to wear tights. The itchy fabric of those drove her crazy. "Maybe it's good for practical purposes, to be married. For taxes, and financial benefits, and two people paying the rent instead of just one."

"You just listed money as all your reasons for marrying someone."

"I mean, am I wrong?"

How many friends from her church back home joked that they would get married to each other by "thirty" just for the sake of being able to afford housing? No way could Em live with her parents while saving up enough to live on her own. They'd already hinted to her that once she graduated, she could kiss her old bedroom goodbye.

Never mind that they'd used what was left of her college fund on the failed salon. She often didn't try to think about her parents and the salon they'd built together. Her mom claimed that within a few years, they'd make back the investment.

They hadn't.

And it broke apart the marriage. Every time Em returned home from a break, she'd watch another string get cut from whatever fragments held together her parents' relationship.

"No, you're not." Noah handed a cheese stick to her. The sign of true friendship that could resist any opposition—shared food. "Still, I think it's awful to force yourself to go through with this. Even if you called off an engagement down the road."

She tore off the top of the stick with her teeth. Cheesy goodness melted in her mouth. At least this made up for her not getting mac and cheese tonight. "What do you mean?"

"I mean that if you think *this* date traumatized you, and don't get me wrong, it sounds super traumatizing—"

Shakiness had filled her limbs when she thought back to it. How easily he shoved her against a wall. Why hadn't she taken those self-defense classes campus offered during her junior year?

"—imagine the mental trauma you'd have to go through if you broke something off like that. I...have an older brother, as you know."

Indeed, she did. Em had met him freshman year, since both brothers happened to attend the same campus.

"During the dating phase alone, he and his girlfriend shared everything with each other. Dark secrets and all. They helped each other through some of their lowest points in life, saw the worst in each other. So, when they broke off their engagement, it was like something shattered in him. He hasn't really hopped into the dating pool again either. Except for a few misfires here and there."

Guilt squeezed her intestines. Could she make a guy, and herself, go through that? "My hands are tied, Noah. Even if I didn't take up the bet, you know that people would put me under this pressure eventually. My parents won't let me live with them after graduation, you know."

"I know." He nodded. "It's funny, really, Em. Most people don't need to take up a twenty-thousand-dollar bet to put themselves through this. How sad is that?"

Sad, she decided.

Very, very sad.

"Does that mean you're going to teach us how to do taxes?"

A master's student, leading their senior seminar class, scrunched her brows at the boy who had just raised his hand in the large arena style classroom. The only one big enough to fit a fraction of her senior class. "I'm sorry? Could you repeat the question?"

Harmony, beside Em, had created a paper Pacman. She grabbed it and started using it to munch on Em's arm. Em batted her away and gestured at her computer. "I'm trying to find you your first match. Stop letting him eat me."

"Yeah, well, Mr. Pacman is jealous. He wants me and only me for himself. Nom nom."

The boy, with his hand still raised, cleared his throat. "Sure. You just said 'Welcome to senior seminar class. Where each week, a master's student will walk you through important things to know for the future.' I'm just making sure that you're going to teach us taxes."

The master's student shoved her blocky glasses up her nose. Today, she was wearing a suit jacket and pencil skirt that didn't fit all that well. Em figured it aged her about ten years. "Umm, well—"

"Or," the boy interrupted her, "is this going to be the type of deal where you teach us stuff that doesn't really help us like imaginary numbers or that 'the mitochondria is the powerhouse of the cell'?"

"Umm, well—"

A cheer from a group of girls in the back dissolved Em's concentration on her laptop screen. She'd have to focus on this later. Maybe during the breakout groups the master's student had mentioned earlier, which would take place halfway through today's class.

A candle flickered in the back, and someone started a chorus of "Going to the Chapel of Love".

Em pinched her nose. Really? A Ring Sing?

Harmony's Pacman nudged Em in the side. "What is happening?" She squinted up at the lighted candle that was making its rounds around the rows. "I'm all for spontaneous singing, but this feels weird. Even for me."

"It's a Ring Sing"

"A what?"

"It usually happens in the dorms. They're not supposed to be interrupting class."

Especially not on the first day. Em grew accustomed to the Ring Sing early on her freshman year in the dorms. Whenever a girl got engaged, everyone on a wing would gather in a circle, sing "Chapel of Love", and pass around a lighted candle. When it reached the engaged girl, she'd blow out the flame and recount her story of her engagement.

This feels early though. What eager beaver proposed on the first day of school?

Em vowed to chuck the candle if it reached her, so the poor master's student could get on with her lecture, but it never did. It reached the eighth girl—a tan blonde with a sparkling ring on her left hand—and she blew out the flame. Several girls in the class whooped and hollered, and the engaged girl stood up.

"Guys, stooop. This is so embarrassing." She giggled at the master's student. "I'm sorry, but I guess—guys stooop—I guess I have to—stop it, stop it, you guys are ridiculous—I guess I have to tell the engagement story."

The master's student clutched at her elbows.

"I mean." She cleared her throat. "We don't have much time to cover today's talk, and the breakout groups are longer today."

"Guys, stop it." The blonde girl batted at one of her friends, who had a phone camera out. Perhaps to document the proposal story. "I'm sorry, but I guess they're insisting. It's tradition after all."

Someone in the front row started chanting "tradition". Everyone, except for Em and Harmony, joined in. Harmony, instead, chorused, "Down with the man."

The master's student hemmed and hawed until the calls of "tradition" grew so loud that the entire student body might as well have broken out into a *Fiddler on the Roof* production. She moved her hands up and down as if to quiet the volume. "Okay, okay, you can tell the story, but try to keep it quick, okay?"

The blonde girl shielded a laugh with her hand. She started talking about how her "besties" had brought her her favorite "pink drink" as a surprise that morning. "And I didn't think today could get any better..."

Harmony leaned in close to whisper, "So why is a Ring Sing such a big deal? Shouldn't we be celebrating people who go on to get their master's degrees, or jobs, or you know, become expert money launderers? There's just so much else to celebrate."

"Editor Girl thought so too." Em tapped her nose once.

"Who?"

"A professional writing major. You may know her. I can't remember her name, but she wrote a whole article for the Mansfield Mirror about it. Here, I'll dig it up." She flipped up her laptop lid and scanned through the Mirror archives. At last, she landed on the article. It was one of the few that Editor Girl had written. Most of the time, she served as a copy editor.

Cha-Ching Sing

An Editorial by Kailani Henreckson

You may have heard of the Ring Sing.

Even if you're a male on campus, no doubt you've witnessed the familiar chorus of "Going to the Chapel of Love". And we should certainly celebrate engagements. Relationships, after all, take hard work and lots of communication.

This, however, gives me pause. Why do we only seem to celebrate couples tying the knot, but not the main reason we've come to Mansfield in the first place: to get a job or to continue in higher education? As I ponder this, I wonder if we should implement a new tradition in the dorms. The Cha-Ching Sing. The beauty of it? It sees no gender. Men and women can participate.

How does it work?

Dormmates will sit in a circle. They'll start to sing, "Money, Money, Money" by ABBA, or the money-song of their choice. They will pass around a stapler. When that stapler reaches a person who accrued a job or master's degree acceptance at another university, the person will staple together the job application form/acceptance letter.

Then they can tell their interview stories.

I hope that we can create more traditions that can include all celebrations. After all, as much as I love a Ring Sing, I want to make sure that we can uplift all people on this campus. Or at least, most.

The blonde girl was still in the middle of her story. "And what would you know, my dorm mates had another surprise for me. Crumbl cookies. Can you believe it? I couldn't eat more than one, of course. Stop it! I'm so tiny, you *know* I couldn't eat more than one—"

Harmony finished the article and *hmph*ed. "Well it's no wonder why they didn't implement the Cha-Ching thing."

"Because most people can't hit ABBA's high notes?"

Harmony's lips twitched. "I mean, yeah, but also because none of the proposed people would ever let that happen."

Proposed people?

Someone beside her shushed them. Em rolled her eyes, scooped up her laptop, and paraded down the steps. She muttered something about a bathroom break to the master's student, who motioned for her to leave through the double doors. Harmony followed behind.

They parked in chairs outside of the room. Em rubbed her nose. "Sorry, can't focus on finding you a match with that story. That poor master's student..." She opened her laptop once more. "Anyway, what do you mean, Harmony?"

Harmony was busy shoving the Pacman origami onto her head like a hat.

"Harmony?"

"Right, whoopsies. Anyway, there's something I learned back home with my church ladies. You ready?"

"I don't know if I'm ever ready for anything with you, Harmony."

Students ambled past. Wind from their stride kicked up some posters on the announcement corkboard. Sure enough, a bright orange paper rested against a thumb tack. Good ol' Noah.

"Okay, well get ready anyway. I noticed how our church didn't really have a singles ministry. Which is weird because they have a women's ministry, a basketball ministry, heck, a pickleball ministry. So, I emailed them."

She took a dramatic pause.

Em clicked on one of the applications. Ooh, this Eli guy had some promise. He liked Star Wars and said that he was into nerdy girls. Maybe she'd found a match for Harmony. Speaking of Harmony, she hadn't talked for thirty seconds.

"You're supposed to ask me what happened."

"No."

"Okay, so what happened was they didn't email me back. So I sent one passive-aggressive email with a smiley face, and may or may not have included a knife emoji. I lose track of my emojis so easily."

Em gasped. "Harmony."

"What? It's like herding cats. Anyway, one of their peeps asked me to come into a meeting. And I was all like 'Yo'. And they were all like, 'Are you trying to amass an army or something'?"

Amass an army? "What? Harmony, that's awful."

"Yeah, they thought I was on some tirade against the church. Didn't help I was in my goth phase. Had a lot of people praying for spirits to come out of me and stuff. Funny, because we're Baptist. Anyway—" Harmony placed another Pacman on her head, since the other one had fallen. "I tried to explain to them that I wasn't trying to attack the church. The guy was sort of sympathetic, but he pulled me aside later and told me why he couldn't go through with it." She sighed. "He talked with the church board, and I guess when they suggested it to a control group, people flipped. The married people were all like, 'Why are we ministering to them? That's just encouraging them to stay single'." A shrug. "I guess they thought they deserved more ministry because they 'actually had some accomplishments to show for it' because they were married and stuff."

Em let the information sink like rocks into her gut. Did married people seriously think that single people deserved to be punished? Because they hadn't "earned" a relationship?

"Anyway." Harmony clicked her tongue. "That's why they'd never do the Cha-Ching thing. Because if everyone's special, no one is special. And people like to feel special. And." She tapped her ring finger. "There's a reason why the class didn't listen to the master's student. I'm an observer of things, Watson." She mimed plucking a monocle off her eye. "And if there's one thing I noticed, it was the absence of something. On her left hand, to be precise. Elementary. Tut-tut."

Em's memory blurred. Did the master's student not have an engagement ring or wedding band? Did people pay attention to those kinds of things? For being in the matchmaking business, she hadn't picked up on as many nuances as she'd hoped. Perhaps Jana had a point. The more she understood her clients, the better. "Are you trying to say that the engaged voices win out over the single voices?"

The usual brightness in Harmony's cheeks dimmed. "Let me put it like this. One of the married people in church told me, 'I love having conversations with single people, but they can't give me marriage advice. That's my rule'. And when I asked her, 'does that mean you can't give advice to single people about being single', she rolled her eyes. She said, 'I have more experience, so I can talk about more things'."

Em rubbed her fingertips up and down the fabric chair. *Did that woman seriously tell Harmony that 'all Christians are equal but some are more equal than others'? What in the* Animal Farm? "Well, Harmony, I'm not going to let that happen to you. Or to me. I think I found your first match. What do you think about your first date being named 'Eli'?"

Chapter Seven

"Gonna be honest, Watson, I'm not wowed by the name Eli." Harmony threw up jazz hands. "Lacks pizzazz."

"Oh my word, Harmony. Also, what's with this Watson business?"

Harmony shrugged. "Might have a brief Holmes phase, we'll see. Now are you sure there aren't any guys in that database with more appealing names like 'Gael' or even 'Rhoshandiatellyneshiaunneveshenk'?"

"What the— No, you can't pick someone based on just their name."

"You can if you want to be"—jazz hands—"pizzazz-ful."

"Okay, Sherlock, how about we take a look at some of his answers, shall we?"

Brightness from her computer screen dried her eyes. Dang, it must've been brighter in the lecture hall for her to have it cranked up this high. She clicked the dim button a few times and then pulled up his answers. "Okay, he says that a platypus is his favorite animal. That seems like something you'd appreciate in a person. I mean, I even had a Perry the Platypus keychain on my backpack sophomore year."

Harmony lifted herself from her chair and hovered behind Em. "Well, Perry the Platypus is a very charming character."

"Says he's nerdy."

"Like the candy? Should I taste his arm to check?"

"Oh my word, do not bite his arm to see if he tastes like Nerds candies."

"I think the most important thing is," Harmony lifted a finger and jabbed it at a water stain in the ceiling, "will he let me be weird?"

Em cocked her head. "What do you mean? You let yourself be weird, Harmony."

Harmony shook her head. For several seconds, perhaps to fan herself with her hair. "Not around Jana I'm not. I have to room with her, you know. And if anyone lacks pizzazz, it's her."

Em's throat constricted. She hadn't realized that Harmony had to stifle parts of herself with her roommate. That made sense, though. Plenty of girls her freshman year received quite a terrible pairing. One—a morning person, clean freak, and passive girl—ended up with a night owl/messy/assertive girl.

She had lamented to Em once, whilst tossing wrappers that littered her dorm room into a bin. "I swear that the school intentionally stuck us with our opposite so we could 'grow'."

That was Mansfield's favorite slogan: "Grow together." This meant that they would force everyone to do activities they didn't like. They even told the students they couldn't lock their dorm rooms during the day because, "it creates a very closed environment, not suitable for growth".

Come to think of it, that seemed dangerous. Making people not put locks on their dorms. Even though dorm rooms were separated by sex, and boys couldn't come over except for sparse Open House hours,

"Oh, Harmony." Em's eyelids squinched. "I know she hates my guts, but if you need to switch, Laila is an absolute gem of a roommate."

Harmony passed her a grateful look. "Can't ask that of you, Watson. It's only two semesters anyway. That's what's important to me, though. Is it a person I'm safe enough to be weird around?"

"Based on the survey results, yes, but I do interview people in person. To make sure they didn't lie. It's a matter of asking the right questions and reading body language."

"Right." Harmony dimmed.

"What's up?"

Harmony lifted one finger and pulled out a device. "Well, it's just that a guy and I hit it off at a professional writing class this morning, and I don't want to let him down."

She pulled open a social media app and scrolled through her followers. At last, she landed on one with the username @robthebuildercanhefixit?

Oh no. No, no, no, no, no. She recognized him right away.

Everything about the man screamed a neck beard from the—well, literal neckbeard—to the trench coat, fedora, darkened round Daredevil sunglasses, and 1800s cane he strolled around campus with, everything about him screamed that he did not understand nor accept social cues. He probably enjoyed talking like some medieval knight half the time. In Em's experience, plenty of guys like him asked for her services. Whenever she met those types for the interview, she got a major "ick" factor from them. Reminiscent of what she'd felt like on her date with Gel Man.

Even if Rob the Builder didn't act like the others, everyone would say she'd cheated when she matched Harmony with him. After all, people often asked her to pair them with someone "in or above their league". Weird as Harmony was, she didn't see her parading around the campus in trench coats calling people "m'lady". Unless she happened to be in an Victorian phase that week.

Now, how to phrase this carefully to Harmony? "Oh, wow, Harmony. He seems cool, but to be honest"—Em winced—"I'm not sensing the pizzazz from him."

Harmony frowned. "You're not?"

"Nope."

"Not even with that cool trench coat?'"

"How about…we give Eli a try? Get it? It rhymes."

Harmony considered this. "Well, I do like motivational phrases that rhyme."

Right as Em clapped her hands to say "great" the doors to the lecture hall banged open. Out popped the master's student. Dark circles highlighted her gray eyes. She waved to the girls.

"Oh, umm." Em motioned to the bathrooms down the hall. "We, er, just got out of those. Whoops. Better get to class."

The master student shook her head. "The proposal story is still going on. I don't blame you ladies. I went ahead and passed out the assignment for this week, but I didn't want you to miss out."

She handed a pink paper sheet to Em. Em read:

Assignment: Due August 31 by 11:59 PM (to be turned in online)

What it is: Meet with one of the master's students on the list below and interview them about their post-college advice. Turn in a 300-word essay on what you learned. Make sure to mention who you interviewed in the essay.

Before Em could scan the list, she found her eyes drifting up. Sure enough, no ring sparkled on the master's student's finger. Had Harmony spoken the truth about single people getting less of a voice? If so, would everyone in that class skip over her and ask another master's student to do the assignment with them?

Em cleared her throat. "I'm so sorry, I'm bad at names. What's yours, again?"

The other smiled. "That's all right. I have no chance of learning all of yours by the end of senior seminar. Especially if I don't get a chance to present." She gestured at the doors. "It's Zuri."

"Zuri. I'm Em. Would you like to get coffee and be interviewed for this?" She lifted the pink paper.

Zuri's cheeks matched the shade. She grinned wider. "I'd be delighted."

Em spied Eli in the student center. He poked a plastic fork into his salad, leaned his elbow against the chair, and threw up a lazy wave toward her. The dark hair and blue eyes screamed about every YA protagonist she'd read back in high school when she actually had time to peruse novels.

She returned his greeting and parked into the chair across from him. Up on the stage platform in the student center, where they occasionally had poetry slam nights, a boy strummed on an acoustic with a flock of girls semi-circled around him.

Something punched her nose. What kind of cologne had Eli doused himself with?

"Sorry I'm late." She motioned behind her. "Got caught up in a philosophy class. Had one of those students who liked the sound of his own voice."

Much as she enjoyed the company of a few philosophy majors on her ex-brother floor, many loved to debate for the sake of argument. They were the kind of students to hold over classes an extra five minutes as they debated with the Bible teacher as to whether "a person is made up of a body and soul" or "if a person is made up of a body, soul, and spirit".

Pretty sure I'm just made up of rage after that class.

"Not a problem." Eli winked. "Probably out stopping Dr. Doof." He made finger guns at her.

"What?"

"You know. You had that Perry the Platypus keychain back when we…" His words stopped. "Don't you remember psych class, sophomore year? We had to work on that one group project with those other three."

She felt her cheeks pink. "Oh, sorry, I'm horrible at remembering people sometimes. Sophomore year feels like forever ago. Anyway, yes, I do think I'm recalling you now."

She didn't. Not one bit. But that seemed to relax Eli a bit.

"As far as that Perry the Platypus keychain." She fiddled with one of the zippers on her bag. "That was a gift from one of my floor-mates. Like, don't get me wrong, I liked the show when I was a kid. But I'm not like a fan, fan. You know?"

His features sank. Did he want her to like a cartoon platypus?

"Sorry, I just assumed"—he speared a piece of romaine—"that you were nerdy and stuff because you liked that show. I misjudged."

"No worries. Speaking of nerdy..."

Her computer emerged from its purple cloth case. She opened the device and pulled up Harmony's survey results. "How would you feel about a girl who is a little over-the-top. Can be extra, but in an adorable way."

Something in his features melted. "Is she a serial killer?"

"No, unless she's in a serial killer phase I guess."

A playful look darted across his face. "That's hot."

Okay, weird response, but at least we're on track to finding some compatibility.

She eyed the next question and tried to ignore the delicious scent from the spicy chipotle ranch on his salad. After this, she'd have to grab a bowl herself. "Okay, and are you okay with an excessive wardrobe? Like, she may or may not show up to a date in a onesie?"

Eli cocked his head. "I mean, that's a little out there. But if she's game, I'm game."

"Great, so all to say, she can be weird around you."

"If she's into freaky, I'm into freaky."

What a weird way to phrase it.

"Amazing." She slammed the laptop shut. "There's a girl named Harmony, and I'd like to set you up on a date with her. Does tomorrow work?"

Eli blinked several times, as though stunned. Em thought back to Jana's last-minute date for her. It did take her a few moments to recover from that initial shock, but she did give Eli about twenty-four hours to prepare.

"Oh, it's with…" Eli snapped out of his stupor. "Sorry, I thought it was with—never mind. But yes, tomorrow should work. Will you be spying, like you always do? I've been told you watch out for the girls on the first date?"

Who'd spilled her trade secret? Fire Girl?

"Um, yes? I usually just like to make sure everything's going fine, and that everyone's comfortable."

"Perfect." He stabbed a tomato with his fork. "Looking forward to seeing you tomorrow, then."

Praise God that Harmony didn't opt for a onesie on this date. Instead, in her new Sherlock Phase, she sported a plaid skirt and hat to match. She lamented the fact that she left her corncob pipe at home.

"Harmony? How do you fit all the costumes into the closet? And how are you able to have so many for certain phases?" Em cocked her head as the two of them headed to the student center, the designated date spot.

Eli had texted Harmony earlier, asking for her Chick-fil-A order. He'd meet the girl at one of the tables.

"You don't tell me your trade secrets. I won't tell you mine."

Harmony then proceeded to skip all the way to the student center, with Em walking behind at a much slower pace. Harmony then held open the door for Em. About twenty students passed through the entrance before Em reached it.

"Umm, thanks Harmony."

"Of course. Can't let a door eat you. In you go."

They stepped inside and weaved around a crowd of students bunched up near the chapel area. Three times a week, most of the student body would meet in there in the mornings for a worship time and a message from some speaker. Her favorite part about it? The stained-glass windows. It painted the students in reds and blues and greens.

They located Eli nearest a column.

He held up two bags dabbed in grease stains. From here, Harmony booped Em's nose, giggled, and skittered off to the table.

Guess she's not one for hugs, then.

Em trailed the line that led to Chick Fil A and ordered an Oreo shake. Every once in a while, as the blenders whirred, she glanced over her shoulder. Harmony appeared to talk a lot with her hands, and Eli laughed. Not a bad start. At least Harmony hadn't thrown him off yet. Part of her wondered if Harmony reined back some of the weirdness on first dates.

Then why was she so herself around me at the Welcome Weekend Bash?

Before they'd headed to bed the night before, Harmony confided that weird people could sometimes sense safe people to be around. Maybe she felt that way around Em.

If so, guilt choked Em. She'd cast judgment on Harmony at first, and it took her a few hours to finally accept the girl as she was.

She retrieved her shake and headed to one of the high-top tables. More than once she noticed that Eli would sneak glances in her direction.

Can't tell if those are cries for help or gratitude.

Someone clapped their tray onto her table. She grinned. "What's up, Noah?"

"Spying on a date?" He hopped up onto the tall chair and thumped a straw against the table until the wrapper peeled.

"If you must know, it's for the Do Good thing. You're welcome."

Noah rolled his eyes and skewered the straw into his drink lid. Something moved in the corner of her eye. She glanced over and spotted Eli beckoning the two of them toward his table. Em and Noah exchanged a look. Then they hopped down and headed toward the seats Eli patted with his palms.

"Figured we could make this a double date."

Noah's eyes widened. "Oh, we're not—"

"Just friends," Em added.

"Well, the more the merrier. Harmony, here"—he chuckled—"was just giving me the rundown of her list of favorite Sherlock Holmes portrayals of all time."

"Ah, yes, thank you dear Mycroft." She aimed her chin toward the ceiling. "Now, onto number thirteen, Sherlock Gnomes."

To Em's surprise, the next hour didn't pass by as painfully as anticipated. Noah had switched the subject to talk about the first week of classes, and everyone shared in their woes of senior projects.

At the end of the date, Eli claimed he had an Art Appreciation project to work on. "But"—he pointed a finger at Em—"if I read your website correctly, we do get the first three dates free, right?"

I mean, if you match with Harmony, you get all of it free. But sure. We'll go with that for now.

Em had made sure not to tell any of Harmony's potential matches that they wouldn't pay the fee. That may have caused some unsavory characters to swoop in, just to get a free service.

Harmony bounced up and down. "Does that mean we can do a second one? Oh, I was so worried ol' Harmony scared you off."

"That's right, Eli. Three dates free."

"And," he thumbed his chin, "will you spy on the next two? To make sure dear Harmony is taken care of?"

I mean... She turned to Harmony. "Would you like me to?"

Harmony nodded no less than fifteen times in rapid succession. "I just feel more comfortable when I have friends close by." She cut a glance to Eli. "No offense. You're really nice. I just feel like I can be more myself if there's someone I know nearby."

"No, no." He splayed his hands. "I'm glad that she's watching. What a good friend she is."

With that, Eli stood, collected his trash, and fled the table. As Harmony squeezed Em's shoulder as a thank you, Em and Noah exchanged a quirky-brow expression.

What just happened?

Chapter Eight

"Do all the matchmaking dates go like that?" Noah asked, holding the door for Em as they exited the student center.

A brisk breeze brushed Em's forehead as they circled the loop around campus. As a sheen of sweat brimmed on her upper lip and forehead. Man, she didn't miss the dorms. "Well." She shoved her clammy fingertips into her shorts pockets. "Go like what, exactly?"

"I mean, are they that awkward? Or was it just—"

"Harmony," they finished together.

She chewed on her lip and dipped her chin at a student she knew who ambled past. "Again, well." Her thumbs rubbed and up down the fabric on her shorts. "A number of first dates can be awkward. It's usually by date two that the couple starts to get comfortable and can figure each other out. So I wasn't worried about that."

When coaching her clients, Em tended to break down the first three dates as such:

- **First Date:** No one is really themselves. As long as no one turns out to be sexist or a murderer, and conversation doesn't stall every few seconds, then it could turn into date number two.

- **Second Date:** Where people "shed their skin" as Laila would say. During this date, people let loose about their preferences and wants. She thought of poor clients who would tell her that their dates revealed they expected eight children in the marriage or no dice—or that they had an unreasonable laundry list of expectations. If the date survived this, then...

- **Third Date:** A date where they determined, "Make this a relationship or nah?" When she'd stepped onto Mansfield, it surprised her that it only took three dates for people to get to this point.

"There's an edge to your voice, Em."

She threw a dismissive wave as they rounded the corner nearest the Prayer Chapel. AKA the designated make out spot for most couples.

Soft piano music drifted from the building.

Huh, someone intended to use that place for its true purpose: worship and prayer. It was a smaller chapel tucked away on another part of campus from the main chapel.

Em sucked on her teeth as a car whirred past. Most student drivers went triple the speed limit signs posted around campus. "I think what weirded me out was the fact that Eli wanted me to watch. Most of the time it's the female who wants a spy."

"Yeah?"

"Yeah. I mean before Laila decided she wanted to be single forever—for a variety of reasons—she would tell me horror stories. About needing to text locations to her girlfriends and take pictures of license plates."

Noah let out a low whistle.

Em's thumbs gravitated to the belt loops in her shorts. "You didn't know this?"

"I mean, I'm in the theater a lot. The girls there are equally busy and don't even have time for Dash Dates most of the year. But yeah, it doesn't work like that for guys. We don't do the license plate thing at all."

"It's sad, really. The worst thing a guy has to worry about on a date is if a girl shaved her pits. A girl has to make sure she's not getting murdered that night."

How often did she worry for her matches? That maybe she didn't vet the guys enough and they'd hidden their true selves. Mom and Dad did that to each other for years. They settled into their actual personalities five years into their marriage—long past when they had their kid.

A shaky breath blew out of her lips.

At least she vetted most boys longer than she had for Eli. If only she hadn't shown up late to that meeting and taken more time to get to know him.

Noah must've sensed her tension. He drifted closer. "I'm sure Harmony is fine, and that Eli is too. Granted, my gauge of men is all the guys in the theater department who think it's okay to wear super tight leggings all the time."

That fissured any stress in her chest. Her shoulders dropped, and she laughed. "Eww, why would they do that?"

When she reached her apartment complex, she waved goodbye to Noah. They embraced in a sweaty hug, but still, she had to admit he didn't smell all that awful, despite the humidity. Using her keycard, she clicked herself inside and almost bumped into Jana in the door way.

"You." Jana held up two index fingers and rubbed them together, like sticks to make firewood. "Shame, shame."

Em quirked a brow and rushed past her to the kitchen. "Okee-dokie, then."

"You, girlie, skipped out on your date midway through. I just got word back from him. He says you got cold feet and noped out."

That jerk. Also, she doubted he would ever use the phrase "nope out", even if held at knifepoint.

Em swung open a cabinet and pulled out a bowl. Cereal for dinner didn't sound all that bad right now. "People skip out on dates all the time, Jana."

"Harmony didn't." Jana gestured at the first room down the hall.

Faint humming sounded from the closed door. This filled Em with a glow. Perhaps Harmony's date had gone better than she thought, if it left Harmony in a sing-y kind of mood.

"That's different." She scanned the options of cereal and landed on Honey-Nut Oats. "Harmony was having a good time—not being told that a woman must not pay and must raise a family and such."

Even in her periphery she spotted the eye roll from Jana. "Most of us suffer through those dates, girlie. We only skip out if we think we're in danger or if an actual emergency arises."

I bet he didn't tell you how he got in my face. Cold shudders ran up her spine. She shook them out and focused on pouring the cereal. *I don't have to prove anything to her.*

"If you keep skipping out on dates, girlie, I'm going to have to call a forfeit from you on the bet. Or, at the very least, inform people that you can't handle the very same dates you put people through."

Excuse me, I vet people, Jana. She would never have set up dates with horror movie villains like this.

Em's teeth clenched so hard she felt it in her molars. Great, she hated the family dentist too. She relaxed her jaw and closed the cereal box. "Fine, Jana, I won't skip out on any others, okay?"

"That's all well and good, but I still don't know if you've learned your lesson. So—as part of my matchmaking business—I'm going to make you go through what every other single person has to go through when they get too picky on dates."

Em's nostrils flared. She eyed the knife set on the countertop. Could she get away with murder? Would Harmony help her mop up the blood?

Granted, Harmony may have had a "serial killer phase" yet to be unearthed.

The silverware drawer banged open. "And what would that be, Jana?"

"Singles group at church. They help singles set *realistic* expectations for their dating life. It starts in thirty minutes."

Em roamed to the fridge. Wan light bathed her face when she opened the door. "How far's the church?"

"About twenty-five minutes."

She slammed the door shut. "Are you kidding me right now?"

"I'd also suggest an outfit change. Best to leave a good impression with the boys there."

Abandoning her cereal bowl on the counter, she huffed and marched to her room. Mid-change into a cute summery dress, she heard a knock at the door. She balled her fist and swung it open. "*What?* Oh." Her fingers relaxed. "Hi, Harmony."

"'Ello, Watson. I hear you're being subjected to a humiliating singles night at a church where some—as they say—'cringey' pastor tells you why you deserve to be alone forever."

"Umm, I guess that's one way to put it."

"Can I join you?"

Em didn't even ask why. Maybe Harmony got a kick out of how people acted at things like this, like some anthropologist would.

Swinging her key ring around her finger, Em motioned for Harmony to follow her out the door. By now, Jana had texted her the address. She plugged it into her GPS, and they whirred off onto the bumpy road.

Twenty-five minutes later—after Harmony recounted for her the highlights of her date and assured her that she had done well with her pick—they arrived at a non-denominational church. The architecture of the building screamed modern, with a lack of color and divots.

They stepped inside, where a swathe of girls gabbed near a name tag station.

Em squeaked a permanent marker across the rectangular label and scrawled her name. Beside her, Harmony drew a stick figure dead in a pool of blood for her name tag.

Lovely.

A shadow surfaced in her periphery. She turned and almost bumped into a guy who wore a tie-dye shirt. "Oops, sorry about that."

"Not a problem." His eyes squinched. "Haven't seen you around here before."

"Oh, yeah, roommate kind of forced me to go."

His expression softened and he snickered. "Yeah, I've heard that before and I—whoops." A girl tugged at the crook of his arm and yanked him away. "See you around, I guess."

Glares surfaced from several of the girls in the group. Em edged away toward a corner, where several posters advertised the international ministries the church supported.

Harmony zoomed toward her with Cheeto dust decorating her fingertips. She must've located a snack table. "Oooo, Em's in trouble."

"Harmony, have you heard of an inside voice before?" Em shied away from the resurgence of glares. "What in the world just happened?"

"Walk with me, Watson." Harmony advanced toward a dark hallway around the corner, and Em followed. "Are you any good at statistics?"

"What?"

"I'll let you in on a secret, Watson."

Harmony located a bench and parked on the arm. Em, like a semi-more-normal person, sat on one of the cushions. "When I'm in my Sherlock phase, I'm actually pretty good at math. After all, the great detective was. I'd hypothesize that there are at least three girls to every one guy here. Meaning—"

She didn't have to finish the sentence. *Competition.* "That's ridiculous." Em eyed the sign-in station for the kids ministry. The church had created a whole booth for that. "It's already a hard enough world for women. Why are we seeing each other as the enemy?"

"I mean, you see it at churches all the time. A new worship leader is on the scene and every girl boxes each other out to get to them. Because they believe there are limited pieces to the male pie. I wonder what male pie tastes like."

Let's not answer that question.

A few moments later, someone with a megaphone called everyone into the sanctuary. Harmony and Em situated themselves toward the back pews.

A worship leader with a mop of hair led them through several songs she didn't know. As he did so, Harmony filled out the prayer request slips found in the pew back pockets. Em squinted. "Harmony." She hissed between one of the songs. "Why are you asking for them to pray for your mad cow disease?"

"Gotta cover all bases. Prayer works in the past, present, and fu-ture—and I *may* have that disease in the future. You don't know."

Five songs later, the worship leader led them in a prayer, where he strummed the acoustic in the background. Lights danced on the stage. Em sympathized with some poor tech booth worker who had to work on a weekday evening.

They sat, and a larger ginger man, who looked to be in his thirties, jumped onto the stage. He held a microphone close to his lips, to the point where his whiskers scratched the windscreen on the mic. "Good evening, everyone."

A smattering of "whoos" and "good evenings" greeted him.

"Aww, c'mon." He rolled his eyes. "You can do better than that. Good evening, everyone."

Em decided within that moment that she absolutely hated him.

Once a louder "Good evening" met him, he nodded. "That's better. Now, tonight, I want to talk about expectations."

A slides presentation behind him showed a modern-style PowerPoint with sans serif font words proclaiming "expectations in dating".

"You all know I like to tell stories, so I'd like to tell one about a young lady who had a meeting with me a few weeks ago. I won't name names, because let's be honest," he planted his free hand on his hips, "this story is pretty embarrassing."

Em shrank into her pew. Something about pastors telling bad stories about others left a bad taste in her mouth. She always wondered why some of them could never tell humiliating tales about themselves.

"Now, this lady comes into my office and she's like, 'Scott, dating is the woorst'." Em winced as his imitation of what a woman sounded like. "And I'm like, 'Huh, okay, tell me more.' And she drapes herself dramatically over her chair and goes, 'Uugh'." He mimed the action. Chuckles bounced off the walls from the singles. "So I said, 'Umm, elaborate.' And she goes, 'All I want is a tall guy who makes lots of money and loves Jesus. What's so hard about thaaat?'"

By now, laughter roared.

Scott sobered and reached for a clicker on an elevated stand. The next slide read, "most singles have unrealistic expectations".

"Of course, I know what you're all thinking. 'Scott has no room to talk. He has a smoking hot wife.' And you'd be right. Stand up for everyone, sweetie."

A young woman, in the front row, rose and tossed a shy wave. Everyone clapped for her.

"But most of you are expecting someone like her. Guys, the Bible says looks fade. Especially—and I'm not trying to be sexist when I say this, it's just the facts—you ladies."

Em's intestines recoiled at this. Sure, yes, the girl in his office may have had an unrealistic expectation about the tall and money-making thing. But books like Song of Solomon existed too. Didn't some level of physical attraction need to exist in a relationship?

"Looks fade, girls. The Bible says it. That's why we're splitting you into breakout groups today, guys and girls. And we're having you each start in chapter one of a book. They'll be available for fifteen dollars. You can pay in cash, or on Venmo, or if you can't pay for it, talk with one of our leaders—"

Em groaned. Seriously? Something else to pay for?

By now, Harmony had filled out all the prayer cards in their row.

"Boys, you'll be reading chapter one of *Taking the Manhood back in Marriage*. I've noticed that a lot of guys in your age range have become passive when it comes to headship. This book will help you to re-embrace the biblical role that has been created for you. And ladies…" He held up a red book with a blocky white font. "For you I have, *Settling for God's Best: How to Overlook Looks and Look Deeper at the Heart*. All right, time for our second point—"

Em shielded her eyes with her hands and leaned onto Harmony's shoulder. "Harmony?"

"Yes?"

"Is this what being tortured feels like?"

Harmony thought about it for a moment. "Nah, I'd take the rack over this."

Chapter Nine

Settling for God's Best: How to Overlook Looks and Look Deeper at the Heart

by Barry E. Smith

Chapter One

There was a young man in my office, and he was in tears. Now, most of the guys in my office had some kind of addiction—if you catch my drift, ladies. I braced myself for the inevitable, "Pastor, I don't know how to stop this. Please help."

I handed him a box of tissues and leaned back in my chair, waiting for the confession. He rubbed his red-rimmed eyes and glanced at me. "Pastor, I'm never going to find a wife, am I?"

I leaned forward. This sounded different than how the start of most meetings went. "Go on, Wilson. Why do you think that? You're a man of God, you help volunteer at the church regularly, and you have a heart for families. You'd make an excellent husband and father someday."

Wilson shook his head. "No, Pastor. Women are looking for, like, Brad Pitt or something. They take one look at me, and I don't have a chance."

For the greater portion of that half hour, I comforted Wilson—wishing I could tell off whatever young lady made him feel this way.

Looks Aren't Everything

One of the hardest truths for us to accept in life, ladies, is that you're not going to be marrying a supermodel. If you do, congratulations, but we always congratulate the exception and follow the rule.

The truth is: if you cry out to God that he hasn't provided your future husband yet, he's probably rolling his eyes at you. He's probably thinking, "Well, gee, Marsha. I sent you ten very nice men, but you turned them down because they didn't have drop-dead gorgeous looks."

Scripture tells us, "Charm is deceitful, and beauty fades."

Did you hear that, ladies?

Beauty *fades*. It doesn't last, and since it doesn't stick around forever, we shouldn't make that a priority.

Odds are, if you can't find a man, you've probably overlooked some true spiritual lookers. In our next section, we'll describe how to manage realistic expectations—so you can finally settle. Settle for the best that God has for you...

"Harmony." Em collapsed onto her bed when they'd returned from the singles group that evening. "Any chance we can dig up that author's address and murder him in his sleep?"

Em counted her blessings that she hadn't spotted Jana upon their return to the apartment that night. Because she may have committed at least one homicide that evening.

She rubbed her eyes to erase the memories that kept surfacing—images of their breakout group where girls went around the circle to read a couple paragraphs each from the book. Or the discussion after, prompted by Scott's "hot wife", about how women needed to create a list of what we expected in a "future husband" and to "cross at least five of those expectations off of said list".

Harmony perched on the corner of the bed. "I mean, you gotta hand it to Jana, Em, this isn't really unusual."

Em stuffed a pillow over her face and groaned into the softness. It muffled her agonized cry. She threw it against the wall, next to her octopus-shaped stuffies. Her parents had gotten those for her birthday. She wasn't sure why, because she'd never stated a love for those sea creatures. "How do you know so much about the dating world, Harmony?"

Harmony shrugged and then ran her fingers up and down the fuzzy blanket on Em's bed. "Honestly, Em, because I've gone through the thick of it. When you told me that you were going to set me up, I was super freaked out. Not only because I was flirting with that guy in the professional writing department—"

Right, Rob the Builder.

"—but because I'd promised myself that I'd never put myself out there again. I swear that one more bad relationship will break me."

This was the most seriously Harmony had spoken to her since they first met at the beginning of Welcome Weekend. Weird people had solemn sides too.

Em winced and sat up in bed. "Girl, I'm sorry I did that. We don't have to keep going with the Eli—"

Harmony shook her head. "The first date was really fun. And the second date tomorrow will be even better."

Shoot, she hadn't realized the two of them already arranged that. Em pulled out her calendar app to make sure she could make that time. Evening seemed free enough.

Wait a minute.

An email from Zuri, the leader of Senior Sem, blinked at the top of her screen with the subject "Meeting Time Tomorrow?".

She tapped the notification and read:

Hi, Emerson,

I just checked my schedule and realized I double-booked myself tomorrow afternoon with another student. She says she can't meet any other time. Is it possible that we can meet in the evening? For an extra incentive, I'm making some scones in my apartment that evening. If you're a fan of blueberry, then you're in luck.

Thank you for understanding, and let me know if sometime around 7pm works.

Sincerely,

Zuri Becker

Light died in Em's phone. She offered a wince-y expression to Harmony. "Sorry, girl, but I may not be able to spy on your date tomorrow. Are you and him going to be okay alone in the—why am I smelling nail polish?"

Harmony had purloined one of the nail polishes off Em's desk and was painting shapes onto her legs. "It's fine. I think Eli was the one who wanted more of a watchful eye anyway." She capped the polish and showed off a sloppy flower. "Besides, the second date is where you can be more yourself. If he can't handle me then..." She paused. "I'll try not to break this time. I'll try."

It was sad that it wasn't even a relationship yet. Would one bad date sour Harmony for a long time? Em chewed on her lip. The word "try" didn't sound all that promising.

Em's backpack hung heavy on her shoulders on the way to the off-campus apartments. Just a mile away, they made for an easy walk from the on-campus halls. Pink clouds formed streaks in the skies. Right before she reached the complex, she rattled off one more text to Harmony.

She'd peppered the poor girl with about ten this morning, filled with last-minute reminders and encouragements.

Em: If you need me to drop everything and run over, I'll do it. Just say the word, and I'll ditch the meeting. I know the August 31 deadline is coming up for the assignment, but maybe I can ask for an extension or something. Or email her the questions.

As she clicked "send", she wondered why she hadn't thought of that before. In-person interviews took way too much effort to set up.

Harmony would know. She'd told Em stories over breakfast that morning of how her journalism department at her previous school would force all newspaper interviews to take place in person, "or at the worst, over a phone call."

"I guess it has something to do with in person interviews being more authentic and less doctored—" She popped a dehydrated Lucky Charms marshmallow into her mouth. Harmony didn't like milk in her cereal. Made it too mushy, she claimed. "The problem, though, is lots of administrative people don't like the paper. Probably because the paper could leak out that they've been hiding things. That they've been using money from the students for things we don't need. So they purposely 'cancel' in-person meetings last minute so that we couldn't get a proper source for that week's article. If we don't have a quote from them, it's just speculation as to what they're doing."

From what Em could gather, the better the title of a person, the more weight their quote held in a news piece.

Within seconds, Harmony responded. First with a knife emoji.

Harmony: Whoops, sorry

Harmony: My emojis get loose sometimes

Harmony: Come back knife-y boy! Yoohoo!

Then another.

Harmony: Anyway, I'll be fine

Harmony: I'm at the place now, and it looks like he's walking up

Harmony: It'll be ice cream, and a potential stabbing *knife emoji*
No biggie

Em convinced herself that she would just have to get used to Harmony associating herself with sharp objects more often. She located the right apartment door and knocked.

Zuri swung it open seconds later and motioned her inside. "Quickly, before Death gets out."

Wondering if she'd somehow entered a dream where people say the most ridiculous things, Em stepped inside and noticed a pile of black floof at her feet. The kitten mewed.

"Sorry about that." Zuri scooped up the kitten. Scents of blueberries warmed the whole apartment. "Death's newly acquired, and he's quite the escape artist."

Mischievous green eyes darted at her. Once again, Death mewed.

"You wanna hold him?"

Em considered herself to be more of a dog person. She missed her ninety-pound white fur baby known as "Bear" back at home. But she did prefer animals to humans, so...

"I would love to." She received Death from Zuri and cradled the now-vibrating fluff pile in her arms. Em traversed to the futon and parked.

"Sorry, it's not much. The apartment, I mean."

As a change of pace, Zuri was sporting harem pants and a tank top today. Although she wasn't technically a *teacher* teacher, Em thought it strange to see a professor in pedestrian clothing.

At least, in a non-frumpy outfit, Zuri could pass for very beautiful. Her body formed pretty angles, the kind that would make even runway models envious.

"Do you have a garbage disposal in your sink?" Em stroked the neck fur on Death.

"Um, yes?"

"Then you're already fancier than me. Campus apartments do skimp on just about everything." Except for AC.

Em had vowed that when she left school, she'd never complain about housing again. It seemed silly to her that her parents used to gripe about having a house near the train tracks by a busy road. She'd take that any day over footsteps and screams pounding the dorm at all hours, thanks to thin walls.

Her phone buzzed, which caused Death to ricochet and zoom toward the hallway, near the bedroom door. She frowned at the device as a picture from Eli surfaced. He'd taken a selfie with Harmony at the ice cream shop. He must have had some poor camera angle skills, because half of her face didn't show up in the photo.

Eli: We wish you were here, haha

Eli: Having a good time!

At least their date appeared to go well thus far. She prayed that he'd let Harmony be more herself. Some of the tension in her temples ebbed.

Zuri sheathed her hands in Peanuts-character mitts, and "Snoopy" yanked open the old oven. She reached in and pulled out a pan full of browned scones. Once she clacked the pan down on the stovetop, she shut off the oven and threw the mitts back into a drawer. "We'll let those cool for a little bit. Now, you wanted to ask me some questions for your senior sem assignment?"

A nod. Em unzipped her bag and pulled out her laptop. She opened it to the instruction sheet for the paper. In boldface, it read, "Make sure to interview the master's student in person."

Ah, now she remembered. That explained why she couldn't email Zuri any interview questions.

"I was wondering"—A Google docs blank document materialized—"since we're allowed to ask about any topic post-graduation...if you'd be willing to talk about what dating's like after college."

Zuri had just parked in a bean bag chair. Her brows drew together. "Oh, erm." Zuri picked at something in her nails. "Wouldn't you rather ask one of the master's students who are currently in a relationship that kind of question?"

She's saying she's not successful at relationships and, therefore, doesn't have room to answer.

"The assignment's all about perspectives, right? I don't see why your perspective is worth less than anyone else's."

"Hmm." Zuri bit a nail bed, realized she was being watched, and clasped her hands in her lap. "Well, I suppose it's better than the questions I got earlier on how to do taxes." She lifted and dropped her shoulders. Chunky bracelets jangled together on her arms. "I mean, no one really knows how to do them. We're all guessing and hoping the IRS doesn't come after us."

Good to know.

Before Em could look at her list of questions, she spotted another message from Eli. He'd sent one of Harmony trying to smash his face with an ice cream cone. He followed this up with a smiley emoji. *Is Harmony's phone not working? Is she having him send these?*

Focus, girl, on the assignment. You have to write three hundred words before midnight.

"Right, umm, I guess my first question is, what's something about dating post-college that you didn't expect."

Zuri considered the question, digested it. "Well, I suppose the first thing would be the unrealistic expectations I've seen in men."

Images flickered from the singles night from less than twenty-four hours ago. "Wait, you said *men* have unrealistic expectations. Not women?"

Zuri bobbled her head from side to side as if saying, "sometimes". "Depends on the woman, but in my personal experience, men are looking for some pretty unrealistic things."

Em's fingertips clattered the keyboard. "Could you elaborate?"

Zuri's features darkened. She opened her mouth, closed it, considered. Proceeded, "Well, this is rather personal, but something I found out is that most men won't date you if you cannot provide them with biological children."

Em's fingers froze.

Yet another text from Eli blinked on the screen. She ignored it, but still spotted the message sent after a photo.

Eli: You're such a good friend for setting us up :)

She blinked, registered. "Hold up, did you say *biological*?"

"Let's just say men are unfamiliar with certain conditions such as PCOS and Endometriosis. These can lead to a high chance that a woman can't have kids. Three men who I dated found out I had one of these conditions and broke it off." Zuri blinked away a glaze in her eyes. "When I mentioned there were options like adoption, foster care, even being spiritual parents to those who we met at the church, they wouldn't hear of it. Said that it was our duty as Christians to 'be fruitful and multiply'."

The last phrase choked her.

Em typed fast and fought the urge to place her hand on Zuri's shoulder in a gesture of comfort. Heat sizzled her skin as another message from Eli popped onto her screen.

Eli: We're thinking about making our third FREE date that dance happening this weekend

Eli: You down to come with that friend of yours?

Eli: So we can make it a double date?

Ugh, I'll deal with that later.

"I'm sorry." Em felt Death weave around her legs. She scooped him up and placed him in her lap. Claws dug through the fabric on her flowy summer pants. Since Zuri was wearing similar pants, Em wondered how she stood claws like this. "We can talk about something else. Just give me a few minutes to change to my initial questions."

"No." Zuri said it soft, fast. Then her expression melted. "I don't get to talk about this all that often. It may be good to do so. Healing even."

Em nodded and nudged Death to his blanket on the futon. Then she returned to her laptop. "Okay, question number two..."

Chapter Ten

"Oh, Em, it's so romantic that the third date is dancing." Harmony flounced around Em's dorm room in a fuchsia tutu skirt. She'd claimed she'd briefly entered her "romantic phase" for tonight's date only. "Everyone knows that dancing leads to love. The movies say so, so it must be true." Harmony's tone sounded tongue-in-cheek.

Em couldn't always detect tones, another gift from autism. But she was rather sure Harmony was being silly here.

The door squeaked open, and Laila gawked at Harmony with wide eyes. "Oh my word, that's a lot of pink."

"Hey, Laila!" Em waved at her from behind a laptop screen. Assignments and Jana's escapades had gotten her far behind reading surveys from potential matches. Several frantic emails lined her inbox, from students waiting to hear that she'd received their information.

If Jana sets me back anymore, she'll run me out of business.

Laila slammed the door and rubbed her eyes. "I think you're going to burn these out of my socket, Harmony."

Harmony halted and frowned down at her hot pink number. "You think it's too much?"

Em closed her laptop lid, eyes dry from hours of work. "I mean, you said that the date went well yesterday, right? And you were plenty yourself then."

When Em returned to the dorm, Harmony had tackled her and told her about how she and Eli talked for hours about their favorite animes and debated the Star Wars series that should've have been technically canon. "He mostly nodded and said, 'mm-hmm' a lot, but he was leaning forward, and you said that body language is good, right?"

Maybe Eli simply didn't understand social cues and thought he needed a spy on all dates, or wanted to exist in group date settings.

Lots of shy kids go to this school. Students ranged from homeschooling backgrounds, to missionary kids, to Christian private school students who had to "leave room for the Holy Spirit" at former Proms and Homecomings. No wonder no one knew how to navigate the dating waters. No one had taught them how to do it.

Laila's teeth sucked in air. She blew it out. "I mean, I'm not going to stop you, girl. But you may want someone to do a little makeup. Even though it's a hoedown, it's probably important to get glammed up."

Every year, after the first week of classes, Mansfield held a "hoedown". Most students arrived in overalls and cowboy hats and would gallop in line dances to their heart's content. Harmony would certainly stand out in her "Pretty in Pink" number.

Harmony parked on Laila's bed, her skirt consuming most of the green bedspread. "To be honest, I had a looong tomboy phase in middle school, so I never really learned."

Laila's red-lipsticked lips twitched. "Lucky for you, I had quite a bit of practice back when I did cheer in high school. Be right back." She left and returned moments later with eyeshadow palettes and brushes in hand. Laila waved one of the latter in the air like a wand. "Also lucky for you, I just shampooed these. So, you'll get some nice clean brushes for today."

Em knew enough about makeup—thanks to her mom's salon—to understand the lotion type stuff Laila rubbed in her palms was a primer.

Harmony shut her eyes, lips barely parting—as though fearful that she'd get a mouthful of the white liquid globs. "Are you going to the hoedown tonight, Laila?"

The other snorted. "Nah, not really my thing. Dances and couples type of things."

Harmony's eyebrows narrowed. Confused.

Em set her laptop at the foot of the bed. "What she means, Harmony, is that she isn't planning on dating anyone anytime soon."

"Ever."

"Right, ever."

There was something beautiful about seeing Harmony's smile, especially when she kept her eyelids closed. "What? That's so cool. Paul and Jesus would've rooted you on. I wish..." Harmony steepled her fingertips in her lap. "I wish I wasn't so into the idea of kissing and stuff. I feel like it would just be easier that way."

Laila pursed her lips and tossed Em a painful look.

Ah, I know that one well.

During their first few semesters at college, Laila would have to explain time and time again to people as to why she didn't have any interest in marriage. People would meet her with cocked heads and dismissive, "Well, you'll change your mind when you find the right guy."

Laila wiped off her hands and rubbed some concealer onto the fingertips. She must've nabbed Harmony's foundation from the bathroom. "I mean, I guess some people could say that. But it's not like I don't feel like I'm in kissing moods, Harmony. That happens to me all the time."

Harmony squinted underneath the foundation slathering. "Hmm?"

"Let's just say I learned that it's probably better for me to be single. I'm not mad about it. It's freeing in a lot of ways. But after a lot of prayer, that's what I decided is best for me personally...I—" Her nose ring wrinkled. "I still get a lot of flak for it though."

When Laila stopped her lathering, Harmony opened her eyes. Laila reached for one of the smallest brushes, rubbed it in one of the circular pink eyeshadow palettes, and tapped the brush to release some of the pigment into the air.

"Why do you think people do that, Laila?"

A soft laugh bubbled in Laila's throat. "People push back against things they don't understand. They've been told by every movie and book that romantic love is the end-all, be-all. So, when someone chooses to stay single, they can't understand it. Close your eyes, please."

Em fought the urge to wrap Laila in a hug. That would, of course, ruin the pink smear she had going on Harmony's upper lid.

"Still, I hope you have a good time tonight." Laila moved the bristles over the bright pink shadow again. "I've heard this is some kind of dream guy, huh?"

Harmony's legs kicked against the thick wooden frame of the bed, almost nailing Laila in the shins. "He's been really checking off all the boxes. I just can't believe it. After all those awful dates, we finally landed on someone nice."

Several layers of makeup later, Harmony was deemed ready enough for the dance. Still, Em offered to curl the girl's hair, until they had to fumigate the room from hairspray fumes.

Arm-in-arm, the two of them headed to the gym, stationed near the dining commons. This was only place on campus large enough to house the thousands of students who would make it out for the hoedown. Even with the large venue, speakers blasted on the lawn for the overflow crowd.

There, in pink cowboy boots, Eli tipped a matching ten-gallon hat at them. Noah lingered nearby. The boys must've arrived at the event first.

Harmony squealed. "Oh my goodness, you remembered what I told you I was going to wear." She clapped her hands and jumped up and down.

Eli's eyes widened upon taking in the dress. "Wow. You weren't kidding about that."

She gave a twirl and the tulle skirt fanned out.

Noah sidled next to Em. Something about this motion caused Eli's expression to twitch. First to solemn, and in an instant, a smile. "What say we dance?" He offered his arm to Harmony. With glee, she took it.

The speakers rumbled the ground with "Cotton-Eye Joe".

None of them could remember the moves quite correctly, and they ended up spinning half the time. Em's mouth ached during the next three line dances from all the jumps, shuffles, and rotations. She had no idea how public-school kids did it—with real dances as opposed to line ones. Her parents had sent her to a private Christian middle school and scooped her out for homeschool when salon funds ran dry.

After the Cupid Shuffle, the speakers announced that it was time for a slow dance between couples. Em and Noah exchanged a look, then dissolved into a fit of giggles.

"Time to sit?" He motioned at a lawn nearby. Students had parked in all available benches.

"Sounds good."

Someone jumped between the two of them—Eli. "I was actually thinking about grabbing me and Harmony a drink." He gestured inside a building next to the gym, the held an indoor basketball court and track. "I hear they have some snacks and such in there. Care to join me to get Noah one, Em?"

"Umm?" She glimpsed Noah, who shrugged. "Sure."

Shakiness filled her calves as they headed toward the doors. Man, she'd need to work out more in the gym if she could find the time. She remembered how a woman at her local Mansfield church had scoffed at her during junior year when Em admitted that she didn't visit the gym on campus all that often. "That's a shame. What I wouldn't give to be able to go to the gym for free."

Em fought the urge to mention to that woman that the membership wasn't technically free. The school charged a $20,000 a year in tuition. And even with her $10,000 academic scholarship, she still paid to attend the school and go to that workout center.

Not to mention I have to maintain a 3.7 GPA or higher, or they'll take away that scholarship. Hence her need to hit the books more than the bench press.

When they reached the doors and stepped inside, she gasped at the cool air. Oh, AC, how she missed it.

She first noticed the lack of students when they stepped onto the indoor track. Spare hurdles lined the lap lanes, she assumed, for the athletic students to practice for their meets. Eli parked onto one of the bleachers stationed against a blue-painted wall. Em frowned at the basketball courts.

"I thought you said there'd be drinks in here."

"Maybe they didn't deliver them yet. We're pretty early in the hoe-down."

Weird.

He patted the bleachers beside him. "I'd like to talk with you about Harmony. Get some advice."

Sourness twisted her stomach, but she didn't know why.

I mean, the matchmaking comes with coaching. And because I've been so busy, I haven't been able to offer Eli as much help as I usually give.

No wonder he'd messaged so much the other day. Maybe he needed someone to hold his hand throughout the process.

She nodded and padded over to the bleachers. Shortness of breath still restricted her lungs, and she prayed they would roll out some drinks with flavor soon so she could disguise the dry smell from her breath. Good thing Noah wasn't an actual date. She would've packed mints or something, had that been the case.

Coolness from the metal bit against her skin. She'd opted for a shorter BoHo-style dress. No overalls existed in her closet, so this was the closest she came to hoedown fashion.

"How can I be of assistance?" She fingered the fringe at the end of her dress.

He sucked in a breath and let it out long and slow. "Okay, this is going to be hard for me to say, so bear with me. And go easy on me, okay?"

Oh boy, he didn't like Harmony and wanted to break it off, didn't he?

Harmony had said something like this would break her, especially after all her bad experiences before. With a shaky breath, Em glanced up into the buzzing lights that circled the indoor track. Everything in here smelled of sweat and gym equipment.

"Okay?" She winced and braced herself for—

"I don't really like Harmony."

She could work with this. Tell Harmony that she could find her another guy. Maybe over a few pints of ice cream or cookie dough and a chick flick, she could help Harmony bounce back. "Okay, that's fine, Eli. I don't expect my clients to like everyone I set them up with—"

"I like you."

Quakes filled her lungs once more, and she choked. It took her several seconds to realize that, yes, he did say that out loud.

She blinked several times. "I'm sorry, what?"

Boys had told her this information before. Thanks to a "no dating until you're eighteen" rule from her parents, she'd dodged most crush admissions in high school. They took her rejection a little hard, but she could blame her parental units for that.

Now...

"I've been smitten with you since psychology class sophomore year." He tucked a strand of hair behind his ear. "I figured you wouldn't notice me. Even when we worked on a group project together, we had separate tasks, and I knew I just didn't have a chance with a girl like you.

You know, someone who is so successful and talented and likes to help others.”

Eli bit his bottom lip.

Oh, goodness, what was happening?

“So when you set up your matchmaking services, I decided to give it a try this year, after I broke things off with someone else.”

Oh no. She pressed her index finger and her thumb against the bridge of her nose and squeezed. *Wake up. Please let me wake up from this.*

“I tried to fill out the survey based on things I thought I knew about you. The platypus thing, for instance. But I guess you misunderstood and set me up with someone else.”

This explained why he wanted her to spy on all his dates. He hoped to spend time with Em, not Harmony.

“I wanted to prove it to you, though. That I could be a nice guy. That I could do whatever my date wanted me to do. Be what she wanted me to be. I proved it with Harmony—” He snatched her hand in his. She tugged it, but his grip tightened. “Let me prove it to you.”

At last he released, and her arm recoiled toward her lap. Shivers ran up her spine from her last experience with Gel Guy. She scooted a few inches away.

“Em?”

“If you wanted to ask me out, why didn’t you do it? Why did you have to hurt my friend in the process?”

In her periphery, he blinked several times. “I assumed she was a client, not a friend. And besides, would you have given a guy like me a chance? Or would you have gone after some Chad who would’ve broken your heart?”

She found it weird how guys on campus would refer to good-looking guys as “Chad”.

Considering his questions, Em searched her mind. Of course, if a guy apart from Noah asked her out to coffee, she wouldn’t have said no. Even with her lack of interest in dates before the bet, she knew from her clients the amount of courage that even asking took. She would've given them at least one date, maybe more.

Wait, why would she have been cool with *Noah* asking her out?

She shrugged off the thought. He was a good friend. At the very least, she'd be comfortable on a date with him.

"I would've, actually. But"—she lifted a finger and rose from her seat—"now that chance is gone. If you wanted to ask me out, you should've done exactly that."

Eli's cheeks pinked, and he shoved himself up. He jumped off the bleachers onto the floor and balled his fists. "You know what, Em? You're just like every other girl on this campus. Not willing to give nice guys a chance." He huffed. "And besides, you're not really that pretty. So I don't know why you think someone like me is beneath you anyway."

With that, he charged out of the room and banged a door shut. Moments later, someone crawled out from underneath the bleachers. Harmony.

She grimaced at Em and waved. "Surprised he didn't see me when I crept under here."

So much shock had overtaken Em that she hadn't either. Her voice cracked. "Oh, Harmony, I'm so sorry. I should've vetted him more, I should've—"

Harmony wicked a tear from beneath her waterline. Streaks from the mascara Laila had put on her formed little rivers down her cheeks. "It's okay, Em. But I think... I think I broke."

Chapter Eleven

DATE #2 FOR EM (September)

"Sorry, I'm a little late."

Em forced a smile at the guy as he parked into his chair. She sneaked a glance at her phone, which now read 6:43. He was supposed to meet her at the English-style pub at six.

"No worries." She swirled her straw in her water. She'd ordered that for both of them. "The wait was fifteen minutes, so I haven't been at the table *too* too long."

Part of her had wanted to hop back into her car around the six-thirty range, but she thought back to how Jana reacted to her the first time she ditched a date. She'd forced Em to go to that awful singles group.

Em had signed up for helping with the set crew on that day every week so she could get out of future meetings. Jana still encouraged her to finish the readings for the book the singles group had assigned. "Every single Christian girl has read a book like that. If you want the full experience, you need to finish it."

Last night's chapter had dealt with meeting the physical needs of a future husband and the biblical grounds for it. She'd fought the urge to gag about seven times.

"Right." The guy picked up a menu and shielded his face with it.

A server nearby bustled to their table and held up a notepad. She tapped her pen against the sheet and cleared her throat. "Have we thought about what we're getting tonight?"

She'd stopped by the low-top no less than five times to ask if Em would like to put in an appetizer. Em winced. From what she learned from her friends who worked in restaurants, the servers only worked a certain number of tables in their section. If someone took forty-five minutes to place an order, that could prevent a high-tipping customer from getting into that table in a timely manner.

"Nope. Not yet."

Itchiness clawed at Em's throat. This happened in uncomfortable situations. She mouthed a sorry to the server who chirped, "No worries." Still, she failed to hide the eye roll as she spun around and headed to another table.

"So." Em fiddled with ends of the British-flag-style tablecloth. Scents of fish and chips and sticky toffee pudding saturated the air. "I hear from Jana that you're a computer science major. Tell me more about why you like that."

He shrugged, face still shrouded by the menu. "I don't know. I've always enjoyed coding, and it makes good money, so it made sense."

"Haha, for sure."

Silence.

At this juncture, most people would ask a "how about you" question. She pretended he had, and squeezed a lemon into her water as she spoke. "Well, I chose PR and Marketing, because I saw how much my parents' business really needed it. I honestly think it could've saved them. I want to do something to help all the little guys out there that get overshadowed by big businesses."

"Mm-hmm."

More silence.

After they finally placed their orders, five minutes later, she decided to kick things off with another question. "So, why did you choose Mansfield? I know everyone has their reasons."

"I got a pretty big scholarship, and my parents went there before." Silence.

"Oh, cool. I went because I absolutely fell in love with the campus when I visited. I loved the small campus feel and how you could get involved in so many activities. And I knew they had a really good PR program. At least, that's what they told me. The representative who stopped by my homeschool co-op really sold it for me. The people, the really good PR major, the—"

"I forgot my wallet. Can you grab the check tonight?"

"Oh, um, sure."

They didn't say more than five words the rest of the evening.

Date #3 for Em (End of September)

Em squinted at this pick from Jana. A guy with nice eyes and a hobo type of beard. She frowned. No matter from which angle she looked at him, the thought of kissing him or even exchanging a hug sent her intestines wriggling.

He cracked a crab Rangoon and handed her the other half. "Now, Em, you were telling me about how you enjoyed helping with the local theater when you were in high school; can you tell me a little more about that?"

He leaned forward and pressed his chin onto his fist. Leaning forward, that meant he liked her.

Thoughts drifted back to the singles group and the assigned reading for that. Nothing about this man screamed attractive to her.

But he was sweet. Should she keep the dates going with him if she writhed at the idea of doing anything physical with him?

"Sure, so I really loved the fact that I could take someone who was shy and really help them break out of their shell—" Oh gosh, Rangoon flecks got lost in the tangles of his beard. A greasy smear of hair on his head sent her questioning how often he shampooed that thing. "—and it was just beautiful to see everyone working together to create a product together. That's what I love to see. People becoming more than they've been before."

"Wow." Sparkles ignited his eyes.

Her nose wrinkled at his scent again. He'd worn cologne, that was for sure, but a musky sort of tone that activated her gag reflex. On second thought, maybe that wasn't cologne. She couldn't tell.

You're being really selfish by not being into this guy.

After all, how many of the dates thus far had ended in disaster? At least this one held a conversation, unlike the British Restaurant Guy.

The man leaned back, eyebrows raised. "Is something wrong?"

"Nothing, I..." Her stomach squeezed. "Can I be honest?"

There was no way she could say, "I'm not attracted to you." No matter how many guy dating experts told females to "tell the truth", the truth stung. She was certain this guy could've attracted other women on campus, just not *her*.

Her mind reeled on how to spin the words in just the right way to communicate the truth, without impaling him.

"Of course."

She winced. "I'm just...don't get me wrong, I'm loving this conversation we're having, but I—"

"You're not feeling it?"

"Yeah." Her shoulders relaxed. "It's not you. Really, it's not. We're just not clicking."

He nodded. His smile faltered the slightest amount, but his face remained pleasant. "I'm glad you told me. If I've learned anything about dating stuff, it's if you try to force it, it'll never work out. Friends?"

She grinned and indicated for the waitress to split the check into two. "Friends sounds great." And friends they stayed, occasionally sending memes and reels back and forth.

She hoped he'd find his perfect girl. He deserved her.

Date #4 for Em (October)

Unknown Number: Is your roommate home?

Em frowned at her device in her apartment. She'd not yet saved the next date's number in her phone. If they made it past Round One, she figured she could give a name to a contact.

"Why's he asking me this?" she said this to no one in particular. All of her apartment-mates had vacated the place for various events. Harmony had gotten caught up in newspaper interviews. As for the other two, Em didn't question. She simply basked in the rare moment of aloneness in the family room.

Leaning her neck against the top of their futon, she rattled a reply.

Em: Haha, we're meeting at the campus coffee shop. Not really sure why it matters if they're home or not.

Three dots filled the screen for a moment. Then his reply.

Unknown Number: I just figured we could hang out at your place for a minute ;) but it might be awkward if you have any apartment-mates home.

Her gut squeezed. *Is he...trying to hook up with me?*

She scanned through her previous conversations with him, in which she'd prompted him to answer his favorite Bible verses, and he'd shared a little bit of his testimony with her. In rare form, Jana had actually given the two of them a little time to talk before the date.

You're a Christian, my dude. Most girls on this campus don't want that.

Em: Haha, sorry, but I don't feel super comfortable with that. Coffee shop in fifteen minutes?

Although everything in her squirmed against going, she figured Jana would hold this against her and force her to return to the singles group. At least, in the TSC, students could keep an eye on the group. In case the guy felt a little handsy.

Sunlight from the blinds in the window behind her warmed her neck as his response buzzed her device.

Unknown Number: I actually remembered I have something else

Unknown Number: Reschedule sometime?

Relief flooded her.

Em: Sure

Neither of them messaged each other again.

"I'm convinced, Noah, that there's not a single decent guy on this campus." She paused when she spotted the eyebrow quirk from Noah. "Okay, not a single *dateable* guy. The guys who want to stay single are chill."

"Thank you." Noah had indicated many times that he had no interest in dating while still in college.

He ducked underneath a decoration on the fourth floor of one of the boys' dorms, Ferrars. As an early October tradition, they'd transformed the floor into a Halloween Open House. The theme this year: *Monsters Inc.* Well, "Scary Monsters", to avoid any copyright issues with a certain major movie company.

"Hello, fellow scarers." One of the floor-mates, in a yeti costume, greeted them. "And welcome to your first day of training on the Fear Floor. Now, usually our business is scaring little children." He tapped his clipboard with a claw. "But we discovered something here at Monsters United. That the screams of college students are far more powerful. In these rooms behind me—" He motioned over his shoulder at the hallways. A few rooms had open doors with decor on the outside, to indicate students could walk into those. "—you will see several situations of the scariest things for college students. We may ask some of you to participate."

A group happened to bunch around Em. They only let ten students into the Open House at one time to avoid overcrowding.

"Finish the Fear Floor and return for some refreshments." In the lobby, several "scary" refreshments rested on tables. Cupcakes featuring bloodshot eyeballs snagged Em's attention. "Good luck, scarers." With a salute, the Yeti sent them off.

Noah inched closer to Em as the group shuffled toward the first room. The word "Deadlines" was etched in red on a piece of cardboard outside of it. "Maybe you should take a tip from Harmony and take a break?"

Ever since the Eli incident, Harmony had asked for Em to set her up on no more dates. Em couldn't blame her. That did leave a vacuum for her Do Good contribution. With the show taking place in less than a week, she'd have to think of something.

Maybe she could take up Harmony on her original offer to bake goods for it. But most of Em's baking escapades set off smoke detectors. She doubted that would be Doing a whole lot of Good for anyone. Except for people who wanted a hospital trip for food poisoning, she supposed.

"And risk not getting that ring by spring? There's twenty thousand dollars on the line, Noah."

"I know, but—"

"So unless you want to get a GoFundMe going, I'm kind of stuck."

His lips clamped shut as they entered the "Deadline" room. Male students had painted streaks of tears onto their faces with blue markers. They wailed and threw papers into the air. Several sheets of past homework assignments were taped to the cinder block walls. Someone had scrawled on them in red marker with words like "Past Due" and "Failure."

They shuffled out and toward the next room, "DTR".

"We will need a volunteer," a monster with a squid hat informed them.

Em raised her hand. "Sure."

"Thank you, dear monster. Now, fellow monsters, we're about to enter the relationships room." Lights flickered above them. Em wondered if they'd assigned one of the students on the floor to toggle the electricity switches on and off the entire night. "Our volunteer here is going to give a DTR to the human found inside. In you go."

She ambled in and found a man sitting on his bed with his head in his hands. As if someone had delivered him bad news. Behind her, she heard someone in the crowd whoop, "Yooo, it's Jeff. Hey, Jeff."

Jeff, who must've been the student on the bed, didn't respond. She couldn't make out much of his face, but the age lines defined themselves more into his forehead. A patch of baldness showed in his hair.

Is he one of the older students here?

"Um, Jeff." She cleared her throat. "I was wondering if we could talk about where you think our relationship is going and—"

Jeff let out a pitiful wail.

The squid monster motioned them back into the hallway and informed them that Jeff's screams would power their city for a week. After a few more rooms, they returned to the larger area for some refreshments.

Noah snickered as he ladled himself some "blood" punch. "I gotta say, Jeff really nailed that DTR room."

"Do you know him?" Em peeled the wrapper off one of the eyeball and gummy worm cupcakes. She popped the "eye" into her mouth and chewed on the gummy texture. Not bad, had a vanilla flavor.

"Yeah, he's a master's student who occasionally auditions for theater. Was sad he didn't show up for Matchmaker auditions, but I guess his thesis is taking him more time than he thought." Noah perched on the couch beside her. He sneaked a gummy worm off of her cupcake and decapitated it with his molars.

"Rude. You owe me another one."

"There's literally a tray of cupcakes, you silly goose."

"Sir, geese are not silly. Have you seen an angry goose? It will kill you."

They spent the next few minutes scrolling through photos on their phones of geese teeth. Noah shuddered. "New fear unlocked... Speaking of fears, it was pretty ironic that they put Jeff in the DTR room."

"Yeah?" She pilfered the gummy worm from the cupcake Noah had grabbed.

He rolled his eyes at her. "You're ridiculous. And yeah, we've had a lot of conversations backstage, and let's just say he's had a pretty terrible time in the dating world."

"Like how?"

"Well, from what he's seemed to indicate, he's run into a lot of baby-crazy girls. Girls who want to stay home and not work and are expecting him to provide the sole income. He says that's a lot of pressure, especially since his Master's isn't exactly in a lucrative field."

She licked a glob off icing off her fingertips. "So, he doesn't want kids?"

"I mean he might, but just not right now. They just aren't a priority for him I guess."

Memories reeled to the scent of blueberry scones and a little black cat. Maybe she couldn't get Harmony a match for Do Good, but that didn't mean she couldn't find one for Zuri.

She nudged her phone out of her pocket—she'd shoved it back in there post goose photos—and pulled up her Notes app. "Can you tell me more about him?"

"I don't like the look in your eyes. What are you up to?"

She shrugged. "Let's just say that if Jeff answers a few questions right, I may be able to help him overcome his fear."

Chapter Twelve

Em: Okay, testing, testing, one, two, three. Levels are looking good.

Em: Now, Jeff, thank you so much for agreeing to do this interview with me. As I've been advised by a fellow apartment-mate who does newspaper work, it's always important to record interviews, so you can get everyone's exact words.

Em: Do you have any issues with me recording this?

Jeff: Umm, nope. Is it picking me up okay?

Em: It's looking good. Once again, thank you for the interview. Since a certain friend of mine was not forthcoming with details about you.

Jeff: About me?

Em: Yeah, he doesn't really approve of the work I do, so he clammed up. I do want to mention that if you're uncomfortable at any time, just to let me know. You don't have to continue if it's not something you're interested in.

Jeff: Right, I remember your email. This is for the matchmaking thing you do, right?

Em: Yuppers.

Jeff: And you said I didn't have to pay, right? Because I do like to support small businesses, but funds are a little tight with school payments.

Em: I gotchu. Trust me, I do get it. This is for Do Good. And I think I have a potential match, but I need to flesh out some things from your initial email, if that's okay.

Jeff: Okay.

Em: For starters, if you're okay with a personal question, how important is having a biological kid for a future marriage? Hypothetically, if a relationship led to marriage.

Jeff: Oh gosh.

Jeff: Well, for starters, I will say that it's not a dealbreaker. I think most people would be sad if they didn't have biological kids. There does seem to be something inherently beautiful about two people creating something together.

Jeff: But I'm also aware that we live in a fallen world. And with that comes health complications, infertility, and couples who can't have kids. That's the beauty of things like adoption or fostering.

Jeff: Does that help answer your question?

Em: Oh yes it does. Okay, number two, if you married someone who is a "career woman" would that be a dealbreaker, or no?

Jeff: Career woman, meaning that she wants to focus on her career instead of staying home or something?

Em: Basically.

Jeff: Oh, yeah, no that's not a dealbreaker. That's something I'd prefer, actually.

Em: Really?

Jeff: Don't get me wrong, I have a high respect for couples who choose to have one parent home and one working. But I will say, that could alleviate some of the pressure if I know that both of us are working—that is, if we happened to have kids in the first place.

UNKNOWN SOURCE: Eeeee

Jeff: Are you...squealing?

Em: Jeff, let's just say this interview is going swimmingly. Just swimmingly.

"Let me get this straight"—Harmony shimmied her hand into long, black opera style gloves. Good thing they'd reached the end of October, and the air had cooled down. Otherwise, she would've melted in those things during the summer—"you're planning to play matchmaker at *Matchmaker*."

"Yes, between two master's students. One knows about it. One doesn't. I got them tickets together."

Em didn't know how Zuri would react to the news about a date prospect. She imagined that perhaps, like Harmony, she'd possibly push back about going out with someone once more. Sometimes people needed a little push, Em had decided

"Hmm." Harmony jiggled into a flapper-style dress. On Laila's dresser, she'd placed a sequin-laden headband, complete with peacock feathers. "This for the Do Good event?"

"Yeah, speaking of, I haven't seen any news articles on it. You guys covering it in next week's paper?"

Although the play would run for four weekends, the Do Good event technically ended on opening night—today. No news coverage meant fewer ticket "sales", despite the tickets going up for free. It was strange for the newspaper not to have covered the play yet. But there were other artistic events happening on campus, and the newspaper only had one section dedicated to the arts. It was either movie reviews, concert reviews, or play reviews. The writers had to take their pick as to which they thought would be most interesting to the student body for that week.

Even Em had slacked on her usual social media posts about the play, thanks to an uptick in homework. She hadn't posted in well over a month. From what she remembered from the seniors last year, they claimed they had less homework. Maybe the professors had gotten wind of this and cracked down harder.

She scrambled to post a quick photo of herself and her new apartment mates (sans Jana, who wanted no part of the photo), and hoped that could help her dwindling follower count.

Harmony pulled up on her black tights and stole at peek at her character shoes. "Next week, yes. Problem is, we've been running into a snag with one of the other articles, and they had to put me on it instead of the Do Good article."

Em rose from her bed and ambled to her mirror. Ah, her lipstick would need a retouching. She uncapped a pink tube and rubbed it onto her lips. "What article?"

"It's on student debt, and oh boy, do I have an interview story to tell you, madam. Mind if I?"

"Go right ahead."

According to Harmony, she'd found herself in the Bursar's office the other afternoon with a notepad in hand and a recording device. The woman spoke to her in clipped tones, fire flashing in her pupils. "It was clear she didn't want me in there. So I tried my highest voice and my brightest smile. Even wore my best suit for an interview outfit."

Em had to hand it to Harmony. Despite her more eccentric closet choices, she did know when to go more business casual or "normal" when situations called for it. No doubt, Harmony would be able to mold well into any future job she landed herself in. She mentioned a hope for editing at a newspaper or publishing house after graduation.

"Anyway, I give her my usual spiel, 'I want to record this meeting, so I can get your exact words. Exact words are important. If you feel uncomfortable at any time, or want to go off the record, I can stop the recorder.'" She slapped the elastic headband onto her head. Then sidled next to Em to glimpse her reflection in the mirror. "Needs a fake mole."

"You *do* realize, Harmony, that *Matchmaker* isn't set in the 1920s, right?"

"Oh, for sure. Just figured that it would be fun to go more flapper tonight. There." She dotted her upper lip with an eyeliner stick. "Perfect, now back to the story." She flopped back onto Laila's bed. "No one has ever taken me up on it before. They usually get comfortable after a few icebreaker questions. But this woman was stiff the whole time. At one point, I asked her how much student debt each student graduates with—you know, the ones who took out loans."

It still astonished Em how many *didn't* take out loans. She wondered how students could even afford one year of tuition her, let alone four. Then again, maybe most parents didn't throw college funds into a failed salon like hers had.

"She stops me. Says, 'Turn off the recording'. And she checks her computer. She says, 'Looks like it's $30,000 is the average'. She pauses and motions for me to stop writing in my journal. 'Actually, write down that it's $28,000'."

Em's eyes widened as she rubbed away some of the mascara fallout on her face. "No."

Harmony nodded. "Sadly, there wasn't much that I could do. The $30,000 part was technically off-the-record. I tried to get her to put it on deep-background, but she wouldn't budge. Threatened to end the interview right there."

From what Em could gather, privacy on newspapers could be divvied into a few categories:

- **On the Record:** "Whatever I say can and will be used against me. My exact words will go on the page, and I will be named as a source."

- **Not for Attribution:** "You can use my words, but please don't name me as a source. I want to be anonymous." The University had put out an article on Title IX the other year, and most students didn't want an attribution for that.

- **On Background:** "You can't even quote me. But you can paraphrase the information I gave to you."

- **Off-the-Record:** "Nothing that I say in this interview can be used in anyway. It's merely to give you additional information. If you interview someone else and they tell you the same stuff, great. Quote them. But not me."

"My gosh, Harmony." Em rubbed a foundation spot that hadn't blended well. "I'm sorry that your hands are tied."

"Eh, happened a lot at the other university. We do have to run it soon, so I may not be able to get another source. But one thing about me is I'm good at digging up information. You have a secret, you will spill it in front of me."

Em wondered how Harmony had this sort of gift. As for Em, her mother would tell her the reason why random people in grocery stores would come up to her and tell her their life stories. "You have a kind face, Em. The kind that tells people, 'Don't worry. I won't judge.'"

As for Harmony... Well, Harmony herself had suggested that some people assumed that weird also meant stupid. Therefore, they could get everything off their chests and figure she couldn't tell a soul.

Harmony wiggled her thumbs in circles around each other, "I love it when people underestimate me. Being the dark horse is fun."

Em shoved her makeup palette onto her dresser. "I look forward to reading both articles, then—the Do Good and whatever you can do with the student debt article. We should probably go." She glimpsed the time on her phone. "Proper theater etiquette is getting there fifteen minutes early."

Plus, she'd placed her, Harmony, and Laila three rows back from Zuri and Jeff. They could play spies the whole first act.

Laila met the two of them at the theater. A crowd bloomed in the atrium as some of the older folks from the Mansfield township community grinned at the photo frames on the wall. The theater made a habit of hanging up pictures from past productions. One couple yipped with glee about a past production of *Finnian's Rainbow*. Perhaps they had performed in it.

An usher in a black polo handed her a program. She flipped to the cast list, where, sure enough, she spotted Noah's name near the top.

Dust motes trickled down when they entered the theater. The school may have invested in the STEM-themed buildings, but many of the art departments lacked the true funding needed for exhibits and productions. Noah and Em had needed to literally scrape the paint off some of the plywood in productions, so the theater could reuse the wood pieces for another one.

Em buried the squeak in her throat when Jeff and Zuri parked in the rows in front of them. Already, the two had begun an animated discussion, one she couldn't hear from this far back. Zuri did have a softer voice. And when Jeff wasn't screaming about DTRs, she imagined he could lower his volume too.

Fifteen minutes later, the lights dimmed, and the director welcomed them to the show. Applause followed her off the wings, and the production started. Scenes blurred together for Em, as she eyed the couple. Occasionally, Zuri would point to something in the program and nudge Jeff with her elbow. He'd nod and lean over for some commentary.

Good, she'd picked an excellent date spot for the two of them. Zuri tended to like intelligent men, and who knew more about theater than

Jeff, who had participated in past productions? She imagined that Jeff would give her details about cast members in the same way Noah did.

"This one's a diva."

"Oh, he's really good. Really broke out of this shell this past year."

"Yep, they type cast her as this type of role in every show. I really wish they'd give her something else to do. She's so talented."

At once, lights flooded the auditorium. Had they reached intermission already?

Laila turned to Em. "So did you understand anything that was happening? It's like watching Shakespeare."

Em shrugged. "Refreshments, anyone?"

Both of her apartment-mates placed orders, and she rose from her seat. She texted Harmony to spy on the couple and send her any developments, then she galumphed up the carpeted steps and into the lobby.

Salty popcorn infiltrated her senses. Ooh, she could go for that right now. Or maybe peanut M&Ms. On the brick wall behind her, several of the Do Good stories displayed. She weaved through the crowd to scan a few of them.

DO GOOD Story: I was really down and the local animal shelter brought me a kitten to my off-campus apartment. We'd been wanting to adopt one for a while, but have been so busy, that no one has a had a chance to go to the local shelter. Thank you, kind animal shelter worker!

DO GOOD Story: Thank you to Candice for the delicious treats you baked for our wing. We really loved the cupcakes.

DO GOOD Story: To that amazing business major who offered to proofread my resume. Since I'm graduating a semester early, you can imagine the stress of applying to jobs. That CV already got me an interview!

Em grinned and shoved her hands into her dress pockets. Although she couldn't have Zuri submit an application like this, her chest warmed at the thought of the two meeting at this production.

The line for concessions had dwindled and she stepped up to the table. One of the students handed her a water bottle, sour gummy worms for Harmony, and a Coke. She paid in cash, and in the corner of her eye, she spotted a figure down the steps, in the hallway that led backstage.

Noah?

With snacks bundled in her arms, she peeked over the steps. He waved her down. She nodded and descended. "Hey."

"Hey." Wind took his breath away. No doubt, even just saying the lines alone for his part must've worn down his voice. "Any chance you could get me a water at concessions? I'll pay you back."

She handed him her bottle. "No worries about the payment. They don't have water bottles backstage?"

"Cast drank it all. Thanks." He unscrewed the cap and drained the bottle of half its contents. Sweat gleamed on his forehead, and his costume stank. No doubt from several hours spent in it during dress rehearsals. She prayed someone in the costume crew would throw it into the washer found in the costume closet.

"You're doing great out there. But Laila is wondering if you're in love with that hat maker in the show or if you hate her. She really can't tell."

"I'm—hold up." His eyes narrowed. Em glanced over her shoulder and spotted Jeff and Zuri, holding hands at the top of the staircase. "Did you... Em, did you do this?"

"What? You're just going to assume that every couple on campus got matched by me?"

Noah rolled his eyes. "You were *bleeding* me for information about Jeff. This has you written all over it."

She folded her arms. "What's the big deal? I did this one for free. Why are you so against me and matchmaking anyway?"

Noah opened his mouth, closed it, considered his words. He sighed and swigged the water once more. "I   you're very good at what you do Em. It's just... You remember my older brother, yes?"

"Yes."

"Okay, well I mentioned a few misfires. Some of those were in Christian dating groups online. Some were for classes he literally paid for. I'll send you the links, but..." He rubbed the white marks in the corners of his eyes. This type of stage makeup would make eyes seem bigger in the stage lights. "I don't think you're trying to take advantage of people, Em. That's not your heart. Still, you have so many gifts and talents. I wish you could use them in other ways."

What did he expect her to do? Money wouldn't just appear in thin air. As much as she'd love to work a job in PR or Marketing after college, she needed to crawl her way out of debt first.

Before she could ask, Noah had spun around. He turned a corner and headed to the backstage area. Gone.

Chapter Thirteen

AFTER OPENING NIGHT, NOAH had sent her three links. One to a group on Facebook, one to a dating coaching site, and one to a singles' retreat. He followed up the messages with:

Noah: I don't ever want to stifle your heart. But do consider that a lot of people take advantage of vulnerable people. Matchmaking services can be taken the wrong way.

Em found Facebook to be a little old-school for her. Most college students didn't log onto it for any purposes, other than to sell products to those in older generations, or to get an easy login code to most sites. She had to request into this group in particular: "Christian Singles in Their 20s and 30s, Looking to Find Their God-Honoring Spouse."

To her surprise, an admin admitted her within the hour. She roamed to the pinned post Noah had texted her about, put up about three years ago.

Post from the Admin

I'm not single, but everyone in this group is. My husband and I created this group to help you to find your kingdom spouse. Now, although we do this on a voluntary basis, we do accept donations for the hard work we do. Venmo information can be found in the comments.

We've noticed that a lot of Guys and Girls complain that there's no good Christians out there. But really, they fall into the same pitfalls. I'll break them down in the Guys and Girls sections. (My husband weighed in on the Guys section.)

Guys If you follow these steps, you'll make yourself a far better candidate for Christian women

Get out of debt: No girl wants a guy with school debt (or any other kind of debt for that matter). We highly recommend Dave Ramsey's course at Financial Peace University to help you to whittle that debt down to zero. Remember, women like financial security. Men are providers.

Work out more: No, we don't expect you to be a Chris Evans, but women do like a man who takes care of himself. So hit the gym and remember that your body is a temple.

Initiate more: Women don't like passive men. That means you ask her on the first date (and pay for it). You tell her "I love you" first. Women want a man who leads.

Girls If you follow these steps, you'll make yourself a far better candidate for Christian men

Lose weight: Sorry, some of you are going to come at me for this. But ladies, let's be honest, if we shed ten or fifteen pounds, we'll be far more desirable to men. Most men want a woman with an active lifestyle.

Smile more: I'll be the first to admit I am not always the best at controlling my expressions. If you frown all the time on dates, men are going to assume you have a bad attitude. Smile more and be more inviting.

Submit more: Some of us are boss babes, and I get it, but we're called to submit to our future husbands. That means letting him hold the door for you. Letting him pay the bill (his pride will be wounded if you don't). And letting him lead you.

Once again, our Venmo info is found in the comments. Any donations are appreciated for the work we do.

Em held back her gag reflex. "Seriously, Noah? Do you think I do this?" She would *never* tell a man to eradicate his debt or a woman to lose weight. "That's how we get eating disorders."

Still, she'd promised him after the show she would read the other sites. *Next stop, the coaching site.*

Are You Having Trouble Getting Past the First Date?

Christians can have a hard time in the dating world. Post-college, it can seem like there aren't any single people at your local church, and that you're missing out on something that everyone else seems to get.

The best way to put your best foot forward is to realize what common mistakes you're making. In this fourteen-week course, dating expert Darren Hiram will walk you through how to keep conversations flowing on dates, how to find someone who shares your values, and how to avoid the typical pitfalls.

Course Cost: $299

"What?" Em's nostrils flared. "Three hundred dollars for a class? What is this, college?"

Yes, she charged five hundred dollars, and coaching was included in that. But this class didn't even guarantee they could match you with someone.

Time for the last link, the dating retreat.

Singles' Retreat: Heading to Cleveland

We've just announced our next retreat location: Cleveland, OH.

You asked, we delivered (so please, for those who submitted the request forms, sign up haha. We put a lot of time into these events). Meet Christian singles and spend time fellowshipping and worshipping together.

Trip Cost: $500 (does not include hotel, food, or travel)

Em shut her laptop. "Okay, Noah, I get it. This stuff feels super sketch." She recalled her ire when she first perused matchmaker sites. Even asked how in the world someone could afford tens of thousands of dollars to *potentially* meet a future husband or wife. But after she'd talked his ear off about what she did for a living, she would have thought that Noah would understand her business wasn't like these ones.

The door to the apartment swung open, and Jana stepped in. She glowered at Em. "A little birdie told me that you skipped out on a date. Shame, shame. I thought we'd been over this."

"Who—oh, hookup guy."

Jana dropped her bags of groceries onto the kitchen table. "Hookup guy?"

"Yeah, first of all, *he* was the one who canceled the date, not me. Second, I don't know who you're having vet these dates, but they need to do a better job. He was planning on getting in my pants!"

"Show me."

Jana was busying herself with sorting the various foods. When she placed a salad kit, in a plastic box, on the table, Em had lifted herself from the couch and scrolled up to the conversation.

"Here."

Jana perched an arm on her hip and scanned the messages. She let out a low whistle.

"See? You guys need to vet better." Even though Jana claimed that she had others picking the "catches" so she could avoid sabotaging Em, Em doubted it. If only she could prove it.

"Yeah, the whistle wasn't for the conversation. I can tell you that yours truly dealt with plenty of guys like that on dating apps, girlie. Plenty would infiltrate the Christian specific ones 'looking for a good time'."

Em's brows furrowed. "Then what—"

Jana held up the screen. "The fact that you, girlie, even entertained a date with this guy after he was clearly trying to hook up with you. You should've blocked him right away. You're lucky he canceled the date."

Oh my word, she couldn't win. *So I'm in trouble if I don't do the whole date with a sketchy guy. But I'm also in trouble if I don't block a sketchy guy too?*

By now, Jana had handed the device back and returned to her grocery organization. She placed the cereals together.

"Sorry, I guess. I'll do better next time."

"I should hope so, but I have the solution for someone who is playing it fast and loose like you."

Jana dug into her pocket and pulled out a pink folded sheet of paper. She handed it to Em, pinched between her two fingers. Em unfolded it and read.

Your Body, Your Sexuality, and Your Faith

Join us in the Fanny Price Chapel this Saturday for an exclusive event that helps us to generate discussions about sexuality and the body and Christ. Men will meet in the Dashwood Performing Arts auditorium and ladies at the Price Chapel. Break times will include light refreshments.

Topics for men: How to overcome addiction and embrace your inner manhood.

Topics for women: How to preserve your purity and be the Ruth to your Boaz.

"Oh my word, seriously? A purity conference, Jana?"

Jana sucked her teeth. "Well, they technically can't call it that anymore because of, ahem, controversy. But yeah, those do exist. Surprised?"

"Yeah, I'm not going to this."

A gasp overtook all of Jana, and she clutched her hand to her chest for dramatic effect. "But *Emerson*, just about every Christian woman has to go through some form of this. Even if they aren't called purity conferences anymore. They've been repackaged."

Em rubbed her temples. She couldn't get out of this one either. Maybe she could bring her laptop with her to work on homework in the meantime. With a sigh, she clocked the time on the sheet. Of course, Jana would only give her ten minutes to get to the chapel. Why would she expect anything less? Everything about that past minute felt staged.

Wanna bet she spoke with hookup guy a while ago, saw this event, and waited for just this moment?

Without even Harmony to accompany her to such an event, she set out. Rain splattered her footsteps on the trek over. She shivered in her jacket and gawked at the substantial crowd of women filtering into the chapel doors. Several of them wore long boho style dresses with long sleeves, all in autumnal colors.

She nestled herself in one of the far back rows. A speaker with highlights in her hair and a round face picked up a mic on the stand. "Hello, ladies. Please fill the front rows. I don't bite, I promise. Front rows, please."

Ugh. Em trudged up to the sixth row from the front. She situated herself in a corner so she could make a quick escape.

"Hi, ladies. I would also ask that you make your way to the middle of the row to let latecomers find seats."

Resolution coursed through Em's veins. Nope, no thank you. She stayed planted in her spot and opened her laptop.

"Also, ladies, we'd like to remind you to put away any devices and be present for today's talk. Thank youuu."

She shoved her laptop back into her case. Okay at this point, that woman had to be targeting her.

Minutes later, a good majority of the seats had occupants. The round-face lady approached the mic once more. "Good morning, princesses and daughters of the Most High." She aimed a finger skyward. "Today we're going to be talking about your precious worth in dating relationships and beyond that. To start." She dug into her dress pockets and pulled out a wad of gum. Its shiny blue wrapper glistened in the chapel lights. "I have an illustration for you today. Who here likes gum?"

Hands raised throughout the rows. "I do too, ladies. This one is a piece of Five gum. You know the kind. The good, good stuff. Now, I need a volunteer."

A redhead in the front row lifted her hand. The woman picked her and everyone in the row whooped and shouted "Go, Claire! Whoo!"

Go-Claire stepped onto the stage, and the woman placed the piece of gum into her hands. "Now, what's your name, sweetie?"

Go-Claire spoke into the mic. "Umm, Claire."

"Claire, I need you to chew this piece of gum as fast as you can for one minute. Ready." The woman held up an Apple watch to time her. "And go!"

One minute later, Claire massaged her jaw and spit the gum into a plastic cup the woman held for her. She returned to her seat, engulfed in the cheers of what had to be her wing-mates.

"Okay, now I'll need a second volunteer to chew this gum again. Anyone?"

No hands lifted.

"Come on, ladies. It's Five gum. The good, good stuff. No one?"

No one.

"That's what I thought. Now, daughters of the Most High, here's the illustration. You are pieces of Five gum." Tassels on her tea-length dress bounced against her legs. "You have so much worth. You are the good, good stuff. But..." She held up the cup. The wad of gum glinted in the light. "If you allow any man—even a brother in Christ, ladies—to chew you up before that wedding night.—and you know what I'm talking about, ladies—this is what you're going to look like to other guys. Notice how we didn't have any volunteers for the second time?"

Heat singed Em's skin as the speaker turned to Ruth, chapter one. Nearby her, a girl turtled into her dress. What if one of the women in here had been "chewed" before? Plenty of women on her wing had shared such stories in years past. What would these types of talks do to them?

After an hour, the woman called for a "break" before the women would return for their second round in Ruth chapter two.

Em stormed out of the auditorium, beating the crowd to the back doors. She flung it open and almost bumped into a man with curly brown hair in a hoodie. Freckles formed connect-the-dots shapes on his nose and cheeks.

"Whoops, sorry."

"No worries." He chuckled. "I ducked out of my session as fast as I could too." He gestured over his shoulder at the windows that were outside of the chapel doors. Rain spattered them, and gray skies formed a halo of light around this man.

"Yeah?"

"Yeah, it was just basically the track coach doing pull-ups and telling us how to be better men. Name's Frankie, yours?"

"Em. Wanna sit down?"

They parked in some chairs nearest the chapel doors. Women sieved past, some talking animatedly about the gum illustration.

"So..." Frankie rubbed his hands on his knees. "You thinking about skipping out of the next session?"

"Ha, I wish. It's...a long story. I had a bet with one of my apartment-mates, so I have to see this thing through."

She bet several little "birdies" existed in the audience, who would snitch on her if she didn't spend the total four hours of the event in that corner seat.

"Oh, I get it." Frankie pulled on the strings of his hoodie. "My RA forced all of us to go. He was heavily hinting to me. Probably thinks I did something in my last relationship that I shouldn't have."

"Yeah?"

"Yeah, a long-distance thing. She's a junior in college too. It lasted two years. We broke up a few weeks ago."

Em's face fell. "Sorry, that sucks."

"It does, but I guess if I do a bunch of pull-ups, it'll solve my problem."

This caused both of them to snicker. They chattered about their woes in their respective sessions. Minutes later, the lights flashed. Everything in Em darkened. Just when she'd started to have a nice conversation with this guy.

Frankie appeared to read her expression. "Tell you what, Em. What say you vouch for me, and I vouch for you. There's enough seats in that place that people won't notice we've been gone. We can both say we saw the other person going back into the session. I hear they're filming them too, if we need to preview some highlights."

Her lip cut up her cheek. "That sounds wonderful, but what are we going to do in the meantime so we don't get caught?"

He flicked a glance over at the coffee table. "Grab a cup and hole ourselves up somewhere? Maybe continue this conversation?"

Her half grin split into a whole one. "That's the best idea I've heard all day."

Chapter Fourteen

RED STRINGS OF YARN blocked Em's entrance to the apartment.

"What in the—"

Someone had configured the thread to zig and zag in every which way. She pinched one of the strings and leaned through one of the holes to see that someone had duct taped the string to the wall.

Oh boy, when the RA went over the apartment at the end of the year, they would charge everyone a fee for peeled paint. Even back in the dorms, they would hand the students a sheet at the beginning of the year to catalogue any scratches or paint-peels they found. Unfortunately, the school had used the blocky furniture for the greater half of thirty years, so everything had received significant scuffs and wear and tear. No matter how hard Em attempted to mark down every scrape—with documented photo evidence—her RA always managed to find a new one and charge her a fee. Her *favorite* had to be her sophomore year, when they'd found a scratch inside a drawer she'd never used.

"Don't touch the lasers!" In the darkness of the kitchen, a figure in a ski mask emerged, holding a Nerf gun.

"The what?"

"The lasers." Harmony tore off the mask and beamed at Em. "I figured for our girls' night that we could have several events. First, an escape room. You have to get through those lasers there without touching them. Second, we—"

Her face fell as she read Em's expression. "Did you—forget about girls' night?"

Em chewed on her lip and sought solace from the window in the family room. Through the blinds, November snowflakes drifted to the earth. These last couple of weeks had blurred together. Now, in mid-November, she'd gone on at least five dates with Frankie. This included a roundabout on the loop.

He hadn't had a DTR with her yet, and she didn't blame him. Coming off the heels of a long relationship, she expected him to take his time. In a few months or so, perhaps he could muster enough courage to stick a label on it.

Still, is it too much to ask him to give me a ring by May? That's six months away, now.

Although many relationships at Mansfield operated at a much quicker pace than that, she couldn't force someone to go faster than they wanted. Nevertheless, they'd had quite a few gatherings and study sessions. This caused her to flake on several commitments. And apparently, tonight, she'd do that again.

"Sorry, Harmony." She winced. "It's a Guys Ask with his floor tonight. I should've double checked on the calendar."

"It's…" Harmony sighed and flicked on the lights. She grabbed a fistful of yarn and yanked on the wall. "It's fine. It seems like you two are all over each other all the time. Even Noah's commented on how much you don't seem to be answering your phone lately."

He had?

Em helped Harmony to untangle the laser strings. No one taught a class on dating relationships. Em had absolutely no gauge about how often a couple should date or spend time together. In fact, back at the dorms, most smitten parties would hang out in the lobby, bingeing shows at all hours. She didn't see certain floormates, because they'd hang out with their "boo" all the time.

She tried to control the objection rising in her throat, and the prickles running up and down her skin. Relationships would mean she would step on *some* toes. Everyone expected her to give them all of her time. She just had to figure out how to juggle one more ball. "Raincheck, but we make it even more epic the next time?"

Harmony didn't say anything, but nodded once.

That wasn't a good sign.

"Talk to me, Harmony. Tell me what's wrong." Em wound the fabric around her fingertips and parked on the futon in the family room.

Harmony tossed her strands onto a pile on the carpet and slumped next to her. "It's stupid. It's going to sound—as the younglings say—petty."

"It's college. We live for petty."

"Fair." Harmony blew out a long breath. "Back at my old school, I had a few friends who ditched me when they started dating people. Saw us as being on different levels and that we didn't have anything to talk about." She blinked several times. "And—and it always started with them going on lots of dates and suddenly not having time anymore. It's almost like, they really wanted to stop hanging out, and they used the dates as—as the younglings would say—an excuse."

"Harmony, *everyone* says 'excuse'."

"Not old people. They get mad at our generation for all of our excuses."

This caused Em to laugh. She sobered and placed a hand on Harmony's shoulder. "I'm so sorry if that felt this way to you. That's not my intention at all. I'm such a routine person that this dating thing is throwing me for a loop."

Even the physical stuff threw her off. People could kiss before they put labels on, right? Because she and Frankie had shared her first one behind the prayer chapel on the second date. It took them a few practices, because the first one felt wet and not right. But by the fourth date, they'd gotten the hang of it.

It seemed that every ten minutes or so that Frankie longed for some form of physical affection, more in the kissing range than anything. He'd even encouraged her to take a love language test so they could better understand how to meet each other's needs. Unsurprisingly, he scored high on physical touch.

Her love language—acts of service—meant that she enjoyed it when someone went out of their way to do something for her such as cleaning the dishes in their apartment or scraping the ice off her windshield in the parking lot. She did notice that Frankie hadn't really done all that many acts of service since they started dating.

I guess you can't do that as often as things like kissing. Maybe I shouldn't expect that much.

Em shifted her focus back to Harmony. "Harmony, I'm sorry it came off that way, but I'm not that kind of person. Just because I'm dating someone and you're not doesn't make us any different. That doesn't make you any less smart or worthy or anything."

Harmony sniffed and rubbed her fist against her eye. "Thanks."

"Tell you what. I'm going to make something. Be right back."

Em raced into her room and pulled up her Google docs. Five minutes later, her printer whirred to life. She entered the room with a warm piece of paper held high.

"What's that?"

"A contract. Read it, sister."

Contract between Parties "Harmony" and "Em"

Parties agree not to ever let relationships get in the way of friendships. As the college kids say, "Sisters before misters."

Parties will not see the other party as lesser-than or unequal due to relationship status.

Parties will carve out time for one another, despite the busyness of relationships.

Parties will celebrate all accomplishments, from rings by spring to cha-chings by spring. Everyone deserves recognition for what they've done, no matter what the relationship status.

Parties will allow for everyone to speak on all conversation topics, despite "experience" or relationship status. Every perspective is helpful and useful.

Parties will throw lots of parties, because I think I've typed the word "parties" way too many times.

Signatures____

(Em)

____

(Harmony)

Harmony pursed her lips and scanned the document once more. "Man, I do love myself some good legalese. Makes for good reading."

"I mean, this document probably would never hold up in court." Em placed a hand over her heart. "But I want us to make a pact that we won't allow relationships to be the reason why we end a friendship."

"That's right. We'll let secret agencies telling us to assassinate each other do the trick. But only then can we end it. Because, you know, one or both of us would be dead."

"Umm, sure, Harmony. Let me see if I can find a working pen."

After scavenging through Laila's supplies, Em found a purple pen that worked. They each took turns signing. When they finished, they hugged.

"Sorry to cut this short, Harmony, but I do really need to get to his dorm for the Guys Ask. You okay if we raincheck, but make the next one epic?"

Harmony nodded, this time her eyes more alight.

Taking that as a better sign, Em rushed to her room to refresh her deodorant and hop into a different outfit. Leggings and a tank top seemed appropriate for an archery date. She shoved on her Doc Martens and shrugged on her winter coat. With a wave goodbye to Harmony, she bustled outdoors.

Dragon's breath trailed her lips as she headed to the guys' dorm. When she arrived, she found a group huddled outside. Someone with a clipboard listed which dates would travel in which cars. To her surprise, she located Noah in the crowd.

"Noah?" She shoved her frozen hands into her pockets. "What are you doing?"

"I live in this dorm." He shrugged. "Well, I sometimes live in this dorm. I guess I sleep in the theater more."

Huh, some part of her had forgotten that seniors could still live in the student housing buildings. Next to him, a platinum blonde shivered in the cold, her legging-cladded legs bobbing back and forth.

Something niggled in Em's gut about seeing Noah with a date, but she released the feeling. Why would she get mad at him for this? She'd started dating someone else, after all, and Guys Ask dates didn't really count as the real thing.

Someone squeezed her shoulder.

Whirling around, she spotted Frankie. He planted a kiss on her lips before she could get out a "hi". Wrapping his arm around her, he tugged her close as the clipboard guy finished listing out all the names.

They shuffled to one of the cars in the side lot. Energy drink cans and pizza boxes littered the floors. She perched her feet on one of the boxes and wrinkled her nose at the scent of stale cheese in the vehicle. The engine chugged to life and the driver nearly rear ended an SUV.

Ah yes, she hadn't missed this. Her freshman year, none of the first years could bring a car to campus—thanks to the limited parking spaces at the school. If anyone ever needed to make a Walmart run or get sup plies off school property, they recruited the help of an upperclassmen.

After that year, Em wondered how anyone at this school managed to pass a driver's test.

Frankie planted no fewer than twenty kisses on her forehead, cheeks, and lips on the twenty-minute drive over. Much as Em appreciated these gestures, she spotted the passenger seat date shrinking in her seat, cheeks pinking. Public displays of affection were never well received at Mansfield.

Several jerky turns later, they arrived at the archery place. A golden retriever—likely the archery place's owner's dog—greeted them at the door. Em gave him the ear scratches the good boy deserved and stepped inside. Stark white walls surrounded several targets. An instructor walked them through how to use one of the bows and gestured to a bucket full of arm guards that were used to prevent strings from snapping against their forearms.

Em grabbed a purple bow and found herself at station number five with Frankie. Each of them would shoot five arrows, and retrieve them when everyone finished.

She notched the arrow on the string, drew back, and fired. *Ouch.* She glanced down at her forearm. A pink streak had formed on her arm.

Frankie seized Em's wrist and kissed the booboo. She winced at how that agitated the pain more and gestured over her shoulder. "I'm going to get one of the arm guards," she said, pulling her arm away from his lips. "Go ahead and shoot without me?"

"Sure thing."

She loped back to the front desk. There, she found Noah with his arm plunged into the arm guard bucket.

"You having a hard time shooting too, champ?" Em raised her voice to be heard over the whistling of arrows.

He laughed and showed off a dark mark on his skin. "Yep, I'm definitely no Legolas."

"Your date kiss it to make it better?"

His nose wrinkled. "No, did yours?"

Shame crept through her gut. Should she feel ashamed about physical contact? Sometimes it did feel a little excessive from Frankie. It seemed that every moment he needed to have a hand on her or plant a kiss somewhere.

But why did Noah always have to act so contrarian to things she did? He'd never done this during freshmen year, prior to the matchmaking stuff. And before she started dating, matchmaking seemed like the only thing he disagreed with.

Then again, they hadn't talked much since she started dating Frankie. Maybe he had to get out any doubts now.

"Something wrong with him kissing it?"

"No, of course not, but—" Noah strapped an arm guard around his wrist. Velcro stuck together. "There are two Frankies on my floor, and I didn't realize which one you were dating until today. You guys haven't exactly posted any photos online."

She tugged an arm guard out of the tangled pile in the bucket and fastened it on.

Of course they hadn't put up any pictures yet. No one did that until they had official relationship labels. Otherwise, parents would pester them for details. Not to mention she could tell in her latest phone calls with her dad that something had gone amiss at home. She could see the doom spelled out for her parents' relationship. If only she could head back home to help them fix that. She was good at fixing things, matching things.

"What's wrong with my Frankie?"

"Nothing right now, Em. But he did just get out of a two-year relationship. Aren't you worried that this is sort of a rebound situation?"

The words punched her in the gut.

Frankie had shared some details about his ex. That he'd met her in an online Christian app, and that they shared five hundred miles of distance between them. They'd visited each other maybe once or twice a month, and he'd almost bought an engagement ring before they broke things off.

"I'm just...trying to protect you. You're my friend, Em. I don't want you to get hurt."

Em tightened the Velcro and winced at the pain of her arm throbbing underneath. "I know what I'm doing."

Anger seethed behind her teeth.

If Noah knew anything about relationships, he would've gotten into one by now. He had no room to talk about this one. Granted, he'd mentioned he avoided relationships because people in the theater tended to be doing stage plays all the time, which led to people feeling neglected. And there was the case of his brother...

She shook the thoughts out of her head and charged back into the room.

Frankie wrapped his arm around her once more and planted a kiss on her forehead and her armguard. As she reached for her bow, he stopped her hand. "Hey, Em, I was going to ask after the date, but in case you have to run off again—"

"Again?"

"It always seems like you have something to get off to. We almost never get to spend enough time together."

Brows knit together. She'd tried to carve out any loose time in her schedule for this guy. How much more could she give?

"Anyway, I was wondering, would you want to make it official?" He grinned. "Boyfriend and girlfriend?"

"I—"

She glanced over her shoulder. Noah leaned against the door frame, arms crossed. Something hot surged in her veins, and she returned her gaze to Frankie. "I think that's a wonderful idea."

Chapter Fifteen

"It's a girls' night." Harmony sang as they headed to the parking lot behind the apartment complex. "We're gonna tear up the towwwn. It's a girls' night. Gonna burn buildings down."

Em clicked her keys, and her car beeped. "We are *not* going to do that last one. Last time I checked, arson is bad, Harmony."

"Not if you're doing it for Jesus. Arson for Jesus!"

Shaking away any thoughts of a T-shirt design with "Arson for Jesus" on the front, coupled by a fire emoji, Em pulled the driver's-side door open. As she did so, her phone buzzed in her pocket. She sighed, pulled out the device, and dug the keys into the ignition. Heaters blasted. "What now, babe?"

A text from Frankie illuminated the screen.

Frankie: Miss you *kissy emoji*

"Oh my word, Frankie. We literally just saw each other."

Right before she'd ducked into her apartment to grab Harmony for the girls' night, he'd kissed her goodbye at her door. It took quite a bit of convincing for him to give her the night off, but she'd insisted that she and Harmony planned this way in advance, right before Thanksgiving break.

He relented and asked her to send him updates throughout the night.

She rattled a text back along the lines of "miss you too", and hoped that would placate him for a while. Handing Harmony the car charger for her phone, she gestured at Harmony's device for the GPS. "Okay, girl, where to?"

"First stop, the movie theater."

Em cocked her head. "Harmony, I thought we were watching a movie back at the apartment. *Clueless*, remember?"

An ancient DVD hookup to the TV and a library rental would give them a one-way ticket to one of Harmony's favorite movies. Next to *Saw*, of course, her ultimate favorite.

Today, Harmony sported a medieval dress. She'd felt more in a medieval phase this late afternoon, it seemed. "We are, but we have to get the popcorn there. Everyone knows movie popcorn is the best at the theater."

No arguments with that. Em attempted to ignore the next five texts from Frankie, that burst onto her device in rapid succession. He tended to send multiple messages at once, and if she didn't respond within half an hour, he'd send a "???".

Harmony played with her trumpet sleeves as Em whirred out of the parking lot and onto the main road. After Harmony blasted some of her "tunes", which were Gregorian chants, they'd arrived at the theater.

When they headed for the shaded doors, a security guard in glasses—weird for November—halted them and jabbed his finger at a sign on the door. "No one under eighteen may enter the theater without a parent or guardian."

Huh, odd. Em vaguely remembered some newspaper article put out by the *Mansfield Mirror* about how a bunch of minors had wreaked havoc at the local theaters, and were now banned from entering without parental supervision.

Em dug into her wallet and pulled out her driver's license. The guard eyed it over his shades, eyebrows arched. "My bad, ladies. Your generation keeps looking younger and younger. You can enter."

They brushed passed him and joined the queue for refreshments. Em leaned over to Harmony and muttered. "Well, that was strange."

Harmony lifted and dropped her shoulders. "Mom says we'll appreciate it when we're older. But if you ask me, we look exactly what we feel like. Young."

Huh, so they did.

It struck her as odd that so many people rooted for college students to find their one and only by twenty-two. The idea of home ownership and investment accounts scared her. Let alone finding a man to spend the entire rest of her life with.

Did Mom feel this way when she married Dad younger than I was?

Images in her mind flashed to Frankie as her phone buzzed. This thing was moving lightning fast. If he proposed to her before spring, would she feel ready then?

She shook away her jitters. She and Frankie had only been dating for a few weeks. Heaven knew she wouldn't have to make that decision for a while.

They approached the counter, and Em breathed in the salty air. Ah, it smelled like childhood and summer $5 movie nights.

"One medium popcorn to go, please!" Harmony rattled her fingertips against the counter. "And please put an embarrassing amount of butter on it. Enough so that it would make a heart shudder for mercy."

Em stopped Harmony from reaching her wallet and pulled out her own credit card instead. "I owe you an epic girls' night."

Harmony pursed her lips. "Okay, but let me get the next two locations. Don't want you spending too much money."

Em tapped her card against the reader. "Two more places?"

"Yeah, you did say epic."

The cashier returned with their popcorn in a plastic grocery bag. Em tied the ends, thanked the worker, and they headed off into the parking lot again. Harmony held the popcorn between her legs as the GPS took them to a candy store in Mansfield township.

Em didn't stop in there all that much, thanks to a creepy poster of a 1950s clown in the display window. But Harmony swore by the quality of the candy.

Before Em could put the car in reverse, another few texts from Frankie buzzed her phone. She groaned and moved to turn her device onto "Do Not Disturb".

Harmony halted her arm. "Do you want me to read you his texts and respond to him for you?"

For a moment, Em considered this. After all, she made a habit not to talk badly about anyone on her message threads, so she didn't say anything mean about Harmony. "Sure, Harmony. Read me his messages, will you?"

"You got it, boss. Okay. 'I love you.' 'Kissy face.' 'Kissy face.' 'Can't wait to hold you again.' 'And kiss you again.' 'And cuddle you again.' 'Miss you.' 'So sad we can't spend time together.' 'Sad face.' 'It's so sad without you by my side.' 'Kissy face' 'Babe?' 'Question mark. Question mark. Question mark.'"

Oh. My. Goodness.

Em gripped the steering wheel to the point where she swore her knuckles would pop.

"Would you like me to respond to him, boss?"

"Sure, tell him, 'Miss you too and I'm going to be out for the evening so sorry if I can't text'."

"Got it." Harmony tapped at the keyboard. "'I'm going to kill you in your sleep and you're going to love every minute of it.'"

"Harmony."

"Yes?"

"Please tell me you didn't actually send that."

"Sadly, I did not. A shame, really. Killing people in their sleep is so much fun."

With that, they found a pothole-filled space in front of the candy shop. They weaved around display cases full of vintage-style wrappers and weird candies in the shape of everyday food from hamburgers to hot dogs. Harmony led her to a soda wall on the back wall and gestured at the Ramune Japanese sodas. "I figure we could each get one. Or twenty each. One or the other."

Em fingered the weird curves of the bottle. "I thought you'd given up your Japan phase, Harmony."

"One never truly gives up their Japan phase when it comes to soda. Besides," she motioned to the row of "weird flavors", "it's this or the ranch-flavored pop."

"Got it. Japan it is."

Em selected a lychee for herself and a green apple for Harmony.

They checked out and returned to the car. Five more buzzes sounded from her phone, and she groaned. Harmony passed her a sympathetic look as they strapped themselves into their seatbelts.

"Maybe...maybe, Em, he needs some boundaries? He sounds like he likes you a lot."

"Loves me."

Harmony hesitated. "Right." She didn't sound so sure.

A few days after the archery date, Frankie had admitted his feelings for her. She'd never experienced love with a guy before. With friends, yes. But with a man? What did that feel like?

His wide eyes had searched hers, pupils darting back and forth. He'd wanted her to repeat it. So she did.

"Yeah, but that's not unusual at Mansfield. I've known plenty of couples who got engaged after only a month of dating." She knew she was justifying it. But what choice did she have? With *that* bet?

According to some of the master's students she'd spoken with, in the "world outside of the Mansfield bubble", couples maybe met up once or twice a week, sometimes more for dates. They didn't have the luxury of colluding after class or all hours in the evening.

"Boundaries." She deflated in her front seat. "I don't even know how to start—"

"By killing him in his sleep."

"Okay, apart from that."

"Hmm." Harmony tapped her finger against her chin. "I'm not the best person to talk about this, because my past boyfriends were...well, weird. And I didn't know how to say no to things like stalking me and throwing baby stuffed animal sharks at me when I worked as a sales associate."

Right, she'd almost forgotten about the shark stalker guy. Em scratched at her arm. "I just... I'm never a person to say no to things. I'd feel selfish if I did."

After all, plenty of chapel speakers had told students to give their all in everything they set out to do, relationships included. If she took time for herself, wouldn't that mean she didn't give one hundred percent effort?

Harmony's dress scrunched in the shoulders when she shrugged. "It's up to you. But I think you should set boundaries or he's gonna keep messaging you like this."

They made their final pit stop at a cookie store before returning to the apartment. Jana, nestled in the arms of her boyfriend Chen, glanced up at them and hit pause on a movie. The screen halted on a couple, discussing something over an afternoon lunch.

Harmony pinked.

So much for boundaries. Never once did Em witness Harmony standing up to her roommate. Jana would let her alarm go off seven times in the morning and would watch Netflix at all hours, without headphones. Harmony never once complained.

Guess we're both bad at standing up for ourselves.

Some sort of motherly instinct kicked in, and Em waved the bagged popcorn in her hands—secure in the grocery to-go bag. "Hey guys, sorry to interrupt your date, but Harmony and I had something scheduled on the calendar for a long time. Any chance you can move it to somewhere else?"

Jana jabbed her chin over at the kitchen. "I didn't see anything on the calendar."

A whiteboard calendar took up the back wall, nearest the sink. There, the four ladies would put their various activities and commitments—and if they planned to have any guests over. On the date for today, it looked as though someone had rubbed out orange markings. Jana must've erased it. Not that they could prove anything.

Em vowed to start taking pictures so she could avoid further gaslighting.

"Besides." Jana snuggled in closer to Chen. "It's the anniversary of the first time we met. I think that would give us dibs over this TV."

Em bunched her fist, but Harmony inched back to the door. "That's fine. I'm sure we can watch it on a laptop and pull it up on some streaming service."

Nope, Em had researched it ahead of time. They'd checked out the DVD at the library because she couldn't find it anywhere on Hulu or Netflix, the only subscriptions she paid for.

"Sorry." Chen winced in what looked like an authentic apologetic manner. "But we're going to be here for a while. After we watch this, we're going to go over the videos from last year's Lip Sync Battle."

Harmony blinked. "Lip Sync Battle?"

Jana giggled and rubbed her hands up and down Chen's chest. "That's right, girlie. That's how Chen and I met. We were in the same dance group."

Ah yes, Em knew the Lip Sync event well. She pulled up the site on her phone and handed it to Harmony to answer the question in Harmony's eyes. They read together.

Lip Sync Battle - Every February, Mansfield holds a Lip Sync Battle competition. Students choreograph elaborate dances and compete for first prize. Some of last year's most popular themes included "Guardians of the Galaxy Soundtrack", "Hercules", "Alice in Wonderland", and "Time Travel".

"It's a huge event." Em returned her device to her pocket. "I'm surprised they didn't tell you about it at the newspaper."

"We follow things on a week-by-week basis. But you said you met a year ago." Harmony pointed at the couple with her ring finger. Just for funzies, Em guessed. "Does that mean they already started practices for this year?"

Jana glanced up at Chen, who did his best to shrug with his arm draped around her. "You know, that's a good question, girlie. I think practices may be starting a little later this year. Something about where Easter falls. We're taking an off-year to focus more on our relationship, but—" Jana arched a brow. "It may not be a bad idea to join."

Em's knees buckled. "Oh, I'm not that good at dancing." Once, her director in middle school had cast her as a principal dancer in *The Music Man*. The director likely needed more dancers, or had gotten her mixed up with someone else from auditions. She learned very quickly in "Shipoopi" that she belonged in the back row forever and ever, amen.

"I wasn't talking to you, girlie." Jana bobbed her chin at Harmony.

"Me?" Harmony pointed at herself. "I mean, I can bust a move called the awkward starfish." She bounced around, flopping her arms.

Awkward sea creature, indeed.

"Right, umm, that's amazing. But what I more so meant was that it's important to join clubs and activities where you'll find guys. At the newspaper, it's mostly girls, but tons of guys sign up for the lip-syncing event. I would've suggested that to Em if she didn't have a boyfriend now."

Em's cheeks warmed. One of the reasons she stuck with Frankie, despite his boundaries? Because it kept her from Jana's "matchmaking."

"Clubs and activities." Harmony sounded out the words as if tasting them.

"Now if you two don't mind." Jana made a shooing motion. "We have an anniversary to celebrate."

Moments later, they found themselves in the hallway once more with their goodies. By now, the popcorn must've gone cold, but the butter would make it all worth it.

Em nodded at the lobby at the end of the hall. "Maybe we can't watch *Clueless*, but we could still get through these snacks—what's that look, Harmony?"

Harmony widened her eyes so much that for a split second, Em did consider whether Harmony was a serial killer, like she claimed to be.

"This is my pleading look, Em. Is it working?"

"Umm, yeah, it is. Please stop it. It's too much."

Harmony's lids reduced to a normal width apart. "Good. Are you...willing to sign up with me for the lip sync battle?"

"Oh gosh." Em pinched her nose. Of course, Harmony would take Jana's words to heart. Plenty of people who dated on this campus suggested that the surefire way to "find a mate" was to do so in an intramural sport or other activity.

People should just do activities for fun, not to find their future spouse.

She recalled what one of her dates stated. *If you try to force it, it'll never work out.*

"I already told you, Harmony. I'm awful at dancing."

"I know but," Harmony dragged her toe of her shoe across the carpet, "I just don't want to do it alone. Pleeeeease. I think, after seeing you and Jana with your dates, that I'm ready to jump back in. I feel like I'm missing out." The wide-eyed look made a return.

Em's phone buzzed several times in her pocket. Thanks to the school's spotty cell services, texts sometimes arrived in batches. She didn't need to look to see who'd sent the messages. *That boundaries talk isn't going to go well with him, is it?*

But if she had a scheduled event—say, three dance practices a night until March—that could give her some breathing room with Frankie. Maybe rekindle some of that original fire she'd felt when she met him at the purity conference.

"Okay, fine, Harmony. I'll do it."

"Yayyyyy. Thankyouthankyouthankyou."

"Just promise me you'll never give me that pitiful look again, okay?" Em pulled up the signup sheet for the Lip Sync Battle on her phone.

"I make no promises, Emerson Levi."

Chapter Sixteen

"I'VE GOT ENOUGH TIGHTS to make an acrobat blush."

As Em and Harmony headed down the carpeted hallway in the performing arts center, Harmony strutted in her hot pink dance tights. Several Amazon packages had awaited Em's apartment mate that morning, including about every shade in the rainbow for hosiery. Part of Em wondered if Harmony rented out her clothes to other students or donated any to the theater department once she finished using them for her brief "phases".

Heaven knows how she can afford it.

Maybe the rent-a-closet option did sound more reasonable. She could've sworn she spotted another student in Harmony's hat that was shaped like a turkey the other day. Just in time for the upcoming Thanksgiving break.

Em would stay on campus for that. No use driving ten hours back home for a three-day reprieve. Laila would stay back too, and the two of them would delight themselves in a Friendsgiving. To her relief, Frankie would head back home to Cleveland.

Finally, I can get some breathing room.

To her surprise, he had not taken the news about the lip sync practices all that hard. He squeezed her shoulder, grinned, said, "If that's what you want to do, babe, I'll be in the front row watching all the performances."

Perhaps the clingy phase had been just like Harmony's outfit choic-es...a mere phase.

They entered a classroom with slick, wooden floors and mirrors covering one end. Brief memories of Em's ballet days flickered in front of her vision. She recalled the five positions of the feet and her dance instructor's groans when she couldn't seem to nail the turns.

Ah, yes, the reason I never kept up with dancing.

A girl with purple hair and a leotard stretched at the barre mounted to the side wall of the classroom. She waved at Em as if she knew her.

Em scrutinized her brain to recall some instance of when she met Purple Hair. Nothing. Oh, how she wished she could recall names better. Saving face, she returned the greeting and stationed herself at the bar. "Hey."

"Hey!" The girl bent down to adjust the elastics of her shoes. She returned to a standing position. "Any chance you got my email? I filled out that survey a few weeks ago."

Shoot, she was a client-hopeful.

"I'm so sorry." Em's grip wrenched the barre. She watched as Harmony spun endlessly in front of the mirrors, pausing periodically to show off her pink tights to a class member. "I've been so busy with schoolwork and upcoming exams—" And nonstop dates with Frankie.

He'd met with her parents on FaceTime the other week. For the first time in ages, a glow illuminated her mother's cheeks, even through the pixelated screen. She'd yearned for Em to find a match since she'd turned sixteen.

At least the parents approve. She recalled several chick flicks of where the parental units would do anything to sabotage a union between two lovers.

"No worries." Purple Hair arced her arm about her head and leaned to the side. "I can imagine that it's a lot to juggle. I wanted to talk with you because I was thinking about rescinding my application."

"Yeah?"

"Yeah." Purple Hair stopped her stretched and dug into the pockets of her shapewear. Once she wedged out a phone, she showed a picture to Em. Ah, the sweet boy from one of her own dates, the one who agreed to stay friends. "I hit it off with him at a Dash Date, and he asked me out to coffee. I don't want to be premature in this, but we're clicking in a lot of ways."

"Please, go for it. He's an absolute sweetheart."

Em made a mental note to cross this girl off the list when she returned home. Spreadsheets full of unresponded-to emails had formed stress headaches in her temples.

"So." Purple Hair moved her feet through the five positions. "What did you think of Juliette's email?"

Juliette, Juliette...

Em pulled out her phone and tapped on a message with that name, to remind herself. The subject line read "Before our first practice"

Hi everyone!

Juliette here, captain of the Mansfield Chorus Girls. For those unfamiliar with what that means—since we go to a larger school by Christian university standards—we're the people who dance at the soccer and volleyball games.

Although I have a lot of dance experience, we don't expect that out of everyone. The whole point of this lip sync battle is to bring students of all abilities together to compete against other dance groups. So let's not be like some of those exclusive groups who only are looking for professional dancers. Y'all know who I'm talking about.

I'll go over the theme with you in our first class, play the soundtrack for you, and then have you do a few counts of eight for me—so I can gauge who we can give some of the more complicated dance moves to.

For class, please bring:

Clothing that is easy to move in. No jeans. Tights are preferred, ladies, if you have them.

Dance shoes are preferred. Tennis shoes really aren't going to cut it. It's honestly preferable for you to go barefoot than in socks (if you don't have dance shoes). We do sweep the floors before each class.

A peppy attitude. This is supposed to be fun. Let's create something beautiful together!

Sincerely,

Juliette

Em clicked off her phone and shoved it into her pocket. Unlike her apartment-mate, she owned no tights, so she'd opted for leggings. "I don't see anything I disagree with?"

Purple Hair nodded, shielded a slight eye roll. "You've never danced with Juliette before, have you?" Em wondered why Purple Hair danced with Juliette in the first place if she didn't appear to like it. Maybe she was good friends with Juliette, or maybe Juliette had blackmail on her. Who knew?

"Nope."

"There's probably a reason she didn't include the theme. Her past few years have been...less-than-exciting ones. And she probably knows that if she tells us the theme, that she'll have people drop out on her."

"Got it."

Speaking of the theme, whispers from the other dancers tickled her ears. She caught snippets of conversations from.

"You think it's going to be something from Disney?"

"I was hoping *Prince of Egypt,* to be honest. Can you imagine doing that plagues song?"

"I heard a rumor that we're doing an 80s mix."

Right on the dot of seven o'clock, a tall girl with a slim physique entered the room. She approached the front and tightened her high ponytail. "Hi, everyone! This is an amazing turnout. Thank you so much for showing up for our first rehearsal. Give yourselves a hand."

Everyone applauded.

"Now, I know you've been all dying to hear what this year's theme is." She splayed her hands, as though in a jazz number. "And I'm so excited to tell you."

People in Em's periphery leaned closer.

"It's 'A Mansfield Love Story'."

The girls nearest to Em deflated. Lights extinguished in the eyes of Purple Hair. Someone nearby whispered. "Ugh, we're never going to win with a theme like that."

Indeed, Em had perused videos of past performances with Harmony during their girls' night. Most of the time, the year's most popular movie or a Disney flick with a thriving soundtrack would take first place. A love story would serve as filler between the better numbers.

"Hear me out." Juliette's eyes widened, hiding bright blue eyeshadow. "We're going to have some T-Swift bops in there and we'll have all the tropes." She raised a hand and ticked each item off on a finger. "Meeting on a dash date, circling the loop, ring by spring. It'll be super meta. Here, I'll let you listen. Maybe the songs can convince you."

Speakers nestled in the corners of the room blasted hits from ten or fifteen years ago. Even the song transitions from one to the next didn't flow in a smooth manner. It was almost as if Juliette had attempted to splice sounds for the first time. When the last song, "Uptown Funk", concluded, a man with beefy hands clapped and whooped near the front of the classroom.

Her boyfriend, I presume.

"Thanks, Chad. Now, I'd love to gauge dance abilities, so you, you, you, you, and"—she pointed at Em—"you, you're my newbies. Why don't you come up here and repeat this count of eight?"

Em's cheeks pinked. "Oh." She cleared her throat. "That's okay, Juliette, I know where I belong. In the back. I'll save you some time."

Juliette perched a bony arm on her hip. *Yeesh, when did this girl last eat a cheeseburger?* "Nonsense. It's important for me to gauge ability. I'll go slow, okay?"

Juliette did not, in fact, go slow. She spun and kicked and leaped to a count of eight two times. "Okay, and now for the arms." Before Em could even cement in her mind the legs portion, Juliette made sweeping gestures with her arms and concluded the series with an open fourth position pose. "All right, your turn."

She clicked on the music, and of course, it went far faster than the example. Em collided with the dancer on her right during the spin and finished with lame jazz hands when she couldn't keep up with the others.

Juliette looked as though someone had squeezed lemon juice in her eyes. The expression melted into something both pitiful and encouraging. "Amazing work. Okay, let's have everyone gather around so we can start working on the first song, 'Love Story' by Taylor Swift."

Half an hour later, Juliette called for a water break. Em uncapped her bottle and meandered into the hallway to escape the humidity of the hot classroom. Who knew that so much spinning could generate so much heat?

As she swigged the metallic-tasting liquid, her pockets vibrated.

"Frankie." She gasped, tightening the water bottle lid. "Not now."

When she dug out the phone, she frowned at the Caller ID. "Tara?"

Em swiped the green button and located an empty classroom. She flicked on the lights. Electricity hummed as Tara's face appeared on the screen. "What's up, Tara?"

When had she last spoken to this wing-mate from freshman year? At the wedding held two summers back? She remembered the beautiful woman parading down the aisle in a mermaid-style gown Some stylist had woven a flower crown into her hair.

"Hey, girl, do you have a minute to talk?" An edge coated Tara's voice.

Em slid onto the floor, resting her neck against the cool mirror glass. "Umm, sure. Is everything okay?"

Tara considered the words, gave one bob of the chin. "Yeah, I think it's going to be. I'm about to announce something on social media, and I figured it would be important for you to know. So you don't get caught off-guard."

Senses heightened. Everything sounded so much louder in the silence.

"What happened?" Em's heartbeat pounded her ribcage.

"I figured, since you were the one to match us. I mean you didn't vet us or anything, but you're the reason it kicked off in the first place—" Tara blinked away a glaze in her eyes. "Maverick and I are getting a divorce. Well." She cleared her throat. "I mean, we already got it. Signed the papers a few weeks ago, but we're announcing it. Officially."

Em gasped. A divorce? The picture-perfect couple? The first ones she'd ever set up? The ones who'd gotten her started in the matchmaking business in the first place?

"I—oh—gosh—sorry." Words crackled in Em's throat.

Tara threw a dismissive wave at the camera. "Listen, girl, I don't blame you at all. I'd been eyeing him for some time, and if you hadn't set me up with him, someone would've. Besides, people, umm, change. You couldn't have predicted that."

Still, Em's throat dried. Couples, ones she'd matched over the years, flickered across her mind. How many others had she paired up who were doomed to fail? "What…what happened, Tara? If you don't mind me asking."

"Everything all at once, I guess." Tara sighed. "I think what it boils down to, Em, is that there's a bubble around Mansfield. What happens in college dating really is not at all like real life."

Many students did use the term "Mansfield bubble". That even sometimes the precipitation seemed to fall on campus in a different way than in the outside town. As if someone had encased the school in some sort of effervescence.

"Little things start to chip away at the relationship when you're waking up next to them. Toothbrushes left face down on the counter. Someone forgot to do the dishes again. Someone forgot about the cell phone bill. Until one day—" Tears pooled in Tara's eyes again. "One day, you realize that you don't really know who you married in the first place." A sour note rang in her voice. "If someone had told me the divorce statistics at Mansfield before my marriage, I probably would've waited a few years before tying that knot."

Something hard got stuck in the back of Em's throat. "Divorce stats?"

"Yeah, I don't remember the exact numbers, but it's bad. When I first saw them, I was like, 'It's a Christian school. Christians aren't supposed to get divorced because the Bible says...blah, blah, blah.' But I guess a lot of marriages fizzle after Mansfield."

Why had no one told her this before? And why was everyone so insistent on seniors finding a ring by spring if they'd lose it within a few years?

"Anyway, girl, I do have to go. I'm sorry if this threw off your day, but I didn't want you to be blindsided."

"No, I...appreciate it. Thanks for letting me know. And *I'm* sorry. Keep me in the loop, okay?"

"You got it." The screen went dark.

Assuming the water break had long-since ended, Em pulled herself up and hobbled her way to the classroom. Perhaps dance for the next hour and a half could purge her of these thoughts, these emotions.

When she stepped inside the classroom, she froze. Rob the Builder had shed his trench coat. Underneath, a T-shirt with a movie poster from Star Wars Episode IV shone in the classroom lights. In the corner of the classroom, Harmony grinned at him. Rob, with his back turned toward her, didn't spy the expression.

Oh, we gotta prevent a disaster.

Juliette called for them to pick a partner of the opposite sex to practice some lifts. Without a moment to lose, Em flew to Harmony. "Hey, Harmony, I think that guy over there, the one in the Muppets T-shirt, was eyeing your pink tights earlier. Think he'd make a good dance partner?"

Harmony eyed him up and down. "Well, I do like Kermit. Especially during my green phases." She saluted Em. "Thanks!"

As Em paired with a shorter man with a linebacker build, she glimpsed Rob. He was left with one of the other unpicked dancers. She squinted at him as he cast a longing glance at Harmony. *Not on my watch, Rob the Builder, not on my watch.*

Chapter Seventeen

"Merry Early Christmas, slash, getting through finals week."

Em lit up like the strings of icicle lights hung over their windowsill when she opened her apartment door. "Noah! Come in."

Present in hand, he didn't budge. "Are you sure your boyfriend is going to be okay with it?"

Em rolled her eyes. She craned her neck over her shoulder and glimpsed Harmony on the futon. The girl had stuffed the largest headphones Em had ever witnessed over her ears. No sound could pass through those things. "We have supervision, you're fine. Besides, it's not like Frankie and I are married."

As Noah stepped in, a thought formed goosebumps up her arms. Would that meant that when she got married, she would have to forfeit any types of friendships with males?

She recalled one talk in a youth group, years ago, where a woman gathered the girls into one room. She was one of two people in charge of the teens. According to Em's parents, the church wouldn't hire her until she got married. And she did, to the other youth pastor.

"Now, girls, I want to tell you a story, okay? There was a young newlywed who walked into my office, and she had held up her phone saying, 'It's so not fair'." The woman mimed shaking a device.

"So I replied, 'Life seldom is.' She shook her head, 'I had this best friend before I got married. We'd go on hikes together and hang out. I knew him before I even met my husband. But he's saying that I can't be with him one-on-one. Group date settings only. He's single. He can't do that.'"

The youth leader clicked her tongue. "She was in dangerous territory, of course. Remember that you cannot hang out with a man one-on-one when you're married, ladies. The temptation is too great."

Would the same happen with her and Noah?

Like the newlywed in the story, she'd known Noah far longer than Frankie. Even Noah had told her tales about jealous theater boyfriends who threatened to deck him when he had to stage kiss their significant others during a production. Could he understand when he'd lost so many female theater friends that way?

She shook away the thoughts. *Not now.* Months still awaited her before she'd have to figure that out.

Noah parked on a chair and admired the view of the Charlie Brown Christmas tree they'd fished out of the dumpster. Strong smells of peppermint hot chocolate invaded the walls of the apartment. Too bad Laila had only made one cup. "How are finals going for you, Em?"

She collapsed into the seat beside him. "I swear that all the teachers are intentionally putting the tests on the last day to keep us here as long as possible."

Didn't help that the RAs wouldn't let anyone stay at campus over winter break, or they'd issue a fine for every hour a student stayed after exams. A ten-hour drive to Raleigh would put Em returning home sometime around four in the morning. But at least Harmony would join her and split the driving.

"Parents are in England this winter break." Harmony had shrugged while taping bows to the apartment walls. "There's a professional writing student who lives in the Triangle. It's a place in North Carolina where three major cities are close together. She can host me for Christmas."

Em did wonder about the international students. Would the school force them to find someone to piggyback for winter break? Unfortunately, even when she lived in the dorms, she didn't have too many international students in her residence hall. She'd never thought to ask.

"Yeah, that sounds about right." Noah held out the present for her. "Merry Christmas."

Her cheeks pinked. "I'm so sorry. I've been so behind, that I haven't had a chance—"

He held up a hand. "That's the point of gifts. You don't expect one in return."

Still, she would have to figure out presents for her parents before her last final. Em often stuffed her parents' stockings on Christmas morning too. She'd figured if she could just make them happy for one day of the year, maybe they'd forget that they hated each other.

If only I could get them enough gifts to stop them from divorcing. Her mind drifted back to Tara.

"Well, open it, you silly goose."

"I just thought you got me a box. Silly me." She honked at him, which caused him to dissolve into chuckles.

"Did you just try to sound like a goose?"

"Yup. If y'all ever have a play with a territorial aquatic bird, I'm a shoo-in."

She ripped at the corners of the paper and pulled the shoebox out slowly. According to Harmony, people who unwrapped gifts in Japan would take longer amounts of time to open gifts. Especially presents from those who mattered most to them.

Once she eased out the box, she popped open the lid. "Oh, Noah!"

A pair of pointe ballet slippers glimmered in the blinking Christmas lights that wound around every wall of the apartment.

"I—have no idea how to wear these. Besides, most of the songs are pop, and these have to be so expensive..."

Noah shrugged. "I found them at a theater rummage sale, so don't worry too much about the cost."

Em gawked at the sheen in the fabric. Rummage sale or not, these couldn't have been used. Em recalled several videos of ballerinas beating the shoes against the floor to get them to soften. No such creases showed themselves in the soles.

He's lying about how much he spent. Noah wasn't much of a liar, except on stage. But he managed to succeed at a fib here or there.

"I figured you could hang it on a hook or something. I just wanted this to show that I support you, no matter what you do. And I figure this could represent that lip sync battle."

Oh, these would hang so lovely over her bed. Although she wasn't the best dancer, she could feel the thought put into them. It was a symbol of his support of her, rather than a practical thing she could use.

"Noah, thank you." They both rose and hugged. "And you do mean that? Anything?"

He palmed his neck. "To be honest, I don't really get the matchmaking stuff. But, Em, if that's what you truly feel called to, then I'm in your corner."

An odd feeling she couldn't figure out ebbed in her ribcage. Good at? Yes. Called to? Now, she wasn't so sure.

"Right, yeah, thanks."

"You have any other Christmas celebrations before you get back home?"

Sort of. She and Frankie had planned a gift exchange. She managed to purchase him some of his favorite snacks at the TSC. Frankie's gift to her was "ten kisses on each cheek." Em tried to bury the resentment that surfaced at this. At the very least, she would've appreciated more a poem or something tangible that didn't leave her cheeks feelings so wet in the cold weather.

As for her roommates, they planned to binge some Hallmark Christmas movies between finals to provide some stress relief. In her spare moments, she'd talk with Noah.

After she and Noah chatted to catch up on the weeks of missed meetings and play prep, they parted ways. Joy glowed in her chest from their conversation.

Married or not, she'd find ways to hang out with every friend. It was a ridiculous expectation to force her to sever all relationships once she tied the knot. Besides, if she could convince Frankie to let her join the lip sync battle, she wouldn't have so much of a battle to keep Noah in her life.

Frankie had, after all, eased up on some of the text messages and calls.

That was a good sign. Right?

Right?

"Dear," Mom motioned to Em's dad, "can you please sit down for once and enjoy unwrapping gifts? We can put the wrapping paper in that trash bag later."

Her mother's tone had an edge this Christmas morning. Fairy lights on the tree winked in and out, and stocking gifts littered her mother's seat on the family room couch.

Chocolate oranges, and candy canes, and whatever else Em could find in gas stations on the drive home made up most of the contents of the knit socks that hung over the fireplace.

"Santa" had forgotten about Em this year, but she didn't mind.

Her parents had weaned her out of childhood things. The minute she got a cell phone and bought a used car from her uncle, they handed her as many bills as they could. Whenever she visited home, she couldn't fight the feeling that they felt she suckled from their bank account too much. Em made a habit of buying her own groceries each week, so they had one less thing to complain about. She even tried to limit her shower time to ten minutes, fifteen max if she had to shave that day. But despite her alarm-setting, it never seemed to be good enough.

Maybe I can convince Harmony's friend to let me use their shower so Mom can't complain about the water bill again.

Her father, bedecked in a Frosty the Snowman sweatshirt, fisted his hips. "Well, I'm just trying to make this more efficient. If you ask me, Christmas takes way too long with us unwrapping gifts individually. Starving children in Africa would be embarrassed to see how much we spend each year."

Ah yes, the starving children in Africa had surfaced once again in Dad's slight Raleigh accent. Never mind that their family had moved here three years ago from Wisconsin. He leaned in hard to the culture.

"There aren't that many gifts." Her mother's voice rose to a near-shriek.

Each person received perhaps seven, and none of the gifts could've been worth more than twenty dollars apiece. Nothing to blush at, but certainly not the piles of presents she'd seen posted by her classmates during her middle school days. Those parents had to have dropped thousands on those baubles. She would have been fine with three gifts, or even one. But her parents had a habit of spending money they didn't need, then complaining about finances.

Cinnamon and vanilla swirled in the air, hinting at the cinnamon roll breakfast Em had prepared and making her stomach gurgle. Her dad had yelled at her earlier that morning for spending extra on ingredients like walnuts for the rolls. *It's my money. I'm not sure why he made such a big deal out of it.*

"That's fine, Dad." She winced. "We can all open our presents at the same time, if that would make you happy."

Em bounced up from the squeaky family room chair and handed everyone a gift each. Within five minutes, they'd torn the paper off everything. Em thanked them for the fuzzy socks and coffee mug featuring an octopus. She'd never really mentioned being into octopi, but maybe they'd found it on a sale rack somewhere. In either case, she'd learned over the years not to complain about presents. It would break out unnecessary fights.

She gathered the wrapping paper, wadded it in a trash bag, and tossed it into the bin in the garage. When she returned, her father had sat in the chair—the farthest seating arrangement away from the couch in the family room.

Her mother clung to the arm of the couch. "So, Em, it seems like ages since we've been able to FaceTime. How's the boy?"

Why was *this* always the first question Em got asked? Academic achievements, matchmaking, none of that ever surfaced in conversation. Only *boys*.

"He's fine." Em answered in a deadpan tone.

It was enough to send mom clapping and yipping. "Oh, sweetie, that's wonderful to hear. Now, can you remind me what his major is?"

"Comp sci, I believe?"

"Oh, computer science." Her mom's eyes widened. "That's what I thought it was. I knew it was one of those pretty lucrative ones. I must say, sweetie, when I spoke with him on the phone, he was an absolute gem."

Em perched on the other end of the couch. Bristles from the Christmas tree jabbed her back. "He was?"

Doubts had surfaced about whether she truly liked Frankie. So many dates had dissolved into fights now, no matter how often she tried to stroke his ego by allowing him to kiss her for the majority of their time together.

Her partner in the lip sync battle classes assured her that relationships went through this. *It's a good thing there's conflict. If there wasn't, you should be worried.*

Some people thought it was odd that Em was sharing her dating woes with a near-stranger from dance class. But maybe that was thanks to the 'tism. She didn't always have a gauge on what information to share with whom.

"Oh, yes, sweetie." Her mother's voice pulled her back. In the corner of the room, Bear the dog panted. He chewed on Em's treat for him, a ball filled with peanut butter—a score found with Walmart delivery. "Frankie seems like he loves you very much, and I think he'll be able to take care of you someday." She winked.

Tension eased in Em's chest. Maybe she'd been making up these worries this whole time. If her parents approved, that had to mean something, right?

The conversation soon fizzled, and she found herself back upstairs in her room. Bear hopped onto her bed, causing the mattress to groan. He slammed his head onto her stomach and thumped his tail against the comforter.

How often had Mom and Dad warned her that the moment she moved out that they'd send this dog along with her? That "he costs too much, and you promised you'd take care of him"?

Yeah, back when we got him when I was a junior in high school.

She patted his head and shivered. Then snuggled under the blankets. At what temperature did Mom and Dad set the thermostat?

Her phone vibrated, and she bit back a groan at the Caller ID. *You're supposed to be excited when your boyfriend calls.*

Granted, he phoned her a lot. Even on the ten-hour drive back home, he'd FaceTimed no less than three times, whenever Harmony manned the wheel. He'd also peppered her with texts. If she saw the words "I miss you" any more times, she might explode like a Christmas cracker.

She sucked in a deep breath, forced a smile, answered. "Hey, Frankie."

"Babyyyy, I miss you so much. Mwah, mwah, mwah."

Oh, goodness, the baby voice. She couldn't stand the baby voice.

To the best of her understanding, she'd always called herself an "old soul". She'd had to act like a grown up long before she turned eighteen. Laila informed her later this meant she was "traumatized."

She remembered arguing with her. "I mean, I don't feel all that traumatized. Some kids are nearly killed by their parents. I didn't have it nearly that hard."

Laila had pursed her lips. "Trauma is trauma, girl."

Em later understood that because she had to mature faster than others, she couldn't really stand for any kind of immature talk or tones. No matter how often she reminded Frankie, he didn't seem to catch on.

I can't force him to change, right? That would make me some kind of monster, making him adjust for me.

"Hey." She lowered her tone and hoped he would pick up on the fact that she didn't feel like being in a playful mood. "How's your Christmas so far?"

"Soooo good babyyyy. Mwah, mwah, mwah. I miss you soooo much."

A pause held them.

"Oh, haha, yeah, I miss you too. Get any fun gifts?" Maybe if she could distract him with another subject, he could get off the I've-been-away-from-my-girlfriend train.

"Yeahhh! I got some headphones." There was the baby voice again. "And some blankets. And some gift carrrds. Yussss."

"Haha, that's great, babe. Gift cards are always great. Where are the gift cards to?"

"Baaaabe. I miss seeing your face and kissing your face." He pouted. "Why do you have to live so far away?"

Seldom did they have a date where he didn't bring up his former girlfriend, who had lived a similar distance from him. Unlike her, Em at least went to the same college as Frankie.

"Haha." Tension clenched in her gut. "Well, thankfully, we get to see each other nine months out of the year, right?"

And then what?

When she graduated, would she have to make frequent drives up from Raleigh? Or if he "put a ring on it", would she have to rent a campus apartment until he got his degree a year later?

Weariness clawed at her eyes.

"Hey, babe." She forced another smile. "I'm pretty tired from all this Christmas stuff today. Is it okay if we chat a little later? Might go take a nap."

"Noooo."

"It won't be that long of a nap." Maybe if she failed to set an alarm, she could blame not talking with him later on that.

He heaved a heavy sigh. "Fiiiine. But I miss you so much. Mwah, mwah, mwah.""Haha, I miss you too."

"You have to kiss me back."

Her intestines writhed. "Umm, sure, babe. Mwah."

"Yaaaay. But don't go, babe."

"Talk soon."

"Noooo..."

She clicked the red button and clapped her neck against her pillow. Oh goodness, that was painful. Why couldn't her conversations with Frankie flow like the ones with her friends? Noah was a guy, and he got through dialogue just fine without any "Noooos" or "I miss yous".

A text blinked on her phone.

Probably Frankie getting mad at me for hanging up.

Nope, one from Harmony.

Harmony: Any chance we could meet tomorrow?

Harmony: I have some pretty bad news

No emojis, nothing.

This must be serious.

Em: How does coffee sound?

Three dots later.

Harmony: Terrible. Coffee probably sounds like an old, gruff person who wants kids off his lawn

Em smiled and closed her eyes for her "nap". *There* was the Harmony she knew and loved.

Chapter Eighteen

"DID YOU JUST BUY one of every single mug?"

Em gawked at Harmony as she carried ten mugs to their table in the squat coffee shop. Bells jingled on Harmony's skirt, and Em realized, seconds later, that the entire outfit resembled a Christmas tree. Small, red ornaments that clung to tinsel fell off the dress and onto the coffee shop floor.

"Indeed, I did. Ho, ho, ho. And now I shall name them. Winnifred—"

Harmony pointed at each much as she designated their monikers. Winnifred had a number of snowflakes on its dark blue exterior.

"Sir Thomas Becket—rest in peace, good sir—Edwina, Malvolio—"

Em peered at her latte art in her cup. The barista had managed to make the foam form the shape of a rose.

"—and of course, Bob."

"Harmony, where do you get the money for this sort of stuff?"

Jingle Bells played in the shop as a coffee grinder screamed. Above hung paper snowflakes that the staff must've cut into various shapes. Lights decorated ferns nestled in the corners by the cream station.

"I'm a mob boss, obviously."

"Do you rent out your clothes or something?"

Harmony's eyes widened. She'd shaded the lids with sparkly green and red eyeshadow. Nice, she'd learned a tip or two from Laila back at the hoedown dance. Or that professional writing major offered to decor her eyes today. "How did you know?"

"Wait, you *do*?"

Harmony dug out her phone. She tapped into the restaurant's WiFi and pulled up a website. Em held back a laugh at the domain name:

She had to re-read the link several times to figure out that it was "Nerdy outfit" and not "Nerd you fit".

Welcome to "Rent a Nerdy Outfit"

Have you ever wanted to put on a play, but can't find the right fit? Or maybe wanted to run around in a chicken costume for no reason? Well, friends, I have you. Or "got you", as the youths say. Peruse the selection below and choose an outfit to "rent". If your order totals $100 or more, pre-taxes, I will ship it to you for free.

Em handed the phone back to Harmony. "Okay, but how did you get so much inventory in the first place?"

Harmony sipped on one of the empty mugs, pinky raised. "Parents used to own a costume shop. They wanted to purge most of what didn't get taken in the 'going out of business sale'."

Got it.

Em fingered one of the snowmen on Harmony's mugs. What had she named this one, again? Edwina? "How was your Christmas? Did you awkwardly sit while people opened presents?"

Harmony shook her head. Tinsel glittered in her hair. "It wasn't awkward. They'd been warned ahead of time, so they made sure to wrap me some presents too. Granted, it was niche stuff, so I don't know if I'll like it."

"Niche stuff?"

"Yeah, like lotions, and body sprays, and pens, and candles."

Em decided not to question that further. She sipped on the foam and winced when the espresso underneath scalded her tongue and obliterated rows of taste buds. "Right, so, you wanted to meet with me. About something serious."

Harmony exhaled long and hard. Her hands shook to the that point Em took pity and fished a granola bar from her purse to give to Harmony.

"Thanks." Harmony bit into the oat and raisin mixture. "Please know that what I'm about to say isn't easy, and I don't really want to say it."

Em's stomach dropped into her intestines. Possibilities whirred through her mind. Would Harmony want to drop their friendship for some reason? Or would she have to move out of the apartment due to the rooming situation with Jana?

Blenders whirred in the background. Harmony crinkled the wrapper and tossed it into one of the mugs. Poor Sir Thomas Becket. "Okay, so let me start this off with a story. Since I'm a writer and stuff."

"Okay?"

"You know how we went to the Christmas open house in your boyfriend's dorm during Dead Week?"

Dead Week was supposed to be a week at the university where teachers assigned no projects, so students could prepare for exams. Most of the professors ignored this rule, but at least the lobby in the library served donuts to midnight studiers.

"Yeah?" She recalled images of poorly decorated Christmas cookies and one of the men on the wing dressed as Father Christmas. Em didn't get much of a chance to explore because Frankie held her captive in the main room. They'd clasped hands on the couch as open-house-goers browsed the Christmas decor and activities.

"So, I could've sworn that your boyfriend said his room was one of the decorated ones. And since Mansfield has an open-door policy, it wasn't exactly locked."

Sourness filled Em's stomach. Where was Harmony going with this?

"Anyway, I went into his room to check on the Christmas decorations. The fact his door didn't have any wrapping paper on it, like the others, should've tipped me off. But something did catch my eye."

Harmony tapped on her eye, accidentally poking her retina. "It was a bunch of Post-It notes." Harmony palmed her eye, reminding Em of some kind of pirate. "And you know me, I love anything neon. Like, I'm the kind of person you never want to take to Vegas. So I thought, 'Hmm, I wonder what he puts on his sticky notes'."

"Harmony."

"Yes?"

"Is this a long story?"

"Sorry, sidetracked. So I look at the sticky notes, and I see an email password. Naturally, I hacked into his inbox."

Alarm shot pinpricks into Em's chest. Her chair squeaked back. "You *what*?"

"I mean, you'd think a comp-sci major would know better than to put his password out for the world to see. It had lot of numbers and special characters, mind you, so at least he knows about password integrity."

Em pinched the bridge of her nose. "Harmony."

"Yes?"

"I'm more surprised at the fact that you *illegally* tapped into an inbox than the fact that he shouldn't have had his password out in the open."

"Oh." Harmony folded her hands on her stomach and bowed her head in shame. "Yeahhh, that obviously wasn't—as the kids say—cool. But in my defense, I am a journalist. The curiosity was killing me."

Girls nearby giggled and showed off their frappe creations. One drink, called "the Grinch", came in a highly pigmented shade of green.

"But we're not here to talk about Harmony's illegal habits." Harmony waved a finger back and forth. "We're here to talk about what I found in your boyfriend's email. I do have—as the youth call it—the screenshots."

Did Harmony hang around grandmas all the time? What was with this youth and kids business?

Harmony shoved her phone to Em from across the table.

Em's throat dried. "Yasmin."

A slow nod from Harmony in the periphery of the phone's glow. "You know her name?"

"Yeah, he talks about his ex every two seconds."

"Then read."

Hey, Frankie,

I know you blocked me on your phone, and I don't really blame you. I got cold feet, and the distance stuff was getting hard—as you know.

There's just something so very different about phone calls than in-person.

I know I saw on social media that you're dating someone else, so I'm sorry if this is overstepping, but should that not work out, I'm wondering if you'd be willing to give us a try again. I don't blame you if you don't answer this email but just throwing myself out there. I'm just a girl standing in front of her ex, asking him to love her again.

Sincerely,

Yasmin

Hey, Yasmin,

I have to be honest, this email threw me way off. I was angry, at first, but I'm going to be honest—I'm a little shaky on the relationship front. Don't get me wrong, I love Em. Super sweet. But something's telling me she's getting cold feet, and I can't help but flashback to what happened between us.

This isn't a "yes, let's get back together." But we can still talk as friends :)

From,

Frankie

Frankie,

Oh, it's so exciting to hear we're friends again. I checked and you've still blocked me on your phone. That's okay, I respect your boundary.

Tell me a little bit more about this girl. Why do you sense that she has cold feet?

My biggest reason was obviously that I'd have to move home states, since you're wanting to get a job in Cleveland. That would mean saying goodbye to family, friends, and so many other things. Now that I've had time to think about it, I'd be willing to do that.

So anyway, is that why she's scared to commit?

Yasmin

Hey, Yasmin,

Sorry, getting ready for finals and Dead Week and all.

Honestly, I'm not sure what it is. She was going on dates with me and stuff and suddenly she's not answering texts, and she's getting busy with lots of clubs and activities. I remember one of our RAs says that people join a lot of things when they want to avoid something. And I can't help but think she's trying to hide from me.

She's mentioned nothing about what we're doing after graduation, so I haven't even talked about her moving to Cleveland. Kinda scared to now.

Frankie

Frankie,

Oh no! That's awful.

I remember that when we were dating, I'd been on the intramural flag football team, but I was willing to give that up to come see you. It's scary to think that someone who is going to your same college won't even give you the time of day.

I'm not trying to sway your opinion of her at all, but that definitely sounds like a boundaries talk you may need to be having with her soon.

Yasmin

Yasmin,

Working on it. She's kind of sensitive, so I have to approach things carefully.

How are things for you? Junior year going okay for you?

Frankie

Frankie,

Oof, so sorry to hear that's she's sensitive. If you remember me right, I was totally fine with taking criticism. That's how relationships grow.

Also, I actually am going to be in town during your finals week. It's a conference that I have to help with for practicum. Don't know if you wanted to grab coffee to catch up on things. Maybe convince you to go for a girl who has thicker skin and also no-longer a fear of traveling a distance for a marriage ;)

Yasmin

Yasmin,

Coffee sounds great. To be honest, I have one ace in the hole, and if that doesn't work, I think the relationship is probably done. Let me go ahead and unblock your number so we can talk over details about meeting up.

Frankie

When Em finished scrolling through the screenshots, she dropped the phone onto the table. Harmony scooped it up with a sympathetic look. "The messages ended there. So we have to assume that either she had to go into witness protection or they started texting."

Anger bubbled underneath Em's skin. Hosts of thoughts swirled in her head. She clocked one of the time stamps in the emails. He'd sent it when she started practicing with the lip sync battle.

When have I ever given an indication that I'm afraid of committing? If she gave him any more of her time, she'd have to forfeit any friendships or calls with her family.

With nowhere to direct the anger to, she rounded on Harmony. "You saw these before now. Why didn't you tell me?"

Harmony chewed on her bottom lip. "It was nearing finals week, and I didn't want you to fail any classes. Plus, there just wasn't a good time to bring it up."

"You spied on my boyfriend's email? Just so you could find something on him? You've been jealous of me this whole time, haven't you?"

Her friend blinked several times. Then Harmony's jaw firmed. "I'm not the enemy in this situation, Em."

Her words sank through Em's ears, down her throat, into her throat. Her skin cooled, and she caressed her coffee cup, which had gone luke-warm. "I'm...sorry, Harmony, you're right. I shouldn't get mad at you because—"

Because what? Her boyfriend was cheating on her?

She had no documented evidence of what happened after the emails, and the emails only showed two things:

1. Her boyfriend thought she was trying to avoid committing to him.

2. His ex was trying to get back together with him by degrading Em's character.

Em slammed her eyelids shut and picked at her skin on her arm. Maybe the pain could distract her from the onslaught of tears. "I don't know what to do, Harmony."

Harmony's voice came out warm, like a winter comfort drink. "Break up with him, Em. That's all that you can do now."

"Yeah, but the emails don't *prove* that he cheated. Besides, there's the—"

The bet. If she ended the relationship now, in the middle of December, that would give her less than five months to find her future husband. She might as well dig the tens of thousands of dollars out of her savings account now and dole it out to her former clients.

"I know it's easier said than done, Em, but," Harmony's nostrils wrinkled when Em opened her eyes, "something I've been told is that when you're with someone, imagine if they break up with you. What will you feel, if they do?"

At first, sad. Definitely sad. From all the kisses he stole, and all the hours spent with him. It seemed silly to think of those kisses as stolen ones, but she'd been uncomfortable of giving so many of them. It was almost like he'd coerced them out of her.

Then? Relief. Just the idea of separating herself from Frankie forced her jaw to unclench and shoulders to drop. Even during these few days apart, she'd finally had room to breathe and not always worry about his hands on her.

Images flickered back to her conversation with Mom, yesterday. Her parents approved of him. What did she miss about him that other people seemed to see?

"I think," Em swirled her cup until the remnants of the foamed-milk rose disappeared, "it's important that I at least confront him about the emails."

Harmony paled. "You're not going to say that I—"

"No, I won't do you dirty like that. I'll simply tell him that I heard he'd been talking with Yasmin. If he went on that coffee date with her, someone had to have spotted her."

Harmony's facial muscles relaxed. "But what if..." They tensed again. "What if, Em, he lies and convinces you that it's all fake? That I somehow doctored emails, or he straight-up denies that it happened?"

Before Em could answer, her phone vibrated in her coat pocket. She tapped the message from her mother.

Mom: Dad and I feel really awful about how tense Christmas was yesterday. As a treat, we'd like to take you on a hike.

Mom: Weather's beautiful for it *sun emoji*.

Indeed, cerulean skies peeked out from behind wisps of clouds, unusual for Christmas in Raleigh this time of year.

Mom: Meet us at the house in fifteen?

Em pocketed the phone and rose from her chair. "I guess."

Chapter Nineteen

Before the hike, Mom suggested a brief manicure session.

"I know it's not like those times in middle school back at the salon, when I used to paint your nails." Her mother clicked on an electric cuticle remover. Bits of skin shaved off of Em's nail beds. "But I figured we haven't been able to do this in forever."

Hope leapt in Em's chest. With Em working most summers, she maybe had time once a week to catch a show with her mom. They'd exchange no conversation during most of those hours. "I did really miss this."

Her mother coated her nails in a clear polish that would make them grow stronger, especially with a healthy layer of paint topping them. "French okay, sweetie?"

"Yeah, French is a good evergreen kind of manicure." She held out her hand, and her mother wrenched a tight grip around her fingers as she painted. "So you said that you and Dad didn't like how Christmas went down yesterday."

In her mother's bathroom, the strong whiff of used bath bombs clouded her senses. Mom *would* use no less than three heavily scented products per day. Now in her mid-fifties, her mother boasted that most people thought she'd reached the age of "thirty-five". Ever since Em's middle school days, her mother had coached her on a healthy skincare routine. She'd gotten used to drug store face sheet masks and the occasional splurge on a clay one.

Her mother sighed, the bags under her eyes darker than usual. Maybe she'd forgotten to put on her eye masks that morning. "Your father and I have a lot of differences. But I think we've managed to find some common ground on something. For now, we'll work together on that." She capped the polish and booped Em's nose. "Not that you have to worry about that, sweet girl."

Em passed her a weak smile. Of course she did,. More than once in her childhood, her mom would joke with her about divorcing her father if *she* didn't act correctly in a situation.

We're going to be late for VBS, Em, don't make me get those divorce papers.

Another B on a report card? Guess your father and I have a done marriage.

Although she'd always follow this up with a one-note laugh, Em's shoulders would scrunch so high, she swore she needed a chiropractor at an early age to work out the stress kinks in her spine.

"Yeah?" She watched the brush dab white paint onto the tips of her fingers. "What are you two working on?"

Her mom lifted a finger to her lips. "Surprises are the best around Christmas, don't you think? Now, why don't you tell me about this lip-syncing competition I've been hearing about while I finish up?"

Em recounted for her about how most practices appeared to go well. At least, from what she could tell. A handful of dancers had dropped out—owing to the theme and song choices—but she'd gotten along well with her dance partner and even nailed one of the lifts.

"Harmony's even having a good time. Although whenever her partner tries to lift her, she yells, jabs him in the ribs, and runs away. I think our choreographer is going to place her in the back with the people who sway back and forth and clap."

Thank heavens Rob the Builder had vacated the group. Perhaps he'd gotten the hints from Em's glares to keep far away.

"That's wonderful, dear. Put your hand under the UV light, please."

Nails dried. Then they piled into the car. Mom suggested Em change into a "nice dress" since "It's not really a hike. It's just a boardwalk and a few dirt paths."

Joy bubbled in her chest. For the first time in an hour she didn't have to think about...

A heavy mood overtook her as trees blurred by the window.

Oh, right, her boyfriend.

Maybe when she met with him after the break, he could explain that he'd texted Yasmin to tell her off. Or maybe his roommate hacked into his inbox and decided to answer emails as him.

They reached the parking lot, and Em leapt out in her Doc Martens. Mom had fought with her on this, telling her to wear ballet flats instead.

"Mom, we still have to walk around. You said hiking."

Her mother had sighed. "Fine, but at least clean off the dirt on those things with a Clorox wipe."

She did so. Although Mom did harbor a fastidiousness when it came to looks and presentation, this felt more nitpicky than usual. The only other times she'd behave this...meticulous...was when Em attended homeschool homecoming and prom.

Although Em didn't have any dates at the time—thanks to the "no boyfriend" rule   her mother would spend hours pinning sparkles into her updo and griping about how Em's hair never could hold a curl well.

If her mother promised her a good time on the hike today, they both had *very* different definitions of what that would look like.

Dad clicked the car to put it in lock, and they all set forth. Bundles of families and groups clogged the trail. Her mother, in her periphery, frowned at this. Em shrugged, leaves skittering from her kicks out.

"What do you expect, Mom? Everyone's on Christmas break, and the weather's nice."

Mom turtled into her jacket and sighed. The eyeroll could be clearly seen in a pool of thick eyeliner and mascara. "Today's not the best day for a crowd here."

"Why?"

"I wish it was more secluded. That's all, sweet girl." Mom squeezed Em's upper arm, and they set off onto the trail.

Even in the dead of winter, everything carried the faint scent of green. Em loitered behind at her dad's slower pace and leaned in to whisper. "So, Dad, I hear you and Mom are working on some kind of project together. You wanna tell me what it is?"

Dad didn't answer but panted as he stuck a walking stick onto the dirt path.

Silence shrouded the three of them until they reached a wooden bridge. A figure in a suit clasped his hands in front of him.

She froze. *Frankie?*

A cameraman hid behind a tree, snapping shots.

Oh gosh, no.

Before she could form more thoughts, someone shoved her from behind. Probably Mom. She stepped onto the bridge, knees rocking.

"Umm, hey, what are you doing here?" She clocked her tone. It sounded like a threat. She followed this up with a smile, and hoped he wouldn't notice or would think her words came out more "dazed".

"Em." He reached out and snatched her hands into his. "These past two months have been amazing. I feel like I've gotten to know you so fast."

Really? Because you didn't ask many questions about me on dates.

Queries would take place in the few breaks between kisses.

"Haha." Could he feel the shaking in her palms? That rattled her intestines? He'd probably mistake it for joy. "You bet. Umm, I think there are people waiting to get onto the bridge, Frankie. Maybe we should move for—"

"They can wait. Em." He dropped down onto one knee. "Marry me?"

Everything within her turned cold. Of course, all signs had pointed to this the moment she spotted him on the bridge. Even before, with the email talking about a last-ditch effort and the manicure...

The manicure.

She glanced over her shoulder at her mom, who beamed at her.

Was this the project that Mom talked about?

That she could hold off on divorcing her dad, if they both worked together on planning a wedding?

Her gaze revolved back to Frankie, who stared up at her, eyes a-question. "Umm, babe," A quaking breath shook her lips. "I...heard that you met up with your ex on campus. Is that true?"

His grip loosened, and he palmed his face. "Oh, no. That...how did you hear about that?"

"A little birdie." She'd take a tip from Jana with this one.

"Babe." He reached forward to scoop her fingers into his once again, but she drew her arms back. "Yasmin blindsided me. I thought it was a friendly meeting to catch up, and I figured, since she was in town..." He shook his head.

Wind whistled in Em's ears and raised the goosebumps on her arms. By now, whispers formed behind her. She caught the words "what" and "taking so long".

"What's between Yasmin and me is nothing. All I see in the future is you."

Em recalled her conversation with Harmony. Everything in his tone dripped with something strange. Almost as if he'd rehearsed this prior. Maybe to Yasmin, she'd bet.

Em spun on her heel and charged away from the bridge. Her mother raced forward and caught her, hands wrenched around her wrists. "What's going on, sweetie?"

"Mom." Em jerked her arms out of the grip and pulled up the screenshots Harmony sent over to her on the car ride to the hiking trail. "Please, read."

Her mother scanned through the photos. Three in, she passed it back. "His hands were tied, sweetie. This is really not the time for this."

She let the words sink in. "I'm sorry, what?"

"Plenty of exes try to do this, when they suspect someone is proposing. Are you going to let one miscommunication get in the way of your future?" She motioned Em close. "He's a computer science major, sweetie. He's going to take care of you, okay?"

Em's ears stung from the tickle of that whisper. She backed away. *Mom's trying to marry me off for money. That's all that matters to her.*

"I need..." Tears pricked the corners of her eyes. She announced to her parents, to Frankie—who was still on the bridge—to the stupid cameraman who didn't even know how to hide himself well. "Time to think. Excuse me."

Em's boots pounded the dirt as she charged back toward the parking lot. Cries of her name followed her, then faded once she put enough distance between herself and them. The group must not have run to catch up with her.

Maybe they'd give her some privacy for once.

She found her family's car and scrunched herself into a small ball beside it, since Mom had locked the car. A family ambled past with quizzical looks. She threw them a wave and pulled out her phone. First, she tried dialing Harmony.

No answer.

Harmony did tell her when they parted at the coffee shop door that her professional writing friend planned to take her laser tagging for the rest of the day.

Okay, Noah. Let's try Noah. He'd know what to do.

She dialed him via video call, and he picked up on the first ring. "Hey, Merry Late Christma—what happened. Oh gosh, Em, are you okay?"

Tears flowed down her cheeks, and she imagined her eyes rimmed with red. Even if she'd accepted the proposal, in this state, the cameraman would've captured some awful portraits.

Why do *they take photos of this? Most girls end up covered in snot or screaming or crying pools of mascara.*

Proposals never worked like the movies, or so she'd heard.

"I'm not okay, Noah. Frankie just proposed."

"Um, oh wow, already? Well, congratulations?"

She showed her ring finger to the camera, and his eyebrows narrowed. His voice shot up, as though relieved. "Oh, wow, you didn't say yes."

"I didn't say anything. I ran away."

"How very movie-esque of you."

The long sleeves of her dress rubbed along her cheeks to wick the moisture. "Haha, but I need some help. Do you mind if I send you screenshots?"

It took him a few moments to scan through all of them. Birds soared ahead in the meantime. To her consolation, no family member had circled back by the time Noah returned. "So, umm, Em. He was cheating on you."

Sniffing, she nodded and braced herself for the next onslaught of tears. Did Harmony feel this way about Eli? Sure, they hadn't gotten that far along in their relationship, but Harmony loved people with all of her being. A heartbreak for her was magnified more than the average being. *I shouldn't have been mad at her for not wanting to jump back into the dating game.*

Heaven knew that Em didn't want to go near a boy after this.

"Are you going back and telling him?" Noah rolled his sleeves. "Or I can go and tell him"—he raised a fist to the camera—"using this."

Em giggled. "Tell him what?"

"That you're not only getting married to him, but that you're done."

Her bottom lip quivered. Could she *email* him that, since he decided to cheat on her in his inbox? Something about saying the words to his face sent shudders up and down her spine. "Well, there's two problems with that, Noah."

He sighed. "There are?"

"First, my parents are basically saying this is what's keeping their marriage together, them planning this wedding for me."

Hurt crossed Noah's face. Then something that resembled pity. "Em, you know that you're not in charge of your parents' marriage."

"I know, but—"

"And what happens after the wedding? Are they going to threaten to divorce until you supply them with grandkids?"

True.

She sniffed again and smeared the contents of her nose onto her dress. Now she really hoped the cameraman had evacuated by now, because she couldn't pose for any glamour shots. "Second, the bet."

"Oh gosh, the bet."

"I mean, maybe I can draw out the proposal until June. And then break it off." It would certainly serve Frankie right. She couldn't imagine herself doing that to someone, though. "Then I can earn the bet money and—"

"Em, do you really think he's going to wait until June to marry you, if you've only been dating for two months?"

She deflated. *No, he wouldn't.*

"Em, listen. Although I can't get you $30,000, you know that I'd do whatever I can to help you if you lost that bet. Don't let that determine your future. Or you're going to end up miserable, like your parents."

Something about his words formed a fire in her bones. "Yeah, you're right. Thanks, Noah. I need to find out what I'm made of, I think."

"You need someplace to stay? In case the fallout goes awry with the parents?"

Shoot, she hadn't considered that.

Although she couldn't imagine her parents would excommunicate her from the family over this, they would give her the silent treatment for days. Perhaps Mom would force her to watch as she signed the divorce papers in the kitchen. "I could ask that friend Harmony's staying with if she can spare an extra guest. I'll text Harmony right now."

Em did so. Harmony, to her surprise, responded.

Harmony: Between games. I'm murdering a bunch of eight-year-olds

Harmony: Just saw your call

Harmony: Oh gosh, she says that yes she'd love to have you

Harmony: I'm so sorry, Em

Harmony: I'll murder an eight-year-old in the next round just for you *heart emoji*

Noah, after checking five more times to make sure that Em was truly okay, hung up but texted her to keep him posted.

"All right." She curled a fist and lifted herself to her feet, brushed loose gravel off her bare calves. "Let's do this."

Chapter Twenty

EM DUG HER SPOON into the tub of chocolate chip cookie dough.

She curled up on the futon in the apartment and watched as fluffy snowflakes cascaded down. Gray skies weighed on her eyelids. But if the gloomy weather hadn't made her tired, the amount of tears she'd shed in the last few hours would. Why did crying make her so tired?

Hard to believe that a few weeks before, she'd marched across that parking lot, into that forest, and told Frankie that she would not, in fact, marry him. Before she could break off their relationship, he'd stormed off and did so over text.

Her molars crunched on a cold chocolate chip as she reached for the carpet to open her "Ethics in Media Communication" textbook. She flipped back to page fifty-six, where she'd gotten stuck the last time.

Interview Etiquette

I remember a tale my journalism professor told us in college. One that I believe will haunt me forever. He told us, "Get the interview no matter what the cost", then proceeded to regale us with the story of how he'd stalked a man on his campus and hounded the poor guy into submission until he relented and agreed to an interview.

Although I believe journalism does require a pursuit of the truth, we still do have to abide by a code of ethics. "What would those ethics be?"

the reader might ask. Below we will explore a list of the Ten Commandments of Journalism ethics.

Em clapped the book shut and rubbed the corners of her eyes. Even a week back into classes after the end of break, she still couldn't get into a groove. She could already sense, from Harmony's silence on the drive back, that she'd worn her friend's patience thin.

No wonder. I crashed the party at her friend's house.

For the first few days, Harmony had supplied her with Arnold Palmers, donuts, and the occasional death threat penned to send to Em's ex. But by the end of week one, Harmony had muttered snippets of annoyance ranging from "bounce back" to "get over it at some point".

She's one to talk. It had taken Harmony how many months just to open herself up again to dating?

Em shoved the spoon into the mound of cookie dough and dug out her phone from her sweats. Maybe she could reward herself with a little social scrolling.

The moment she tapped on Instagram, regret built in her chest. A photo of Eli, kneeling on the ground, in front of a girl with hands clasped to her mouth, burned Em's eyes. Despite herself, she read the caption.

She said yes!

Katherine, it's so hard to believe that we met just a few months ago, but I've enjoyed getting to know you. The late-night conversations, coffee shop dates, and the time we've spent together has made my heart happy. Every, every minute.

You make me want to become a better man every day, and I cannot wait to do this life together with you. Love you always.

"You've got to be kidding me." Indignation lit a fire in her bones. She cast a glance at the popcorn ceiling and hoped her gaze could burn through heaven. "Seriously, God? Where's the justice in this?"

A man who used Harmony to get to Em got a happy ending?

According to Harmony on their drive back to school, Frankie too had posted on social media. He announced his new relationship with Yasmin via a photo of them at the campus coffee shop. Considering that she hadn't made the drive back to Indiana yet, this confirmed they'd met up while Em and Frankie still dated.

By now, Frankie had blocked Em on everything. Even email.

Good.

When some of Em's clients didn't work out with their matches, they claimed they would doomscroll for hours, watching updates on their ex's pages. Em recalled a conversation with one of them in the dining commons.

"Part of me wants to be happy for them. After all, when you fall in love with someone, you want the best for them." The boy had swirled a spoon into his ice cream cup. With no milkshake joints nearby the campus, the students improvised by stirring the soft serve into submission. "The other part of me wants her to experience all the hurt that she made me go through."

Em unrolled herself, grabbed the spoon, and staggered to the sink. Piles of dishes stunk on the sides, spilling into the drying racks. The first week of the second semester had hit all the apartment-mates hard. Even Jana skipped her usual gym runs for bubble tea from time to time.

Em scrubbed some bowls that had cereal caked onto them. Three dishes in, she gave up. "Ugh, what's wrong with me?"

Mom used to call her "bounce-back" Em. In middle school, when she played on the basketball team—a sport her mother pushed her into that didn't last that long—she'd always jump back up from the floor, no matter what knocked her down. One game in particular left her with a hefty nosebleed and a possible concussion when a girl decked the back of her neck with the ball. Still, she rose.

Down seven, up eight. Just like the Bible verse said. People fell down seven times and would get up eight times. And she scored her tenth basket right after that. Coach had to call a time out, just so they could staunch the bleeding that didn't seem to stop.

"If I can get through stuff like that," she cupped her elbows and tugged her arms inward to hug herself, "why is this so much harder?"

Seldom did an hour pass by where a memory of Frankie wouldn't surface. Much as he grated her nerves, it felt as though he'd stolen something that didn't belong to him. Even though he'd dropped off some of her gifts to him at her door and offered financial compensation for her time—via a sticky note on the door frame—none of those filled the cavern in Em's chest.

Maybe I should look into the counseling center on campus.

According to a *Mirror* article, though, they'd been backed up for weeks. Most students, if lucky, could see an on-campus therapist once a month.

Besides, what would Mom say?

Mom hadn't sent so much as two texts since the event. Except for one very long paragraph, twenty minutes after Em told her, "I'm staying with a friend. Take me back home so I can pack a bag."

Mom: If you had been upset with the relationship in the first place, you should've told myself and your father. We feel lied to, and it's very embarrassing to pull together a whole proposal if your daughter isn't even interested in the guy in the first place. Now, we're having to mend the friendships we've made with his parents. What's more is that I feel very hurt that you don't think you can stay with us after this. You're always one to run away from conflict. You hide from it. Handle this like a grown up and come back home.

The "handle this like a grown up" line sucker punched her in the gut. Mom always included something like that when Em hung up on her to prevent getting a scolding or a lecture.

A squeak sounded from the apartment door, followed by peals of laughter. Jana, and to Em's surprise, Harmony entered, jiggling cups full of eyes. Remnants of tapioca boba rested at the bottom of their plastic vessels.

Harmony, why are you hanging out with Jana?

Once they flicked on the lights, Harmony's eyes narrowed at Em. She threw a quick wave, and her voice exited in unusual, clipped tones. "Hi, Em." Her eyes roved to the cookie dough container, still stationed on the futon. "You still holing up in here?"

Jana and Harmony shared a look, an eye roll.

Prickles ran up and down Em's skin. *Keep it together, Em. Together.*

She'd already tried to talk in chipper tones and didn't bring up Frankie with Harmony since the awkward drive. Now, she apparently wasn't even allowed to grieve alone either.

"Just working on some homework." Em gestured at the textbook and bumped her voice up an octave from its gruffer timbre. Her face felt tight. Shoot. Tears did that. No doubt Harmony had detected the puffiness and the red-rimmed eyes. "Homework's been absolutely insane this time around, don't you think?"

"Mhmm." Now, Harmony avoided eye contact. She jiggled her cup and ambled to the trash can. Halted. "Em, isn't it your turn to take out the trash?"

Em winced at the pile of paper towels and plates that had filled the can to the brim, to the point where the lid didn't even shut anymore. "So it is. I'll get on it this afternoon, I promise."

Harmony wrinkled her nose at the dish pile and glared at Em.

That wasn't me. Laila's been experimenting with lots of recipes. Not that Em would complain. Laila's potato soup attempt kept her warm for the first few days when she couldn't muster the energy to trek across campus in the cold to the dining commons.

"Right. Pretty sure you've said that before." Harmony suckled on her straw to get the last remnants of her tea and marched toward her door.

Just before the door slammed, Em heard her toss the cup into her small room trash can.

Part of her wanted to confront Harmony. Over what, though? Perhaps she deserved some of Harmony's cold shoulder, for all the trouble she'd put her through during winter break.

Em shuffled to the trash can and popped off the lid. Jana, still planted by the door frame, sucked on her ice. "What's with the weird looks, girlie? Harmony and I are roommates. We're allowed to hang out from time to time."

"I didn't say anything."

Various stenches from the bag assaulted her nose. Did someone in their apartment cook fish? No salmon or cod bubbled up in her memory. She yanked the bag out and tied up the strings.

"Besides." Jana's ice clicked once more. "We found some common ground."

"Well, that's great," Em muttered through gritted teeth. She hoisted the bag over her shoulder, as if she was Garbage Santa Claus. "Glad to see you two are getting along."

She slipped on her flip flops, headed into the hallway, and padded outside of the apartment, into the cold. Blustery winds bit her cheeks. Why did she have to go from the warmer North Carolina temperatures straight into this? January in Indiana felt like a punishment.

When she returned, Jana had not budged from her spot.

"You need to stand or something, Jana?"

"Nope." Jana lifted her eyes from her phone. "Need to ask you a question. Bet still on?"

Em sighed, then trudged to the kitchen sink to pull out a fresh trash bag. She fluffed it out. *Not now, Jana.*

"Because if you *aren't,* then we need to make good on paying all those people back."

Gas money alone had cleared out her checking account on the way over here. Already she had to dip into savings for meals and amenities, because she hadn't matched many people this past semester. Even of those she did, only some made it to the second date and few to the third. And she wouldn't get paid until that third date.

Em sighed. That didn't leave her with much of a choice, did it? Bounce Back Em would have to resurrect. "I'm no quitter."

"Glad to hear, because I have a date set up for you in the TSC." Jana glanced at her phone. "And you have just enough time to make it over."

Of course I do.

Em glimpsed her outfit. A baggy hoodie and messy bun wouldn't cut it for the best first impression. A sniff test revealed that she'd at least had enough sense to slather on some deodorant this morning. Heaven knew she'd made good use of dry shampoo these past few weeks. *Well, I guess he'll have to take me as I am.*

"Do I at least get a name?"

She did not. But she did get a photo.

Not too bad looking, Em thought. Although she didn't often experience an attraction to guys who came in a shade that pale, she'd make an exception for this one. His blond hair and blue eyes struck her in the photo.

Huddling herself into her hoodie, she waddled over to the TSC, flip flops and all.

Thawing her frost-covered toes, she entered the toasty building. Good thing Harmony suggested a pedicure day close to the end of winter break. Toe polish would stand the test of time. Even a nuclear explosion couldn't strip that layer of paint.

Em spotted Blond Boy near the coffee shop. Alas, he did not go for the hoodie vibe at all. Instead, he'd packed himself into a cozy sweater and khakis.

She waved. "Hey, sorry, I was just informed about this date. I can go back and get changed if you'd prefer."

"No need. This is fine."

Oh ho, she detected an accent. German?

Em dug her wallet out of her pockets and glanced inside. Ten dollars remained, thanks to the toll roads on the way to school. She held up the cash. "How about I handle this one for being the hot mess that I am?"

Blond Boy grinned. "That is very kind."

They placed their orders. Blond Boy must've learned not to make the paying person spend much, because they each asked for a "small" version of their favorite drinks.

Mom used to tell Em horror stories of past dates in her college years where the date would order the most expensive item on the menu. *"You always want to match the price of what the other person orders. If they get something that's $5, you do that too. $20, same deal."*

Em's chest tightened as she collected the smaller and warmer version of her chai latte. Could her parents ever reconcile with her? And did she even want that? *I felt like some 1800s bride being traded in for cattle.*

She could excuse them wanting her to have a husband who made *some* money. Or at least, didn't sit on the couch all day. But for them to choose a mate solely due to how they could get their leech of a daughter off their hands? *Maybe someday, but not now.*

Em decided in that moment that forgiveness and reconciliation were two different things.

Forgiveness: She could let go of what her parents did to her and let God handle it from there.

Reconciliation: Both parties had to come together and admit what they did wrong.

Knowing her parents, they'd create a million excuses as to how they had no fault and how they "were only looking after our baby girl".

Blond Boy positioned himself at a high-top table, and she joined him on the other end. Drinking a sip of the chai, she released a content sigh. Cinnamon and nutmeg, the good stuff.

"So." She set the cup down on the table. "Did I detect an accent?"

"Munich." He grinned. "I am on a full ride here for tennis."

Ah yes, the school did recruit quite a few international students for their sports programs. The downside? They'd require those students to stay an extra year, meaning they couldn't enter the workforce until they'd reached at least twenty-three.

"Well, that's awesome. Tell me a little bit more about yourself."

"What would you like to know?"

Conversation already flowed in a natural sense. She didn't know the dating practices of Germans, but perhaps he'd adapted to school culture and would be open to a proposal after five months of dating. *Em, that's dumb, stop planning your future. You know where that got you last time.*

"Umm, how about favorite Bible verse? That's a fan-favorite I like to ask."

Blond Boy pinked.

"What's wrong?"

"Erm—I am not a Christian."

All light vanished within her. "Oh."

Plenty of girls on her wing in previous years had dated boys outside of the faith. From what they'd indicated to Em, although those relationships worked for some people, it entailed lots of passionate fights involving faith and values. *I don't know if I could compromise in that area.*

"But." Blond Boy lifted a finger and sipped on his Americano. "Perhaps you can convince me I am wrong." He grinned. "Many girls have tried."

"You mean, missionary date?" Some students believed that they could "flirt to convert" their dates and convince them to become a Christian before they got married. "Sorry, but... I don't know if I could do that. That's sort of a non-negotiable for me, personally."

Blond Boy shrugged. "I understand. Thanks for paying." He nodded to her, ejected himself from his seat, and carried his beverage with him out of the TSC.

For some reason, even though this date was the shortest, it hurt the most.

Chapter Twenty-One

"Okay, miss mopey." Laila slammed the door to the apartment and jabbed a finger at Em. "I hear you've already missed two lip sync battle rehearsals this week. It's time for a girls' day."

Em rubbed her eyes in bed and glimpsed her phone. *11:06 on a Tuesday?*

"My partner's been out sick anyway. There's no need for me to show up."

"Mhmm, get changed, girl." Laila flung open Em's closet doors and pulled shirts off the hangers.

"I'm going to miss class. You know they take off for attendance."

"Taken care of." Laila balled up a shirt and tossed it at Em's face.

When Em unburied herself from it, she sat up in bed. "What do you mean, 'taken care of'?"

"I took the liberty of emailing your professors this morning. You sounded really pitiful too…"

Laila read from her own device:

Hey,

Feeling down for the count. Throwing up non-stop. I'd normally go to the Health Center, but I don't even think I can drive a car. My apartment mates can vouch for my condition, and my roommate has already quarantined herself to the family room couch.

Let me know how I can make up for missed classwork.

~ Em

"You lied?"

True, Em did hate their school's way of making them walk a mile to the Health Center, just for a doctor to gaslight them and tell them, "You seem fine enough to me. Go to class. No health slip for you."

Still, breaking the eleventh commandment to *skip class*?

"Here's the deal, girl." Laila perched on the corner of Em's bed and patted Em's blanketed shins with her palm. "You *are* technically sick. This is depression if I've ever seen it."

Em snorted. "Ha, I'm not depressed."

"When's the last time you brushed your teeth?"

"That's personal." Em made sure not to widen her lips too much when she talked, in case Laila could detect the onion breath. "Besides, depressed people have it way worse than me. I'm just in a rut, that's all."

"Mhmm. Still sick. And unfortunately, because society doesn't take mental health seriously, we're going to have to fake you being 'real sick'." She tossed up air quotes. "So get changed, and we're going to spend today getting your mind off of things."

Em clutched the balled shirt. If she knew anything about Laila, once that woman set her mind to something... "Fine, but I hope someone's taking good notes in Journalism Ethics, because that teacher has about seventy slides a class, and it's hard to keep up."

Once Em shimmied into jeans and a flowy dress shirt, she followed Laila into the parking lot and climbed into the front seat. A fresh evergreen air freshener, in the shape of a pine tree, dangled from the driver's mirror on a string.

"Where to?" Em fastened her seatbelt.

Laila shrugged. "Didn't think I'd get you this far. Let's see what Indiana has to offer us."

Not much, apparently. They found themselves in a museum dedicated to quilting twenty minutes later. After Laila paid the hefty admission fee—well, hefty for looking at literal blanket displays—their footsteps clapped against the slick, hardwood floor.

"Since you won't go to therapy," Laila threw a withering glare at Em, "I figure this could be a Rorschach test of sorts." She jabbed her thumb over her shoulder, at a pink quilt with triangles. "Now, Em, what do you see in this?"

Em snickered. "Oh, I see Frankie! Frankie! Oh, it's too much, Laila!" She clutched at her chest and feigned a heart attack.

"Girl, be real."

"I dunno. Triangles. Triangles in the shape of Frankie."

Laila wagged a finger at her. "If you don't take this journey through the quilts seriously, I'm going to have to take you to the Museum of Plungers, and then you'll be sorry you skipped Quilt Therapy."

Em doubted that Indiana even had a museum dedicated to the un-clogging of toilets. Nevertheless, she acquiesced. Several carpets later, she and Laila stopped dissolving into giggles and found themselves admiring the stitchwork, the hours it would take to puzzle-piece the various shapes together and create a beautiful work.

"You know." Em stared at a blue quilt with Mona Lisa's face etched into one of the fabric circles. "I wish people would work this way."

"Yeah? You want us all stuck on quilts?"

"No, I mean. I guess if you're a weirdo or something—"

Harmony would probably say something to the effect of that. Oh, Harmony...why hadn't she said two words to Em since they returned to campus?

"—what I *mean* is that every piece in a quilt is important. And if only we saw other people that way. That we'd all fall apart without each other."

One of the chapel speakers in recent weeks had talked about the passage in 1 Corinthians, that every Christian made up one body of the church, and every part had equal importance. So why did so many eyes say to the hands "I don't need you"? Or livers say to the intestines, "I'm a more important Christian than you"?

Imagine a world where singles, married Christians, divorcees, widows...all saw each other as equally important.

Laila drank in these words, a sad sort of look behind her eyes. "Because." She huffed and ambled to a pink carpet, full of geometric squares. "Because people don't like equal. People like power, pyramids, ladders, control. And most of all, people hate change."

Em thumbed her jeans pockets and frowned at the Mona Lisa. She couldn't argue against that.

They thanked the older woman at the front desk when they left the museum, and read off the names stamped onto the brick walk outside. Snow covered several of the letters. Her autistic side liked to catch small details, even when they didn't matter much. After their museum trek, Laila suggested a lunch-stop at IHOP, since Em had forgotten breakfast once again that morning.

Em didn't mind. Theater folks at Mansfield stopped by this pancake joint all the time after shows. It was one of the few restaurants in the area that could seat fifty-something cast and crew members at one time. When she arrived, scents of bacon and eggs dizzied her brain. Fingertips clutched to her side. Could she feel ribs now? How much had she eaten in the last few weeks? Even *Harmony* had gotten tired of coaxing Em to down three meals a day over winter break.

She thought back to Frankie's social media post. *God, is it bad that I want him to hurt as much as I am hurting?*

A waitress with a tight ponytail led them to a booth. Em perused a menu, sticky with syrup from the last customers. Someone in the back must not have wiped down this thing well. Eyeing the pancake creations, she selected the "Cinnestack", when the server returned to place their orders.

Two ice waters slid onto the table moments later. She mused about how ice water paired terribly with January weather.

"Hey." Laila cupped her drink between her palms. Fingerprints formed shapes when she released her grip. "How are you feeling?"

"Do you really want to know?'

Laila shielded an eye roll. "Yes, girl, I really want to know. I wouldn't have asked otherwise."

Some people didn't want to know that information. If you said anything other than "fine" or "good", they'd still respond with a "good to hear."

"I feel—" Em searched for the word as a boy at another table played with the various syrup containers. She wondered who would pour something like "strawberry" or "blueberry" onto a flavored pancake. "—lonely."

"Gotcha."

Em picked at loose skin on her hands. "Which sounds stupid, because you're literally dedicating a whole day to spend time with me. You're skipping class for me. So I'm selfish for feeling lonely."

Pancakes arrived in the silence. Laila sawed into her strawberry stack. "It's normal to feel lonely, Em." She swallowed a wad of pancakes and triangled her stack even more with her knife. "I feel it all the time."

Huh. Em hadn't considered this. With Laila's choice to stay single, Em assumed this meant her roommate had a world's worth of confidence in herself and her own company.

"And you know what?" Laila pointed her knife at Em. "I know plenty of married people who are super lonely too."

"You do?"

Images of her parents surfaced. Em knew people like that too.

Laila speared a sugary strawberry with a fork. "Loneliness is our gauge that the world isn't the way it's supposed to be. That we're built for something more. That's we're supposed to be more—"

"Together, united. Relationship status or not."

"Exactly."

Em tore into her pancake and melted along with the cinnamon flavor. For the first time in a while, she felt hungry.

After their IHOP visit, they browsed a few bookstores and grabbed a bubble tea to go. Laila refused any payment for their time together, insisting that they'd not had a roommate date in ages and that this more than made up for lost time.

"Maybe when I get the money, I can pay you back." Em chewed on a tapioca boba as they drove past the school entrance. "Or get you for the next time. So this isn't hanging over my head for forever, you know?"

Laila gripped the steering wheel tighter, until white showed in her knuckles. "Listen, relationships don't work like that. They're not transactional, girl."

"I know, but—"

Laila slowed to a halt and flipped on her hazards. She perched an elbow on her seat, after she put the car in park. "Listen, I may be choosing to be single, but I used to date people. There was this one person I went out with for a while who was a piece of work."

Em leaned closer, enthralled by the story. Her roomie didn't talk much about her dating days.

"This person would buy everything for me on dates. Wouldn't let me pay at all. Came from a rich family, so Mama was padding the wallet, if you know what I'm saying."

"Never worked a day in their life, got it."

"This was also my senior year of high school, and I was super naive, but I just figured, 'Okay, that's nice that they're paying for things. Really sweet.' So then it's time for the Homecoming dance, and I've made it very clear to this person that I don't want to kiss until marriage." Laila snorted. "I mean, if you know what I've done in the past, you know I made it wayyy past kissing, but at the time, I thought that was what I was supposed to do."

Her fingertips fiddled with one of her braids. "After the dance my date goes on and on about how much tickets cost for this thing. How much a corsage is. How much it cost to rent a limo. Then we get to my front porch." She sucked in a deep breath, exhaled. "I won't forget what he said to me. My date looked me dead in the eyes, looked at my lips, and said, 'Well, you know what I want'."

You know what I want.

Em clapped her hands to her mouth. "Oh, Laila, that's awful."

"It was. And after I gave this person what he wanted, I lived by this idea that that's what relationships were. Someone paid for you, you owed them something. Most of the time, something physical. Thankfully, I learned better. Chose to be single. So—" Laila locked eyes with her roommate. "If I pay a bill, take you out somewhere, take care of you...it's because I want to and expect nothing in return. Okay?"

Em nodded.

The ignition fired up, and Laila steered them back to the apartment parking lot. Em wrapped her in the tightest hug she could muster before they returned indoors.

Laughter from Harmony pealed all the way into the hallway. *Great, she's hanging out with Jana again, isn't she?*

Keys jingled as Em dug them into the lock and twisted the door open.

Instead of Jana, Noah was parked on the couch beside Harmony. Soft noise from a video played, and the two laughed. Light spilled into the apartment, and Noah glanced up. All of him softened when he spotted Em. "Hey, you're back! Harmony wasn't sure where you went."

Harmony didn't look up from her phone, but kept scrolling videos. She plugged her headphones in, so all sound muted.

"Noah." Em clutched her arm as Laila brushed past her, saying something about catching up on some homework. "What are you doing here?"

"Wanted to check in on you. You weren't in class today."

Oh, right, she did have a Gen Ed Bible class with Noah on Tuesdays. It was odd for seniors to still be taking Gen Eds. But the school required so many extra classes, especially for Bible classes. Plus, Noah had so many theater classes that he'd skipped out on the core curriculum until now.

He dug into his bookbag, nearest their TV stand, and pulled out a laptop. "I can send you the notes. Although you didn't miss much. Some Ethics Bowl student decided it was a good time to debate about the Cosmological Argument, so we didn't get through more than five slides."

Ah yes, Ethics Bowl. Every year, several of the philosophy students would compete against other schools to debate the moral implications of certain political bills or acts. *Too bad they bring that fighting spirit into the classroom with them.*

"Notes would be great, thank you."

"You're looking better." He tapped his cheeks. "You have some color again."

He wrapped her in a warm hug, and they suspended there for several moments. When he released, she caught a slight glare from Harmony, who had watched the embrace. *What's that about?*

"Well, I should be going." Noah shrugged on his coat and looped his backpack onto one shoulder. "Have a few lines to memorize for the upcoming student-directed plays. Oh, and also." Noah cocked his head at Em. "Birdie told me that you're still keeping on the bet."

Okay, is there someone literally named Birdie on this campus?

Em splayed her hands. "I don't need a lecture."

"No, I wasn't planning on giving one. But, if you want to avoid a certain singles group, my church happens to have a young adults Bible study the same night. Might be worth swinging by."

Right, Jana's singles group. Didn't she make mention earlier that week that Em would need to start heading there again to "work on herself for her future husband"?

Noah made finger guns, clicked his tongue, then disappeared from the apartment.

Harmony shed her earphones and headed to the kitchen. She pulled open the snack cabinet moments later.

Should I poke the bear? "Hey, Harmony. How was your afternoon?"

"Fine." Cold, clipped tones. Something had gone wrong.

"That sounds fun!" Time to bring back that chipper voice. "What did you d—"

"Noah and I are really hitting it off."

"What?"

Harmony locked eyes with Em. Some icy resoluteness made the pupils appear blacker and stonier than usual. "Noah stopped by to check in on you, but he and I started flirting." She popped a Cheez-it into her mouth and sashayed to her room. Before she slammed the door, she called out. "Just thought you should know."

Chapter Twenty-Two

"Are you sure they won't kill me if they see me with you?" Em hid behind Noah's torso when they entered the small church building. The lobby smelled of stale powdered donuts and old coffee.

"Who will kill you?"

"Girls. They'll think I'm trying to steal one of the few guys here."

When he whirled around, quirking a quizzical brow, she explained what happened at the name tag station at the other singles group.

"If looks could kill."

Noah let out a low whistle. "Well, it doesn't work like that here. I mean, we *do* have a name tag station," he gestured at a table with scattered "Hello I'm..." tags and permanent markers, "but none of that competition stuff."

Dubious, she moved with shaky steps toward the name tags. Uncapping a pen, the permanent marker scent dazed her senses for a moment.

Why do they always make these markers smell so strong?

Permanent things gave off the most distinctive odors, she decided. The school hallways when they smelled like summer. Old books in the archives section of the library and their almondy pages.

"Em?"

She glanced up as she slapped her tag onto the chest of her floral dress shirt. Zuri waved, releasing her grip from Jeff's hand. Jeff was absorbed into a group of guys, who spoke in muffled tones.

"Zuri? What are you doing here?"

Noah did tell her that the young adults group would host people ages eighteen to thirty-eight, but from what she could tell from the people who filtered in the doors before her, most of the crowd consisted of college students. Thirty-eight seemed like a long way to go. But perhaps in a college town where master's students could be various ages, it made sense.

"Well." Zuri unsheathed an orange marker and scrawled her name in beautiful cursive that Em couldn't read. Why did they stop teaching that in grade schools again? "I'm actually leading this group."

"You are?"

Em had always assumed that young adults was synonymous with "single Christians who can't find a date". Many churches back home would do something like that. Why would someone, who found their "other", lead a thing like this?

"Indeed." Zuri placed her name on her flowy skirt. Some people didn't like name tags on shirts, Em guessed. "I realized, when I was single, that there were so few resources for people who weren't married in the church."

"So you started a group here?" Em leaned against the table.

"Yes, but it was only after I complained to a lot of my married friends. They'd sort of roll their eyes and say, 'Single people are always griping. If they want something to be done, they should do it themselves.'"

"That doesn't seem right." Em chewed on her lip. "If someone's being oppressed, telling them, 'Well go fix it,' is almost worse than not doing anything at all."

"I thought so too." Zuri bobbed her chin and shoved herself away from the table. "Then I figured, maybe I'm called for such a time as this to pave that path, since it had fallen on deaf ears in the marriage communities. And here we are."

"Ah, Esther. One of two women that we're allowed to talk about in women's Bible studies. The other one being Ruth."

This caused Zuri to snicker. "You know, those ladies were—by our church standards today—pretty scandalous. Definitely not fitting our definitions of biblical womanhood."

Em cocked her head. "Really?"

"Yeah, Ruth initiated about everything in her relationship and was a working woman. Definitely wouldn't fly in certain circles today. And Esther was essentially forced to have sex outside of marriage, and saved an entire nation from genocide. Today we'd wag our fingers at them and tell them to 'sit down and let the men take it from here'."

Huh, how many times did people tell her a skewed version of certain women in the Bible? Most women viewed Esther and Ruth as "submissive women" who "gave their all to their husbands".

Someone whistled for Zuri, and she lifted a finger to Em. "We're about to get started. Go ahead and grab a seat in classroom B."

Down the hall, Em noticed that each of the rooms had a different name attached to them. Abraham for Classroom A. Boaz for Classroom B. A little way off, Esther received the E classroom.

When Em found a seat in the classroom, her heart sank as other attendees entered. All women. Would this feel just like the singles group when they parted them into breakout groups, to tell the women how to "work on themselves" to finally land that husband?

A few girls, in long skirts, introduced themselves to Em. They talked about their education major and how the classroom assignments for this semester about did them in. Em always sympathized with the soon-to-be-teachers and believed they should earn far more income than they would make.

Zuri entered and waved at everyone. Em's shoulders relaxed. If Zuri led the discussion, at least she wouldn't dive into topics like submissiveness or homemaking.

At the previous breakout at the singles group, their instructor had listed several reasons as to why Christian women couldn't find husbands. *Nine times out of ten, it's because you're not doing something correctly.*

Something told Em that those statistics had to be skewed. Sometimes God didn't allow someone to get into a relationship because the other needed to work on themselves. Or because the timing wasn't quite right.

"Okay, everyone, please open to Job Chapter 40."

Job? So no Ruth or Esther today, after all. Sometimes pastors threw in a Mary or Martha to mix things up.

"Does anyone want to read it?"

One of the long-skirt girls volunteered, and they read together the chapter about God answering Job's cries for help. Em recalled Job from her Old Testament class. Job, an upstanding man, did everything right. Satan ruined his life anyway and took away his family, his home, and his health. Job's friends kept trying to find out what Job did wrong to earn this punishment. *I feel you, Job.*

Eli and Frankie ended up in relationships, while she had been cast aside.

"Now." Zuri clapped her hands in her lap. "At the end of Job, we see that God's furious with Job's friends. Why do you think that is?"

Someone in a wheelchair and wearing flared pants raised her hand. "Because they'd been trying to find out what he did wrong instead of comforting him. And in the end, Job didn't do anything wrong."

"Excellent answer. And a good point that in the beginning, we see them comforting him in silence. But then they tell him to buck up and figure out how he ticked off God."

Images of Harmony flickered. Was she acting the same way toward Em? Sure, Em needed to find ways to recover and heal without depending on friends. But did Harmony believe that Em deserved her "divine punishment"?

"What can we take away from this passage when we think about Job's friends? Yes, Em?"

Em dropped a shaky hand. "Maybe that we shouldn't assume that someone's being punished when they go through hard things. That at a moment's notice, the same stuff can happen to us."

"Good, I love that. Anyone else, yes?"

The girl with the flared pants answered again. "Maybe the dangers of giving unasked advice. Don't get me wrong, I've gotten some great advice. Though sometimes, it feels like people think they have to be the savior in the situation, when really, there's no easy fix."

Ten minutes of discussion later, Zuri called for a prayer time. "This conversation has been amazing, ladies, and I'd love to keep it going next time we meet. Since this is the first time we're back from break, I figured we could take a little longer to hear what's going on in your lives. Prayer requests or praise reports?"

The girl in the flared pants raised her left hand. A jewel sparkled on the finger.

"Okay, I can go first. I know most of you know, but for those who are new, I did get engaged this weekend!"

Claps and cheers echoed in the room. Em applauded along with them but clenched her gut, bracing for the next poor girl who had to follow that up.

One of the ones in the long skirt lifted her hand. "I also have a praise report." She rubbed her fingers up and down her knees, perhaps to dry off some sweat. Em got clammy hands from time to time. "I...managed to land an internship for practicum after forty applications."

To Em's surprise, the classroom roared with applause, the same caliber as for the girl before. *Harmony would be proud. A ring sing and cha-ching sing—each receiving their due recognition.*

Hope wilted in her chest. *Oh, Harmony.*

They finished the night with prayer and regrouped with the boys for a brief time of worship. Men and women parked together in the pews and lifted their hands up in praise during each of the numbers.

Joy glimmered like a light. In Em's chest, in her skull, in the tips of her toes. *Is this what heaven feels like?*

On the way back to her car, she clicked the unlock button, paused at the front door. "Noah."

"Mm?" He was halfway into the passenger seat and popped back out of the vehicle.

"Why can't it always be like this?"

Noah blinked. Lips twitched. "Someday, Em." He slid back into his seat. "Someday."

Is it Halloween or what? Because there's definitely a lot of ghosting happening.

For Jana's next method of matchmaking, she signed Em up for a dating app. "Sometimes, you have to find guys from outside of your school. Especially when you're a senior and your options are limited."

Em frowned as she swiped left on all the profiles of men holding up fish or the heads of deer they'd shot. *She's got a point, Em.*

Senior women seldom went after anyone younger than a junior. After all, with graduation on their heels, that would mean doing distance with someone younger. Even at a school with thousands of students, the waters emptied of their eligible population by the time senior year rolled around.

Once more, she flicked through the photos Jana selected for her, all pulled from Instagram. At least her apartment-mate chose decent ones.

Name: Emerson, call me "Em"

Bio: I love Jesus and love to help on campus wherever I can. Also, apparently, I'm a semi-mediocre dancer and am competing in a lip sync battle? Swipe right if you love dogs, the Lord, and are looking for something long-term.

A notification buzzed. Someone super-liked her. She scanned the profile. Aww, a man with a stocky build hugged a dog in his photo, a golden retriever.

Bear would have so many fun play dates with that good boy. She paused. *Am I really choosing someone based on my dog?*

Yes, yes, she was. Her thumb slid to the right, and a message from him popped up right away.

Dog Man: Hey, hope you're having a great week! :)

Dog Man: I see you're from Mansfield too

Scanning his profile, she determined he was a junior, but one who would graduate a semester early. Communications major. At least he'd be able to hold a conversation.

Em: Haha, what are the odds?

Dog Man: Probably because the dating culture here suuuucks, so we defaulted to dating apps

Em: You got that right.

Dog Man: Also, you're that matchmaker, right? That's super cool

Three more dots.

Dog Man: Any chance we could talk about it over coffee?

Dog Man: Maybe this evening?

Her heart catapulted into her throat. Choking on the beat, she checked her calendar.

Em: I could meet after dance practice. May be a bit sweaty, though

Dog Man: Ayyyy I have practice tonight too :) so we'll both be gross

Dog Man: You ready to lose? Bet your theme can't beat Encanto

His group chose *Encanto*? Of course they'd take the trophy with that. Still, she messaged back.

Em: Those are fighting words

Sweat dried onto Em's forehead as she entered the TSC with her dancing shoes hooked to her index fingers. She'd slipped into sneakers after practice and rolled on extra deodorant to compensate.

Dog Man parked at a high-top table and motioned at two drinks. "I took the liberty of asking the barista what you get." He slid the warm chai to her. "Says you stop here a lot."

"Well, this is where I spy on my match-ees." She sipped the warm cinnamon and let out a soft moan. "Sorry, but hot drinks do something to me."

"Haha, relatable content. You know my ex-girlfriend used to be really into chai."

"Yeah?" She tilted her head.

"Yeah, until I proposed, she accepted, and then I found out she was cheating on me with my best friend. Haha."

Em's eyes widened as Dog Man drank in a deep sip of his steaming drink. *Did people...share that much information on the first date?* "Oh, wow, umm, I'm really sorry about that."

"Oh, it's fine. Nothing beats the time that my mom told me she didn't love me and I'm the reason she didn't love Dad anymore, and why she drove away from home and never called me and my siblings after that." Dog Man's laughter stung her ears.

Commotion in the TSC dizzied her brain, and sympathy tugged at her heart.

Now I have to go on a second date with this guy. If he's opening up to me this much already, I would be a monster to not, right?

"Wow, you've certainly been through quite a bit, haven't you?"

"Nah, that's nothing. There was also that time where my ex-best friend tried to kill me in the parking lot, when I found out what he did to my fiancée. Whew. You wanna see the scar from the gunshot wound?"

By the time Em returned to her apartment building, she never wanted to see a movie that involved firearms ever again. She rubbed her temples from the migraine that had settled in and detected a tightness in her gut. How had she clenched her intestines the whole date?

Not all dates are the same, Em. Sometimes people just might be more comfortable with sharing their life with you.

Why, then, couldn't she shake this feeling? The same one that had overcome her when Gel Hair confronted her outside the ice cream shop?

You felt taken advantage of. Like free therapy.

Had she done that to Harmony?

She glimpsed the hallway and the shut first door. Light spilled out from underneath it. Considering Jana worked out at this hour, that meant Harmony had to be in there.

I should leave her alone if she's putting up a boundary.

Opening the dating app, she checked for messages from Dog Man. Nothing.

She typed a couple out.

Em: Hey, had fun! I'm sorry you've been through so much.

Em: Maybe we could try coffee again? And keep the conversation going?

Five minutes later, he unswiped her.

Chapter Twenty-Three

"Do I look like a haunted house to you, Laila?"

Laila tossed a quizzical glance over her shoulder as the two descended the steps of the Dining Commons. Understanding dawned, and she swiveled back. "Is this about Ghost Boy?"

"You mean Dog Boy, yes. The one who I went on a date with yesterday, and then he cut off all communication."

"I can't keep them straight." They reached the bottom of the steps, and Laila scooped up two plates. She handed Em a yellow one. "He's not worth rental space in your head, girl."

Broccoli steamed in warmers nearby. Em scooped vegetables onto her plate and ducked further into her sweater. She'd already worn thin the patience of Harmony. Could she afford to lose Laila too? "Sorry, I can drop it."

"Girl, listen." Laila clicked tongs before she grabbed a baked potato wrapped in foil. Em mirrored her. "I'm your friend, so I'm here to listen. I just don't think these guys are worth even giving a moment's thought to. They're trash and should therefore be thrown into the trash can in your mind."

Em envisioned a trash icon, like the one featured on computer screens, somewhere in her brain space. She peeled open the potato and reached for the ranch dressing at the salad station. Then she parked next to Laila at one of the empty tables.

"Did you just put ranch on your potato?"

"Don't judge me."

"No promises."

Neither of them wanted to make a grocery store run—owing to the amount of time alone it would take to defrost the car windshield. Since Mansfield made the students sign up for a minimum of five meal tickets per week, after their freshman year, they decided to make use of a meal they didn't have to cook themselves.

"Let me tell you what I think happened." Laila waved her fork in the air, forming an invisible circle. "He told you too much way too fast, got scared, and then decided to cut ties right away."

Em poked holes into her potato to let the ranch seep deeper. "But I wasn't being judgy at all. I listened and was sympathetic."

"Doesn't matter. I can tell you that I used to go on plenty of dates with people who lacked emotional boundaries."

"*Emotional* boundaries?"

Laila peered at her. "You've never heard of—you know what, we were talking about this in one of my classes. Let me pull up the screenshot."

Em's roommate scanned through her camera roll until a slide from a classroom appeared. She handed the device Em, and Em's fingers pinched the screen to enlarge the words.

Types of Boundaries (and examples of breaking them):

Physical/Sexual: "I know you said you didn't want to kiss, but I'm going to kiss you anyway. And I'll make you feel guilty in the process if you don't do it."

Emotional: "I know you're going through a hard time, but I'm going to dump all of my emotional garbage for the week onto you without asking."

Spiritual: "I'm going to tell you that you're being a 'heretic' or 'not Christlike' when you're doing something that inconveniences me. I'll convince you that something that isn't a sin is."

Intellectual: "I'm going to make you feel like your thoughts and ideas are worthless or stupid, simply because I do not agree with them."

Material: "You have something (food/money/materials) that I want, and I'm going to guilt you into sharing it with me."

Time: "I will make you feel ashamed that you spend your time with anyone but me. This may include me degrading the activities you do that give you joy."

Em clicked off the phone and returned it to its owner. Her fork siphoned out a piece of potato onto her tongue. *Mm, that ranch-y tang, delicious!* "I had no idea there were so many types of boundaries, Laila."

"Most people don't, and boundary-pushers don't want you to know about them. That's why people get angry when you tell them 'no'. They're used to getting told 'yes'."

Then Dog Boy had invaded her emotional boundaries. No wonder she felt the need to continue the date, despite him asking her almost no questions about herself over coffee.

"What's the balance then?" Em peeled off a piece of the skin of the potato and dipped it into the ranch. A little soggy, but still flavorful. "Because you obviously don't want people sharing *no* information on dates either. That's how you get married couples who know nothing about each other." Her thoughts drifted to Tara and Maverick. *Did they choose not to unmask themselves until they reached their wedding night?*

"Isn't that the question?" Laila sipped on an orange soda. Bubbles fizzed when she set the cup down. "I think people know when they push boundaries for starters. They'll pretend they don't. But when the 'no' comes out, that's when you see the real them."

Em thought back to her mother.

Before the engagement disaster, when they'd get into fights, her mother would text her nonstop, until Em relented and kept the relationship going. Messages would pepper her phone like:

Mom: I love you so much and am so proud of all the things you do. You're such a hard worker, and I brag about you to all my friends. I am so lucky to have you in my life.

Mom: I was watching our show today, "Survivor," and thought of you. Included one of your favorite clips in this.

Mom: I think we should have a day together, just us, when you're back home. When you're feeling up to starting our conversations again, I can't wait. I'm also sending a gift package your way.

Gifts, messages, everything would confuse Em. To the point where she thought, *Maybe what Mom did wasn't so bad.*

Thank God Mom had held off communication this time around. She could heal, for once.

A boy with a buzz cut approached their table. He tugged at the ends of his sweater and pushed his glasses up his nose. "Excuse me, but," he motioned to Em, "would you happen to be Em Levi, the matchmaker?"

"Yeah?" She wedged her fork into the potato. It was starting to go cold. Maybe the DC didn't cook them long enough. "Although I'm not sure how much of that matchmaking stuff I've been up to."

Thanks to her depression that hadn't ebbed all the way away, she hadn't checked her survey responses for weeks.

"Sure, sure. I was just wondering... My wing's having a Dash Date. Would you like to go to laser tag?"

She eyed him up and down. Not totally her type, but if his character showed to be beautiful, she could see herself being attracted to him. Her lips twitched. "That sounds great."

An hour later, she found herself in a minivan with her date the next seat over. He didn't talk much, so Christian worship songs hummed through the speakers for the rest of the drive. When they arrived at the laser tag place, her date paid for their first game ticket. Neon paint splattered the walls, floors, and even the ceilings. Some sections existed under a black light, to bring out the fluorescence all the more. Em halted at the front station, whilst choosing her username.

Noah entered the building, and hooked on his arm? Harmony. She'd clad herself in all-black today, including a fake katana, which the workers made her check in at the coat station. Harmony didn't pass Em a single glance as Noah paid for her ticket. Instead, she parked at a table near a concessions stand. Hot dogs rotated underneath bright lights.

"So, Em." Buzz Cut cleared his throat behind her. "Wanna get ready for the first game?"

"On it." She tapped the suggested username of "Ghost". The worker, in a black polo and with the saddest-looking eyes, handed her a keycard to insert into her laser gun. She hopped off the steps and joined her date in the gun room. A heavy vest slumped onto her shoulders, and she strapped herself in. Nineties techno music blasted in the background as a worker instructed them on the rules of the place.

"No running, no jumping, no crouching, no decking someone with your gun and running away—and yes, we have photos posted of the kid who did that. He's not allowed back in, no matter how many disguises he wears."

Are we sure that Harmony didn't do that the last time she went laser-tagging?

Speaking of, Harmony snuggled close to Noah and rested her head on his shoulder. In the darkness, Em couldn't read Noah's reaction to this. Something sizzled in her gut, though.

Why?

Nothing about Harmony and Noah clicked, that was why. They didn't work. Although Noah dealt with plenty of eccentric people in theater, he never expressed an interest for any of them.

She gripped her gun tighter and almost jumped when her date tapped her shoulder. "So I was wondering if you could tell me a little bit more about the matchmaking stuff you do."

Doors opened to the laser tag area. "Umm, can we discuss this afterward?"

Before she could collect a response, she joined the group as they filtered into the room. She found a hiding place behind some mirrored walls and waited for the beeping to stop. Once it did, the game would commence.

"I mean," her date's voice tickled her ear, "we can talk right here."

The beeping ceased. A figure in black shifted nearby. Em lifted her gun and aimed. Moments later, Harmony's vest lit up with green lights, the color of the enemy team. She'd struck true.

Without a moment to lose, before Harmony's vest would stop vibrating, Em darted to the ramps that led to the upstairs hideouts. Lasers pew-pewed past her. She aimed and struck the two soldiers at the top. They yelped and skittered down the other ramps.

She squatted and peered through bars in the top railings. Her date found her and squatted beside her. "Do you maybe offer a friends and family discount? Maybe you can give it for free if someone pays for your laser tag game?"

Ach, a laser nailed her in the shoulder from somewhere else in the arena. Buzzes ran up and down her spine. She whirled around and stared up at Buzz Cut. "Do you mind? We're on an *actual* date here. You can't just ask me to go find you another one."

When her vest stopped quivering, she aimed her holster at her date's chest. Aimed. Pulled the trigger.

His vest sprung to life. Orange lights winked in and out. "Hey, I'm on *your* team."

"Not anymore. Don't follow me."

Several techno jams and several "kills" later, the lights clicked, and they returned to the suit area. She shed hers and huffed all her way out to the lobby. According to a TV screen perched above the check in desk, she'd scored fifth highest in the round.

"Rough game?" A girl munched on a hot dog slathered in mustard.

Em pinched her nose. "I don't want to overshare." She glimpsed over her shoulder as her ex-date checked himself in for a second game.

"Sister, I live for the tea."

With that permission, Em regaled her with the tale about how her date solely asked her out to get free services for the matchmaking business.

Hot Dog Girl dabbed her lips with a napkin, crumpled the paper, and binned the garbage. "Ooh, I've heard this story before."

Em's fingertips clacked against the tabletop. A mistake, she learned a second later. Some sticky substance lived there now, not to be wiped away until the graveyard shift. "You have?"

"Mhmm, have a friend who did the Mansfield film program. Is making quite the name for herself in Hollywood. She says she has people asking her on dates all the time. Only to find out that they're asking her, 'Oh can you please get me an audition' or 'Can you please convince them to hire me on as a PA'?"

Em wrinkled her nose. "Ugh, that's horrible. Why do people think that they can get away with that?"

Hot Dog Girl wiped her hands onto her pants. "It's all in the mentality." She tapped her temple with two fingers. "If you think everyone is there to do something for you, you're going to act like it."

Saying no more, Hot Dog girl shrugged and headed to the front desk.

Harmony panted nearby and palmed her forehead. Some people decided to sit out the next round and make use of the air hockey and foosball tables in the lobby.

I wonder if Harmony thought I was being a user. Because the two of them danced in different numbers during the lip sync practices, they never had a chance to discuss winter break.

Collecting herself, Em rose and parked nearer to Harmony. "Hey, Harmony. Saw you got second place. That's amazing."

A shrug from Harmony.

"Um, I was wondering if we could talk about winter break. I wanted to apologize for—"

"Noah really likes me."

"What?"

With a dismissive flap of the hand, Harmony gestured at the suit room. Noah had filtered through the doors for round two, it seemed. According to the scoreboard, he'd placed near last in the first one. *Poor guy. Probably is too nice to shoot people.*

"Umm, okay, congratulations? I was trying to say something, before—"

"He was even talking about getting coffee. Since this is the first date, and that's the second, I can imagine there's a loop-walk in the future."

Prickles ran up and down Em's fingertips. She couldn't control who Noah liked. Although in her professional opinion, she wouldn't have matched Harmony with him in a million years.

"All right-y then. Is that all?" Em asked.

Harmony chewed on a nail bed. Sucked on some blood. "I just figured you may want to know that I am in no need of your services anymore. In fact, I'm doing very well on my own, considering *he* asked me on this Dash Date."

Em blinked several times. Stupid tears, making a resurgence now.

Why did this hurt so much? Because it came from Harmony? The very same girl who Em comforted when Eli revealed his true colors.

What about our contract? To always treat each other well, no matter what our relationship status?

Harmony appeared to read her mind and stood. "I've been advised by some people to keep my distance. Because we're in different parts of life, Em. It may be better for you to give me some space, until you get your life together too."

Excuse me?

Her apartment-mate had just told her that they couldn't hold a conversation until Em got on her level. So much for the girl who left senior sem and informed Em about the inequality between engaged Christians and single ones. *You became like them, Harmony.*

Em rose from her seat, leg wobbly. "Harmony, wait."

A hand flew up from Harmony, and she marched over to the check-in desk.

Chapter Twenty-Four

I'm going to find my future husband for Valentine's Day if it kills me.

Em glimpsed the clock on the oven in the kitchen. Yeesh, 5:15 am. How long had she stayed up scrolling? After returning from a lip sync practice that went until midnight—one week out from the show—Em finished the last of her homework assignments and started swiping right on the Christian dating app.

It did strike her as odd that the lip sync battle performances would take place on V-Day itself, but presale tickets had skyrocketed. The show had nearly sold out of all seats within the first few hours. *Maybe it's a good date idea to take someone to a performance like that.*

Thankfully, the last show ended by 8 pm, so that could leave time for a significant other to grab a milkshake after in the TSC.

Burning overtook her stomach. When had she last eaten?

She pushed herself off the futon and roved to the kitchen table. On it, a silver pan with baklava glistened in her phone flashlight's beams. Em had nibbled on some of the corners that night. A little Post-It note, in beautiful handwriting beside it read, "For Em Only."

Maybe Laila would force her to consume more this way. Throughout the past few days, different treats and snacks would make an appearance on the table, all baked goodies.

Prying one of the pieces out of the pan, Em slapped it onto a small plate. Honey dripped from her fingers. She licked the stickiness off and opened the kitchen silverware drawer as gingerly as possible. Every sound in this apartment amplified in the early hours of morning. And she'd promised a now-snoring Laila that she'd head to bed around one in the morning.

Nuts and a sweet cinnamon drizzle crunched between her molars. *Oh man, I have a good roomie.*

She fought the urge to somehow pay Laila back for this and returned to her phone. A man with arm tattoos and a gentle grin materialized on the screen. *Oooh, he looks promising.*

She swiped right, and they matched.

Weariness weighed on her eyelids, and she collapsed onto the couch. Although Em didn't remember falling asleep, minutes later—or so it seemed—dawn bled through the blinds in a pink February sunrise. Prying her eyes open, she checked her phone.

A notification from Tattoo Guy dinged.

Tattoo Guy: Man, you were up early this morning :)

Tattoo Guy: Turning in a last-minute assignment?

She shielded a yawn and stumbled into the kitchen to pop a pod into their Keurig machine. Although the groan from it may wake up her apartment mates, she didn't care. Most of them had 9 am classes anyway, thirty minutes from now.

Toasty coffee with a hint of blueberry flavoring, in hand, she returned to the couch and hit a reply.

Em: Lip sync battle practice, actually. It's crazy how much Mansfield takes the tradition of people dancing and pretending to sing songs. Have you been to one of the shows?

Em: Our teacher's been pretty ridiculous about late-night practices

Em didn't even have a chance to worry about confronting Harmony at those rehearsals—not that she wanted to—because Juliette ran them through numbers until their mouths dried from dehydration and ribs hurt from the lifts and panting. Much as Harmony enjoyed dancing with her partner, she swore he bruised something in her torso every time he hoisted her in the air.

Three gray dots winked on and off. Then Tattoo Guy replied.

Tattoo Guy: Guess that means no late-night dates. Any chance we could go for a lunch in the TSC? If you're not too busy :)

She responded in the affirmative and slapped her head against the small pillow on the futon, drifting off until noon.

Praising the Lord that she didn't have any morning classes, she slipped into a comfortable dress and leggings and set off into the bitter cold, toward the TSC. Knee-high boots hugged her calves all the way as a girl hustled past in a sleeping-bag style coat. Although ridiculous-looking, many students would bundle up from head to toe, as though regular inhabitants of the Alaskan tundra. Wind tunnels whistled through the lack of trees and spread-out buildings. Tears pricked the corners of Em's eyes from the icy gusts by the time she reached the entrance. She yanked on the door and joined the winding line for the food.

Tattoo Guy informed her, via text, that he'd already secured a table. No Chick-fil-A today, it seemed. The queue alone for that would take another twenty minutes.

She shuffled out of line and ambled toward the grab-and-go section. She'd never tried the sushi from Mansfield before, but she picked up a Philadelphia roll that claimed to have been made that morning. At the checkout, she handed the woman her card and then padded toward the staircase.

On the second level, carpet muffled her steps. She glanced back and winced. Wet shoe tracks followed her all the way up the stairs. Salt services at the campus lacked a great deal. During exams of her freshman year, they didn't even bother when a blizzard hit campus. Students slid to the academic buildings, calling Mansfield an "ice rink".

Tattooed arms waved her over to couches, nearest the counseling center. Em waved back, sat, and peeled off the plastic lid to her sushi.

Tattoo Guy wrinkled his nose at it. "You actually trust the raw fish here?"

She shrugged. "Never had it." Rice grazed her tongue.

"I just couldn't after my roommate was puking all night."

Mid-cream cheese bite, she stared at the half-eaten piece and placed it back into the container. Who needed to eat on dates, anyway? Her stomach often contracted during these meetings, and she couldn't get in all that much food, owing to nervousness.

"So." Tattoo Guy speared a tomato on his salad. Feta cheese decorated the romaine lettuce. "How have things been going with the lip sync battle? We auditioned for it last year but didn't make it in."

Although they hadn't polished everything yet, the judges wanted to make sure that no "scandalous dance moves" existed. They'd advised Juliette to take out some of the more "Dirty Dancing" lifts, but their group made it on to the final round.

I wonder which ones they rejected, then if our theme made it in?

"Yeah?" She set the sushi case on the table in front of them.

"Yeah, was surprised, too, because the theme was Super Mario Bros. But I guess Luigi got way into some of the moves, and the judges thought it was 'too inappropriate'."

Em sniggered at the thought of a plumber in green overalls tearing it up on the dance floor. Tattoo Guy laughed along with her. "Yeah, this school can be pretty ridiculous sometimes, can't it?"

"You're telling me. If Luigi was a girl, they would've thrown a conniption. I'm surprised they even were mad a guy did that."

"Luigi *was* a girl."

"Ah, that checks out, hold on—" She peered at her phone. It hadn't stopped buzzing for the past minute or so. Three missed calls from Dad littered the screen.

Dad? He never made contact. Even when her parents spoke with her, Mom would initiate everything.

She winced at Tattoo Guy. "Do you mind? This might be an emergency."

Tattoo Guy's eyes shot to his forehead. "Is everything okay?"

"I hope so." She rose and headed down the hallway. "I won't be long."

Once out of earshot distance, she dialed Dad again and shut herself into one of the dark conference meeting rooms.

"Hello?"

"Dad?"

"Oh, hey, Em." An edge rested in his voice. Did a medical emergency happen? A quick scan of her memories reviewed her schedule. Would Juliette kill her if she missed tonight's practice? "Is now a good time?"

She parked in a chair.

"Is everything okay, Dad?"

"I—no, Em. It's not. There's no easy way to tell you this, and we were going to wait until your lip sync battle had finished. But your mother is posting the news on Facebook today and—"

Her stomach bottomed. She knew the words before he even spoke them.

"Dad," she cut him off, "actually, now's really not a good time. I'm super stressed from schoolwork, and honestly, bombed a test in my apologetics class yesterday, and—"

"Em."

"Plus, I got maybe three hours of sleep last night."

"Em."

"And I'm on a date right now with a guy, so now's not a really good time to..." Something watery overtook her voice. She swallowed it down. "To tell me that you and Mom are getting a divorce. That's why you called me, right?"

Dead silence on the other end. She tapped her fingertips against the table, then dug them into her arms. "You never call to check in. Ask about me. But you decided to call about this, right?" She blinked rapidly. "And you decide to break this silent treatment you and Mom have been giving me by telling me this, right?"

"Em." His voice fractured. "I'm sorry."

She hung up.

Spasms filled her gut from held-back tears. By now, her date had to speculate about the nature of the phone call. She gathered herself, wiping away her tears and checking her reflection in her phone camera. Her face didn't appear too blotchy. *It's all a dream. You can feel more when the date is over. Keep yourself together, girl.*

Sniffing, she bumped back the seat and returned to the couch.

Tattoo Guy slurped through a straw of some drink full of ice. He set the cup down and smiled at her. "Hey, was it something serious—" He paused. Frowned. "Something happened, didn't it?"

Dang it, she didn't hide her expressions well. So much for Noah's encouragements for her to take up acting again.

She banded her arms across her chest and sunk into her original seat. "I—it was something pretty heavy, but I don't want to mention it on a first date, you know?"

A la Laila's talk on emotional boundaries, this man didn't deserve to be dumped on. She fiddled with the ends of her dress.

"No, really, Em. It's okay to tell me."

Her eyes met his deep, brown ones. A shaky breath rattled her rib cage. "Okay, umm." She screwed up her face to block out any potential tears. Embarrassing for a first date to see how blotchy her skin turned when she cried. "There's no easy way to say this, but my parents are planning on getting divorced."

"Oh." Tattoo Guy whistled. "Umm, wow."

"Yeah, they've been having a rough go of things in the last few years. Married young, I think, and had kids too fast, and—"

Tattoo Guy bounced up from the couch, aiming his steps toward the staircase.

"—oh, are you getting a refill, or?"

All of him slumped, as if caught. He spun around and squinched his eyelids in a look that resembled pity. "Em, I don't know how to say this without adding more hurt. But there was something mentioned at a talk that my youth pastor gave a while back, and I think it would be really dangerous if I ignored it."

Knots formed in her intestines. She rubbed her fingers up and down her leggings. "What talk?"

"He said that kids who have parents who are addicts, kids who have parents who are divorced...that 'they're automatic red flags'. His words, not mine."

Air punched out of her lungs. "I—" Her bottom lip quivered. "You know I have no control over what just happened, right? If anything, I tried my best to help them keep the marriage together."

"I'm sure you did." His voice dropped into a soft tone. The kind her father had used with her moments before. "But I need to trust the Spirit on this one."

The Holy Spirit?

Guess what, jerk face, I have a relationship with Him too. Are you trying to say He's punishing me by my parents' divorce?

"Goodbye, Em. I'll be praying for you." He vanished down the staircase.

Hollowness caverned her chest. Glimpsing over her shoulders both ways, she found no one in the area. Good.

She doubled over and cried into her knees. Letting out loud sobs, until hiccups overtook her from her breathing fast. Heartbeats pounded in her temples, and dizziness caused her skull to swim.

Someone tapped her shoulder.

Rubbing the snot away from her nose with a crumbled napkin, she unwound herself. She glanced at the person behind her. Worry lines had deepened on Zuri's forehead. Em smeared her long sleeves over her cheeks to collect the remaining tears. "I'm—I'm, *hic,* sorry, Zuri. I can, *hic,* go someplace else to cry."

Zuri lifted one finger to indicate she'd be right back. Five minutes later, by the time the hiccups disappeared, Zuri returned with a large, steaming chai. "A comfort drink. Now, why don't you tell me what happened?"

For some reason, it was so much harder to get the words out than to think the phrase, "My parents are getting divorced". But somehow the words came out anyway in a beautiful contradiction. Within minutes, Em had spilled out all the information about their marriage, along with the bet, her woes with Harmony, and the terrible dates these past few months.

Her gut squeezed. Oh man, she'd violated so many of Zuri's emotional boundaries.

"Sorry. That was a lot. I shouldn't have told you that much." She sipped on the cinnamon foam in the drink, surprised it had lasted this long with the length of her monologue.

"No, Em. There's nothing to be sorry about. I asked. First of all—" Zuri spread out her arms. "—is it okay if I give you a hug?"

Em nodded and leaned into the embrace. Some of the pain ebbed.

"Okay, second of all," Zuri released, "there's a lot to unpack. Something you may want to explore with the counseling center on the divorce front. When you're ready, of course."

This earned another nod from Em. After the lip sync battle next week, she'd have plenty of time open in her schedule for them to fit her in.

"I don't know if I can address everything since I do have a senior seminar to lead in about fifteen minutes." Zuri put away her phone after checking the time. "But since I do know Noah from our young adults group, let's discuss him. And this spat you have going with Harmony."

"What's there to discuss? Harmony's been acting weird and has been rubbing in the fact that he's into her or something."

Granted, since the fight at the laser tag arena, she hadn't spotted the two of them together. Noah did mention participating in the student-directed play, so maybe his rehearsals couldn't afford him much time for coffee.

"You say *rubbing in*. Is this referring to the fact that Harmony is dating someone and you're not."

"Yes."

"There's an edge to your voice, Em. Is there something more? Maybe something to do with Noah?"

Noah?

Em's eyebrows scrunched together. What did he have to do with... "Are you trying to say that I have...feelings for Noah, and that's why I'm jealous?"

Zuri shrugged. "Worth exploring. I don't think Harmony would've been making such a big deal about the fact if she didn't think you were competition."

Competition?

"We're—we've been friends this whole time. If he wanted to ask me out, I mean, if he was even interested, why didn't he?"

Words stuck in her throat. Did she like Noah? Had she this whole time?

Zuri rose from the couch. "My lips are sealed on these matters, but let's just say, lots of little birdies talk to me." Zuri winked and strode off toward the staircase.

Chapter Twenty-Five

ONLY AT COLLEGE COULD a band of boys in space alien outfits seem normal.

They roamed past and headed to the TSC stage to practice. Lines of students wrapped around the building for the 6 pm performance. Already they'd done the earlier show, the 3 pm, and the cast could grab a brief dinner before the final show.

Tray in hand, Em parked across from Juliette, who frowned at her from behind her salad fork. "Are you eating Chick–fil-A before our final performance? All that grease before you start dancing and running around again?"

Em dipped a fry into Chick-fil-A sauce. "It's the Lord's fries. He'll carry me through." Salt freckled her tongue as she swallowed. Even if her stomach regretted this later, she wouldn't.

"How'd you think that first performance went?" Juliette chewed on a nail bed. "Do you think the crowd loved it?"

Even though Em couldn't spot anyone in the blur of faces in that dark auditorium, the applause sounded modest. No one had been wowed by the theme, but a few chuckles happened during the more relatable numbers. Someone afterward thanked the group for their "nostalgic" music choices.

Truth didn't always work in situations like this, so Em grinned. "I think they really appreciated it, Juliette. Think I even saw some people swaying along to 'Shut Up and Dance with Me'."

This caused her dance instructor's face to light up as she crunched on a crouton. "Think we have a chance of winning?"

Ha. Em shrugged. "Who knows? Although, I will say that *Encanto* group knocked it out the park."

And they did. Whoever played Dolores sashayed that red skirt as if tomorrow didn't exist. The tight choreography, the audience singing along to the "Bruno" song, even Em knew the winner before the judges would announce it at the 6 pm show.

Speaking of, Dog Man—who played Mariano—beelined toward their table.

Dryness clogged her throat. These past few days she had been mulling over her feelings for Noah, and Lord knew she couldn't stand for any more drama. Not after the parental divorce announcement.

"Hey, Em."

"Umm, hi. Good job?"

"Thanks, umm, you too. I just wanted to say..." Dog Man steepled his fingertips. "Sorry for ending things like that. I feel awful about it, and it's been eating me alive ever since."

Juliette, behind her, glared at him. He shrunk underneath her gaze.

"Oh, umm." Em cleared her throat from a fry that had gone wayward in the windpipe. "Thanks."

Dog Man saluted them and bolted back to the Encanto group, parked at a large booth.

"Ugh." Juliette stabbed her salad with a significant force.

Em sipped on her sweet tea. "What's up?"

"Lemme guess, he took you out on a date. Maybe a few? And then did something awful like ghosted you, or dumped and ran, or something like that?"

"Yeah, how did you—"

Juliette held up a hand and swigged from her water bottle. "Let's just say that I've seen it happen before. Guys tend to apologize for one of three reasons. One." She tallied each off of her long, beautiful fingers. "They want to get back together with you and will say whatever it takes to do so. Even will claim that they'll do things differently this time." Two fingers lifted. "They will do it to clear their conscience. They say sorry, cool. They're off scot-free and can go mess up some second girl or three." Her ring finger joined the other two. "They're genuinely sorry. But that's rarer."

Em blew out a low whistle. Although part of her hoped that the actions some of her dates committed would fester into guilt and shame, she knew better than that.

Vengeance is the Lord's. In His time, they would figure out how they'd hurt girls. And over time, would hopefully become better people.

A shadow loomed over Em's shoulder. Clenching her gut in anticipation for a return of Dog Man, she turned around.

Instead of "Mariano's" cheap knock off, Harmony stood with a cookie from the dorm in her hand. "Em, I—" She placed the cookie on a napkin and tossed it onto the table. "I gotta stop baking these for you and actually apologize."

This caused Em to blink several times. *Baking these?*

Oh wait, did she mean the baked goods she'd find every morning? Did Harmony make those instead of Laila? Em probably should've asked, but Laila dipped in and out of the apartment so often, that Em never had the chance to bring it up.

"You made me the treats?"

"Yes, and—" Harmony slumped into the chair beside Em. "It's because I was a big chicken and was afraid to apologize. But sorrys aren't gifts and flowers, they're words. Words that stick with you forever."

True.

How often did Mom try to make up for one of her screaming matches at Em with a care package or Venmo transfer to "grab herself a Crumbl cookie"?

You can't buy apologies.

"I..." Harmony blinked and pinched her nose. "Obviously started hanging out with Jana after winter break. As you can imagine, introvert me can get peopled out after a time—and much as I love you, Em—I was peopled out."

Em could understand. Even back in middle school, she'd spent a summer at camp with one of her best friends at the time. By the end of the month, she wanted to strangle her. They didn't talk much after that August.

Is that what having a husband is like? Wanting to kill him half the time?

Harmony continued. "She, of course, took advantage of the fact that I was annoyed and said things like, 'She's using you', and 'You can find a match so much better for yourself'."

Prickles poked Em's skin. Of course Jana did. Why should she expect anything less by this point?

"I don't know how Jana landed on the idea of Noah, but she tried to tell me that he was super into me. So when he actually asked me on a Dash Date, I thought that was the case." Harmony chewed on her lip. "Turns out, he wanted to ask you, but one of his floormates beat him to it. He understood most theater girls were busy, so he picked the only other person he sort-of knew. Me."

Something about the fact that Noah wanted to ask *her* brightened Em's chest. Yes, they defaulted to making each other go on their floor dates in the past. But Noah had the pick of the litter with others he knew. Most single girls in the theater would've said yes if asked. *Does he...maybe like me?*

"Anyway, I'm a massive hypocrite. Here we made this pact that we wouldn't be condescending to each other, despite relationship status. And I did just that. I became the monster." Harmony fisted her hands and raised them to the sky like Godzilla. "All to say, I'm sorry, Em. I get if you never want to be friends with me again, or if you want to axe me to death and give me a Viking's funeral on the campus lake—"

"Harmony, Harmony." Em squeezed her arm. "Of course I forgive you. And no, I'm not setting your body on fire in a boat."

"Oh, c'mon. It's such an epic way to go."

Harmony brightened at Em's words, and the two of them hugged. When they released, Em poked at her fries, which had turned cold. "Besides, it was on me for being all moody during Christmas break. You guys were kind enough to take me in."

"I think." Harmony nibbled on the napkin-wrapped cookie. "This is really all on Jana. She's been cooking something up. But don't worry. I have a secret project I'm working on. She won't know what hit her."

"Is this secret project legal?"

"Mostly."

Twenty minutes later, Juliette rounded up the group to head backstage. They would head on second after the hit starting number "Bohemian Rhapsody". The group contorted themselves in every way possible to Queen songs.

No wonder they placed us second. A palette cleanser between good numbers.

Taylor Swift's "Love Story" strummed in the background to acoustic guitar. A few sparse whoops sounded from the audience as the cast, in overalls, swayed onto the stage.

The "lovers", played by Juliette and her boyfriend, swung in and out of each other's arms to Rihanna's "Airplanes". Juliette had played them the program dozens of times, to the point where Em had the various songs memorized and stuck in her head at various points of the day. Clips from multiple songs would tell the love story of campus. And Juliette had compiled a track that easily transitioned from one song to the next.

Em's hands swooped up and down to, she guessed, imitate an airplane. Juliette claimed that the lighted gloves they had on their hands would look really cool when the lights went pitch black. The audience confirmed this when they whooped and hollered at the "firefly effect" of the illuminated fingers.

She and the background dancers clicked those off and darted backstage for the next number as the "lovers" kicked it solo for "Just the Way You Are" by Bruno Mars. Harmony and Em zipped each other into their cowgirl dresses and yippie-kay-yayed onto the stage for "Cotton Eye Joe". Beams blinked in and out for the "whoop" "whoop" "whoop" lyrics. Rhythmic claps from the audience thundered in the echoing auditorium.

She had to hand it to Mansfield students, they knew how to hype a group up, even one of the worst dance numbers in the show.

After she hurtled backstage, when "Stuck Like Glue" turned on, she and Harmony laced each other into multi-colored bridesmaid dresses for the final number. Heaven knew why Juliette picked out costumes with corsets, but she said she liked the "look" from the stage.

"Firework" from Katy Perry thrummed through the speakers. Em bounced on the balls of her feet, scuffed the bottoms of her shoes, checking for traction. Then she swung her arms across her body. Kicking her leg back, she nodded at her partner and raced across the stage. Leaped. He held her up, and the audience whooped. One girl, in a shorter bridesmaid dress, was tossed up into the air basket toss style, and a "groomsmen" landed a flip.

For some reason, throws and flips always got the audience giddy.

Juliette, strapped into a *Swan Lake*-style white dress paraded "down the aisle" with her boyfriend to "I Think I Wanna Marry You".

When they reached the end, the boyfriend dropped to one knee and pulled out an actual ring. The music cut off, and an MC handed him a mic. Harmony and Em exchanged wide-eyed glances.

Juliette clasped her hands to her mouth as he spoke. Hollers from the audience broke up most of his words, but Em did catch the, "Will you marry me?"

Tears sparkled in Juliette's eyes. "Yes. Yes!"

After the couple kissed, she swooped her arms around his neck, and they spun around. The audience roared for sixty seconds straight in the blackout. Although the *Encanto* group would probably win, their group had made Mansfield history.

Em's dance group filtered into the now-empty TSC and bounced up and down in a chant. "Ju-li-ette. Ju-li-ette."

Someone found an LED candle from backstage of the chapel that adjoined the student center, from the Queen Group, and passed it around. Everyone sang, "Going to the Chapel of Love". Juliette "blew" out the candle when it reached her by shutting off the battery.

She waved her hands as if to indicate "no, no". "First of all." She set the candle down on a table. "Y'all already know the proposal story because you literally witnessed it. So there's no point in me telling it."

Laughter rippled around the group.

"Second of all, although the ring was a nice surprise." She pulled her now-fiancé in and kissed him. "This is *our* night. We accomplished something together. So this ring sing is for all of us. For the hard work we just did."

Everyone agreed and let out a loud cheer.

When the event finished—and *Encanto* did, in fact, win—the crowd spilled out of the auditorium. Several rushed to the groups to congratulate them on a job well done. A certain man in a trench coat tapped his cane against the floor, angling toward Harmony.

Harmony shared a glance with Em and squeezed her hand.

"I know you don't approve but," Harmony chewed on her bottom lip, "is there any way you can go over with me to talk with Rob?"

Em pressed Harmony's fingers back. "Fine. Let's go, you little player."

This caused the two to giggle as they skipped over to Rob. He tipped his hat at Em and then Harmony. "You, ladies, did an excellent job. Although I was remiss to leave the group early, I am so happy I was in that front row to watch the performance."

Harmony gasped and bounced up and down. "You were in the *front* row? You had to have come early, then to get that seat."

"Indeed." He smiled. "Set up a tent at 3 am, first in line."

Mansfield had this ugly habit of students skipping class, solely to get the best spot at prime basketball games or dance events. Never mind that they broke the school commandments in doing this. It struck Em that Rob the Builder must've done this for Harmony. Despite Harmony rejecting any advances thus far.

Well...Em forcing Harmony to reject any advances...

"Did you have a favorite number?" Harmony twirled a strand of her hair in her fingers. Oh boy, this girl was head over heels. "Besides ours, of course?"

"Hmm." Rob tapped his chin. "I did enjoy all of them. I must say, however, that the *Encanto* number did not deserve that win. If not your group, then certainly the one with all the Queen songs."

Em liked this guy already.

"If this is not too forward," Rob the Builder clutched his cane as he made a slight bow to Em, "I was wondering if you'd like to join me for some milkshakes at that delightful restaurant in the TSC." He nodded at Chick-fil-A, a few yards away. "My treat, of course."

A gasp filled all of Harmony. To the point where she must've forgotten to breathe, because a loud exhale sounded ten seconds after.

"Oh, Em." She pulled Em to the side, out of Rob's earshot. He pretended to be interested in his Daredevil glasses. "Can we? You can supervise to make sure we don't get into too much trouble."

Something buzzed in Em's pocket. Shoot, did she not turn that thing on "Do Not Disturb" during the performance? Fishing out her phone, she read a text from Noah.

Noah: Caught your performance before I had to go to practice :) Leave it to my director to schedule something on both Lip-Sync day and Valentine's Day

Noah: You did amazing! So excited to continue to support whatever you do :)

Fire set her chest alight. If Harmony felt the same way that she did about Noah right now...

Harmony stared at her wide-eyed again in her attempt at a "pleading" look. Em shoved her away and laughed. "To be honest, Harmony, I probably should head to the auditorium. Have something I need to take care of." She nodded at Rob, then back at Harmony. "Go get 'em, girl."

Chapter Twenty-Six

WHAT'S ESSENTIAL WHEN CONFESSING your love to your best friend? A chocolate Oreo shake. Yes, a combination of the two flavors in one.

Em waited until Rob and Harmony had placed their orders, so she could give them some space, then asked the worker if she could combine the chocolate and sandwich cookie flavors. A blender whirred, and Em glanced over her shoulder. Harmony leaned in at her high-top table with Rob talking with his hands. Literally. He'd formed his hands into Pac-man puppets and spoke to Harmony with them.

They're perfect together, aren't they? Although Em wouldn't have matched the two, she couldn't argue against divine providence or plan.

Once she retrieved her beverage from the worker, she poked a straw through the lid and set off toward the auditorium. Heat patched all over her body to the point where she had to shed her winter coat outside. She tossed it on a bench in the lobby of the theater and thumped up the carpeted steps. Shaky fingertips gripped the handrailing on the way up.

Should I do this?

Em halted, midway up.

What if he doesn't feel the same way?

How often did she hear stories of people reading into friendships the wrong way? That the flirtatious tone a person took was just the normal timbre of their voice?

She puffed out a breath. Only one way to find out.

When she reached the top of the stairs, a woman in a black T-shirt shoved her way out of the double doors that led into the theater itself. She halted when she spotted Em. "Emerson?" She squinted through her glasses. "Is that you?"

Shoot, what name belonged to this woman?

Em settled on Stage Manager. Vague memories of this woman on a headset backstage existed in the back of Em's mind. "Hey...you. Yeah, sorry, I've been absent from the theater a lot this year. Been so busy."

"You're the one who helped out with sets and costumes for so many years, so it's no worries if you need to take a break from time to time. Not a theater major or minor, right?"

A dim light buzzed overhead. How much did the school invest into this theater? Pennies?

"Nope. Marketing and PR."

Stage Manager's eyes widened.

"What?" Em cocked her head.

"Oh nothing. I—had an idea. But I don't want to ask free work out of you."

By now, Em's intestines had tied themselves into Gordian knots. Maybe postponing confessing her love to Noah wasn't the worst idea in the world. "I wouldn't mind, actually. What do you need?"

"Follow me to the computer lab?"

Both the journalism and music departments conjoined spaces in this long sprawl of edifice. They stepped into a dark classroom, and Stage Manager flicked on the lights. Large Mac computers filled every available desk space.

This must be where the newspaper people put together the Mirror.

Stage Manager slid into a rolling chair and booted up the computer. Once she put in her password, she dug up Canva. An atrocious, bright yellow poster stung Em's eyes. Once she squinted through the pain, she read the blocky orange letters.

Student-Directed Plays

What: *Come see your fellow students direct plays, such as "The Boys Next Door," "Antigone", "The Glass Menagerie", "A Dream Play", and "A Woman in Mind"*

When: *March 21, 22, 23, 24, 25 at 7 pm. Each night will have a different play.*

How Much: *$5 per play, or $20 to see all of them*

"Ticket sales have been way down this year. I know it's February, but we started sending emails in January. We were going to post these around the music hall, but we have limited budgets we're operating under. So it has to be just perfect."

Em thumbed her chin. "Well, for starters, let's work on your color palette."

Minutes on the analog clock ticked by as Em pulled up InDesign and created a play poster, complete with silhouettes and easy-to-read fonts.

"You sure you're not a graphic design major?"

She lifted and dropped her shoulders. "We take a few classes on that. This is nothing compared to what those students could do, but this should work. The second thing—the *marketing* thing—is that you don't really have much of an appeal for people to come to these performances."

Stage Manager rubbed her thumbs on the space bar key. By now, her computer had gone dead from lack of use. "I mean, we told them to come support their fellow peers. What more motivation is there?"

"Trust me, you learn a lot about people in marketing classes."

"What do you learn about them?"

"People often suck."

Some of the film students lamented that they had a hard time selling tickets for the film festivals that took place on campus. Even when they cast fellow students, including them in their mini-movies and shorts, it was never enough to draw a crowd.

Stage Manager fiddled with a pen that had apparently been in her pants pockets. "See, at other schools, they make it a requirement for class to attend theater stuff. We don't do that here."

"True, but"—an idea struck—"what if you collaborate with the English teachers?"

"Collaborate?"

"Sure." Em scooted her chair back, shot up from it, and moved to the front of the classroom to pace. A Journalism Ethics poster bullet-pointed behind her, the "Art of an Interview" lecture. "What if you could convince teachers to give extra credit for students attending a play? To the point where they could bump up one number in a grade."

Stage Manager considered the idea. Her chair swiveled back and forth in semi-circles. "You know, that could be a big incentive." She tapped the pen against her cheek. "I know so many people who get 89.5 in their classes, so close to that 90. That could be a huge push to sell tickets. But—" The pen aimed at Em. "What's the incentive for English professors? Why would they let their students do this?"

Good question.

Electricity hummed in and out of the fluorescent lights in the building. Dead flies clumped in the glass in the corners. When had they last cleaned those out? *I swear that everything in the creative departments is twenty years out-of-date...wait a minute.* "What if you give a portion of ticket sales to the English department? I'm sure their budget could use a boost."

"Hmm, but we're already operating on next-to-nothing."

"Right, but more people being required to go means more performances, which means—"

"More ticket sales. Oh my gosh, you're a genius."

After they proofread the poster a zillion times to check for typos and missed commas, they sent fifty documents to the printer. Warm papers toasted Em's fingertips when she retrieved them from the output tray. Together with the Stage Manager, she pinned the fliers to the cork boards in the music department hallway. Somewhere in the distance, a soprano sang a selection from an operetta in a practice room.

Creativity never sleeps.

Other pages, advertising senior performances and handbell concerts, crowded their play posters. Em wondered how many of these events would receive more audience members with some font work and a social media push.

I wonder if the school would ever hire someone to market these types of programs.

In her periphery, a figure in a hoodie approached. She turned, and her heart choked her throat.

"Em?" Noah eyed the posters and then her. "What are you doing here? I thought you'd head back to the apartments after the lip sync thing."

"I—umm."

Stage Manager scooped the rest of the papers into her arms and carried them away, saying something about letting the two of them catch up.

Em cupped her elbows and fought every urge to tear down the hall-way, screaming like a banshee. "Hey, Noah. Long time no see."

"No kidding, between my play and your dance stuff. Practice just let out, pretty late too." He threw a thumb over his shoulder. "I'd normally suggest we catch up over milkshakes, but I think the TSC is closed by now."

The restaurants would be, at least. Em would have considered offering some of her milkshake to him, but she had a more pressing thing to do in this moment.

Silence cloaked them for a few moments. The soprano moved onto "Queen of the Night". The *ooo-ooo-ooo-ooo-AHH-AHH-AHH-AHHs* formed an awkward tension headache in the back of Em's skull.

"Soooo." Noah drew out the word. "I may get back to the dorm to—"

Now or never, girl.

"Noah, I have something to say."

She winced as he stumbled backwards, as if her words had tripped his soles. He cleared his throat. "Oh, umm, sure."

Em shut her eyes. She didn't want to know what he looked like when she said this. "I—erm. It's okay if this isn't how you feel at all. And I hope this doesn't make things weird between us, but I—"

"You like me too?"

Too? Her eyelids flew open. Shakiness overtook her knees, and her abdomen quivered. Why did the movies never portray it like this? The loudness of her heartbeat against the silence? How if a wind blew over her, she might knock into the linoleum floor. "You—" Her mouth dried. "Umm, what?"

"Follow me." He beelined down the hallway. Flickering lights followed his wake.

Dazed, her mind kicked into gear moments later and commanded her legs to move. She raced past a newspaper stand and back toward the media side of the building. By now, Noah had ducked into the computer lab and flicked on the lights again.

Right, Stage Manager must've turned those off at one point.

Em stepped into the room, and a computer whirred to life. Fans blew on the inside to keep it cool, probably from overuse throughout the day. "What are you—"

Noah held up a hand. "In theater, we believe in showing, not telling."

Moments later, he pulled up the browser and landed on a GoFundMe page. He motioned Em over, and she read while he scrolled, slowly.

Donate to My Friend's Student Debt Fund

$9,012 raised of $30,000 goal

Hi, everyone! I'm a theater student at Mansfield and just about to graduate. I have this amazing friend who took on some student debt and a not-so-amazing bet.

Before we get into what the bet is, there's something you should know about her. She loves helping people. She's not a theater major or minor but is in our theater all hours helping with sets and props and about everything. She'd give you the shirt off her back if immodesty wasn't against our student handbook.

Now, onto the bet. My friend's very good at matching people on dates. And let's just say, there was someone on campus who didn't like what she was doing. She made my friend take on a bet that she'd have to find herself a husband by the end of senior year, or she'd have to pay $30,000—long story.

My friend is beautiful, drop-dead gorgeous some might say. Still, she's a senior in college. I'd hate for her to have to rush some relationship and marriage for the sake of getting out of student debt. College tuition is already ridiculous without having to worry about finding the right guy. Donate to this fund so my friend doesn't have to end up in an arranged marriage.

Em's heart warmed in her chest so much that she could've toasted s'mores. *He thinks I'm drop-dead gorgeous.*

Noah leaned back in his chair. "I was hoping to get more people to donate before I showed you this, but I guess now's as good a time as any."

"Noah." She gasped. "How did you get that many donations?"

"Some people in the marketing department helped with me get the word out, but let's just say, you've helped a lot of people over the years Em. So we got a lot of shares—and I guess a lot of sympathetic parents on Facebook."

Ugh, of course it happened on Facebook. She rarely checked that. Nine thousand dollars couldn't cover her debt if she owed her clients by May. But at least it could put her in less debt than before.

Tears stung her eyes. So many emotions had run through her in the last twenty-four hours that it felt like all of them surged at once.

"Oh, Em." Noah rose from his chair and wrapped her in a warm hug. They hung there forever, and he kissed her forehead. The warm imprint of it burned.

"I'm just..." She wiped away the moisture along her lower lash line and parked in a chair. Her legs wouldn't hold her up much longer. "So confused. You said the word 'friend' around me so many times that I was convinced you never wanted to date anyone in college."

He palmed his neck. "I mean, I didn't. Until you stole my heart, of course." A sigh dropped him further into his chair, when he returned to it.

Stole his heart?

Tingles ran up and down her spine. Why didn't she notice the signs before? He'd purposely skipped practice to go to Dash Dates and Open Houses with her, swung by her apartment to check in after the Winter Break depression. No busy theater guy would go out of the way to do all those things. Let alone create a fund for her to get her out of the bet with Jana.

"You have to understand that a lot of girls in the theater department were friends with me. The moment they admitted feelings and I didn't feel the same way, it got awkward. They stopped talking to me, and when I developed strong feelings for you—" He cut off. Not that he needed to finish.

Friendships tended to shatter at Mansfield the moment someone admitted a crush. Except for the one date at the Chinese restaurant with the kind guy, Em planned to speak to none of her previous dates.

"Okay, so—" Em picked at dirt under her nails. Not the most romantic for a time like this. Where was a forced manicure from her mom when she needed one? "Now that we've established that said parties in this room may or may not have strong feelings for one another, what happens now?"

A finger hooked under her chin and lifted her face up to him. Oh, she could get lost in those eyes forever. "Well, we might want to try this for a start."

He pulled her in, and they kissed.

Chapter Twenty-Seven

"Noah? Are you trying to propose to me using a Ring-pop?"

"In my defense." Knee-down in the grass by the lake, he raised a finger in the air. "The theater costume shop workers wouldn't let me use one of the prop rings. I'm saving up for a real one."

A late-March breeze rippled the water. Thank goodness, Noah hadn't asked for a cameraman to hide out nearby. He'd picked a day where no one else hung out by the waters. Secluded and alone.

"Babe." Em tapped his arm, as though instructing him to lower it, and sat on the grass beside him. Sand from the volleyball pit entangled with her fingers. Some player must've kicked the grains out to here. "Is this about the bet?"

"I meeean." He placed the ring on the grass and tore his fingers through his curly hair. "It would be nice to have a $30,000 bonus right now. And besides, we have about a month until finals."

Then graduation.

Em drank in the scents of spring and grinned as ducks who swam circlets in the waters. Unusual for March, the temperature had toasted to a nice sixty-something degrees.

"Babe."

"Yes, Em?"

"Listen, I'd love for you to propose to me sometime down the road. But"—she sucked on her teeth—"not now. It's been a month."

Although not unusual for the timeline at Mansfield, especially because Noah and Em had known each other for years, this would cause some eyebrows to lift. Underclassmen would whisper as they passed by that the two of them were clearly eager to "get it on" during their wedding night.

"You sure, love?"

Em nodded and laced her fingers into his. "Marriage sounds wonderful, but maybe a year or two down the road. Once we've been able to have a taste of the real world for a while."

Several of her classmates—including them—had applied for jobs. Noah had landed one at a regional theater in the area. There, he'd serve as a technical assistant for their shows. And maybe after a while, manage to secure a few parts in auditions. "It's a big, big world outside of Mansfield," he'd informed her. "We start at square one again. It doesn't matter if you've landed leads in every production in college. No one cares."

As for Em, several departments had banded together and begged the university to create a role for her that could help them boost ticket sales for events. Thanks to Em's help, the seats had overflowed for the student-directed plays, with the collaboration with the English department. After speaking with someone in HR in an informational interview, Em had a few emails in her inbox about what that role would look like.

Surprised Mansfield went for it.

Could've been because Harmony's article on the Average Student Debt perked some ears. Although Harmony ran the "$28,000" number in the article, some anonymous source leaked that it was really $30,000. It wasn't the number that was the big deal. It was more the fact that the school had tried to cover it up.

Parents demanded that the bursar's office release a spending report, because they'd lied in the interview with Harmony. When the school relented and posted the reports, several students dropped out for the next semester. With numbers down, they'd need a PR miracle. Enter Em.

It's not ideal, doing marketing for a sketchy school. But the small departments, and the professors who really care—those are the people I'm going to bat for.

When Harmony heard that Em and Noah would stick around in the area, she asked if Em needed a roommate in her apartment. They'd split the rent until either Em or Harmony married off to their new boyfriends. Perhaps at the same time.

Speaking of Harmony, she charged up the sidewalk in a chicken onesie and raced down the hill toward the lake. She reached the couple and doubled over, gripping her knees while she panted.

Em laughed. "I, umm, rain checked the proposal if that's why you were running here, Harmony."

Harmony shook her head. Moments later, she regained oxygen. "I figured you'd tell Noah the idea is stupid." She shook her finger at Noah. "Besides, I have news about Jana."

"Jana?" Em sat up straighter in the grass.

"I have news about the project I was doing on her."

Ah yes, the potentially illegal project.

Harmony shoved her hands into the pockets of the chicken. "I had an inkling, dear Watson, that Jana was purposely sabotaging your bet. And that all her little "birdies" were really her telling guys to act like jerks on dates. So you'd burn out and cry 'uncle'."

"What's with this Watson business, Harmony? Are you a chicken or Sherlock? Pick a line."

"Wow." Harmony triangled her hands on her hips. "That's very species-ist of you to assume a chicken cannot be a detective, Em."

Noah giggled. "I'm not even going to ask."

"Anyway, after some perhaps illegal, perhaps legal snooping—you can't prove anything—I procured enough evidence to assert the veracity of my hypothesis."

This earned a head tilt from Noah. "What?"

Em leaned into his shoulder. "She's saying that Jana purposely sabotaged the bet."

"Got it."

In an avian fashion, Harmony waddled back and forth when she paced. "When I confronted Jana with the evidence, she called off the bet. Even," Harmony dug into the pockets and pulled out a check, "gave a portion of the money she owed on the bet to your honeymoon fund."

Em unfolded the check. Sure enough "Honeymoon Fund" was scrawled in the "what for" section.

As for the amount... Her jaw sank.

Noah whistled. "Five thousand dollars. That's a modest Europe or Caribbean trip."

On a budget, but yes.

"Man, I'd never have thought that Jana would buckle." Em drew her knees to her chest. "It's scary to think what she'll be like when she leaves college. How she'll treat single people. Acting like they haven't gone through enough hardship or earned it enough."

"I mean." Harmony parked nearby the couple and tied grass strands into bows. "There are a lot of Janas out there, but there are a lot of people like us, too. It'll take some time, but we can slowly make the world a more tolerable place."

Em leaned in closer to Noah and basked in the warmth of his chest. Working together was a comforting thought, indeed.

Discussion Guide

FORBOOK CLUBS OR PERSONAL reflection. Warning, spoilers ahead, so each of thequestions will be divvied up by chapter to avoid revealing too much.

CHAPTER ONE

1. Em is asked to spy on the dates of girls for their safety. In your opinion, has dating, evenChristian dating, become dangerous for women?

2. Some of Em's former male clients explained that women had unrealistic expectations to the point where they'd even reject a guy if he didn't wear glasses. Why do some people have unrealistic expectations in the world of dating? How can we remedy this inour own dating relationships?

CHAPTER TWO

1. Jana is a character who has a chip on her shoulder. She had to fight for her relationship, and she thinks everyone should go through exactly what she went through. Why do some people gatekeep dating? Is this a dangerous idea?

2. Although Jana goes about it the wrong way, she does have a point that it seems like Em is taking advantage of single people and desperation. Do you think that companies or individuals take advantage of vulnerable groups? Why or why not?

CHAPTER THREE

1. Em discovers that she has minimal flirting skills—due to a lack of practice and because she grew up in a sheltered environment. Why do you think the pressures are so heavy onChristians to know how to date intuitively if they're never taught? What are some ways we can remedy this?

2. Harmony is a lot forEm to take in at first, but she sees the potential in her and her dating prospects. Why do you think people are quick to reject those who are a little odd or different?

CHAPTER FOUR

1. Em helps a shy couple come together and form a perfect match. Is it necessary for friends to help orchestrate some relationships (not all) for people who have cold feet or fear of rejection?

2. Noah tells Em that she can "help a lot of things". I.e., she has gifts and talents but is using them for the wrong purposes. What are the dangers of using a good gift for harm or for the wrong reasons?

CHAPTER FIVE

1. Em goes out with a very old-fashioned man. He mentions how dating relationships are pointless if the couple never has children when they get married. Is this a fair statement?Why or why not?

2. Em experiences a brief physical assault altercation with this man. Thankfully, she finds a way to part ways and never interact with him again, but why do you think these types of actions can be common in Christian dating? How can we prevent this from happening?

CHAPTER SIX

1. Em mentions financial safety as her main reason to pursue the bet. Why do you think some people date for financial security? Is this a good idea? Why or why not?

2. The engaged voice wins out over the unengaged teacher in this chapter. In your experience, have you seen a hierarchy in Christian circles based on relationship status? How canwe push back against the idea of "all Christians are equal, but some are more equal than others"?

CHAPTER SEVEN

1. Em stereotypes all people who are like Rob the Builder and instantly decides that he's not a good fit for her friend. What are ways that we can stop ourselves from making quick judgments about the appearance of others?

2. Harmony states that she wants to feel comfortable and to be herself around whoever she dates. Why is it so important to be our true selves in relationships?

CHAPTER EIGHT

1. Em experiences some cattiness at the singles event when she interacts with one of the few men there. Why do Christian females often see each other as competition? How can we better uplift one another instead?

2. At the singles event, Em—and the other females are told to settle. What's the difference between "non-negotiables" and unrealistic expectations?

CHAPTER NINE

1. Physical attraction, to some level, is important in a relationship. Why do you think some Christians have toned down the need for this? Should it be prioritized more?

2. Zuri says that several men have rejected her based on her inability to produce biological children. Why do you think women might be rejected based on their ability to reproduce? What do you think about this sort of rejection?

CHAPTER TEN

1. Eli tried to morph himself to be anything that Em wanted him to be. And when she rejected him, he turned on her. Should we need to give up ourselves to be whatever our significant other wants?

2. Harmony claims that the breakup broke her. Why do you think people experience so much burnout in relationships?

CHAPTER ELEVEN

1. On one of Em's dates, she loves the character of the guy but isn't attracted to him, no matter how hard she tries. They end up friends in the end. Why is it important to see friendship as a viable option if a match doesn't work out? Why do you think people refer to it as the "friend zone" and a worst-case scenario?

2. We learn that Jeff, a master's student, has a fear of commitment because so many women want him to be the main breadwinner. Is it fair to put pressure on one person to make all the money in a relationship? Why or why not? Is it okay for one person to be the breadwinner?

CHAPTER TWELVE

1. Why are truth tellers important?

2. Why do you think Noah is so against Em setting up people, even for free? Are there times when it's okay to set someone up on a date? When is it overstepping?

CHAPTER THIRTEEN

1. Em finds herself in a no-win situation where she's in trouble if she cancels a date but is also in trouble if she doesn't cancel a date. Have you seen examples of double standards in Christian dating?

2. What are some potential pitfalls of illustrations like the gum one in chapter thirteen?

CHAPTER FOURTEEN

1. Harmony is worried Em will drop their friendship because they're in different places in life. Do you think this happens sometimes when Christians start dating or get married?

2. Em's boyfriend seems pretty codependent. Although time and touch are gifts, he seems to be demanding it all the time from her and not reciprocating in her love language. Do you think codependent relationships have become more commonplace? Why or why not?

CHAPTER FIFTEEN

1. Em sees that so manyChristians are expected to get married early on. Although there's nothing wrong with marrying young, why do you think this has become the norm or expectation for couples?

2. Em has a hard time making boundaries with her boyfriend and decides to sign up for an activity instead to enforce them without having a boundaries talk. Is it difficult for you to have a boundaries talk? Why or why not? Why might it be important?

CHAPTER SIXTEEN

1. Our main character is shocked by the divorce rate at her school. She soon learns that the divorce rate among Christians isn't all that different from the trend. Why do you think divorce happens frequently in Christian circles? Can things be done to prevent it?

2. Tara mentions that the school exists in a bubble, and that once couples encounter real life, some of them fall apart. What are some ways that Christian dating can be like abubble? How can people better prepare real life beyond dating?

CHAPTER SEVENTEEN

1. Em is saddened by the fact that most people advise her not to have male friends when she gets married. Are there possible downsides to limiting who we can be friends with?Is there value in limiting opposite sex friendships after marriage? Why or why not?

2. Although Em doesn't look forward to her conversations with Frankie, she tries to change her mind when her parents absolutely love him. How can opinions affect how people perceive their relationships?

CHAPTER EIGHTEEN

1. Yasmin is clearly trying to convince Frankie that Em is no good for him. How should exes be treated when it comes to relationships?

2. Harmony has a hard time telling Em the truth. When she does, Em releases her anger on her. Would you want to be told if a close friend saw red flags in your relationship? Why or why not?

CHAPTER NINETEEN

1. Em's parents want her to get married to anyone, to the point where they'll purposely overlook faults. Why should we want the best for our single friends when it comes to relationships—even if that means waiting more?

2. Her parents often triangulated, using Em as the only reason why they kept their marriage together, but controlling Em's actions in the process. Why is how we communicate with our children so important in marriage? How can we avoid the mistakes that Em's parents make?

CHAPTER TWENTY

1. Em has a hard time bouncing back and throwing herself into relationships, after heartbreak. Are there pros or cons in trying to force someone to date when they're healing?

2. Em is scared to tellHarmony how she's feeling because she's worried she'll annoy her friend. Why is it important that we know that people heal at different paces?

CHAPTER TWENTY-ONE

1. Loneliness is often the reason people dive into relationships before they're ready. How can we recognize the signs of loneliness, and better take care of each other?

2. Some romantic relationships can become transactional. "I did this, so you owe me this." Why do you think this happens? Is this a healthy function of relationships? Why or why not?

CHAPTER TWENTY-TWO

1. Sometimes marriedChristians will say single Christians have to stop complaining about being oppressed and do something about it. Is this a helpful attitude? Why or why not?

2. Em meets with a guy who overshares, and she feels obligated to keep the conversation going. What does a healthy amount of sharing look like in Christian dating?

CHAPTER TWENTY-THREE

1. Laila introduces Em to several types of boundaries. Although this chapter hones emotional boundaries, why is it important for every Christian relationship to know all the types of boundaries?

2. Harmony now sees herself as better than Em, because of relationship status. How can friendships be destroyed by the idea that a relationship puts you on a different level than a single friend?

CHAPTER TWENTY-FOUR

1. Valentine's Day can be tough for singles, to the point where they'll try to get with any date they can, not to be alone on that day. How can we make this holiday more inclusive?

2. Tattoo Guy refuses to date Em because her parents divorced. Why might people reject potential girlfriends or boyfriends on things that are outside of their control?

CHAPTER TWENTY-FIVE

1. We learn about apologies in this chapter—real ones and fake ones. What constitutes a real apology? What is important to you in an apology?

2. Em sees that Rob theBuilder is a genuinely nice guy, despite the stereotypes associated with people like him. Why is character important in relationships?

CHAPTER TWENTY-SIX

1. Em starts to discover her talents can be better used for good. What differentiates a good use of a talent from a bad one?

2. Why do so many friendships shut down the minute someone admits they like the other? How can friendships be better prioritized even after a rejection?

CHAPTER TWENTY-SEVEN

1. Now that you've finished the book, what was the biggest takeaway that stuck out to you?

2. Which character's story do you relate to the most? And why?

Emma and its Inspiration

MANY OF MY BOOKS and plays have been modern versions of some beloved stories. Some of these include *The Phantom of the Opera*, The Book of Daniel, The Book of Esther, The Book of Ruth, and The Book of Nehemiah. When given the opportunity to write a modern-day version of *Emma*, I jumped at the chance.

My first introduction to the book came from *Clueless*, one of my dad's favorite movies. I admired the lead actress and thought they did an excellent job touching on *Emma*'s themes, whilst creating a story with its own legs.

When I finally read *Emma*, it had me howling. Austen has such a way with her wit, and I love the political and social commentary she imbues in the pages.

For those unfamiliar with *Emma*, it falls under the genre of "comedy of manners." In other words, "This book is going to make fun of dating mores of the time."

I took that concept and ran with it. My dating experiences mostly happened in the Christian world, and although some examples in the book may seem a little out-there, they really aren't all that far away from what I've gone through and what I've heard from others. Names, details, and some other things got switched around. But sadly, most of the ideas we are presented with remained the same.

Emma herself in the book is not the most likeable character. Sorry, Austen. So I did want to find ways to make her a little more sympathetic.

Some people may also get annoyed at Noah for constantly trying to argue with Em. Something to be noted is that the relationship between love interests in Emma is very similar. Perhaps, in that story, he sees the best in her and wishes that she could aim for her potential.

As for the inspirations, this is probably one of the "loosely based" types of renditions. We do see many of the same characters—pulling the same stunts—but I figured a Christian college setting would take on a world of its own. Enough to pull the story somewhat out of its source material.

I know some of the satirical nature of this book may not be to everyone's taste, and that's okay. I hope that some of it made you laugh, just as Austen's book would've earned some definitive chuckles from her audience at the time.

The topic of dating, relationships, and marriage is quite a loaded one. Probably because it is so personal to all of us. Rejection stings. Cheating can break us. And we often find our worth tied in who shows us affection.

Know that I did try to nod to the original source material whilst trying to cover a breadth of the experiences I've seen in this world. And thank you for reading this and bearing with me as I passionately pen this.

A Note from the Author

I COULD FILL AN entire book with just my own dating experiences. And although we got a sampling in this story, you didn't get everything. This is not the place to air out dirty laundry or call out certain men...although some may deserve a shout out in here. Instead, I hope that this book can shed light on just how rough Christian singles have it.

When still single, I made a vow to advocate for any singles in the Christian world. That meant dating singles, single singles, and singles who planned to stay single for the rest of their lives. It blew me away that Paul, and *literally* Jesus advocated for staying single. And yet, the pressures for singles to get with someone, anyone, "were abusive", as one person who shared their story confided.

In the process of writing this book, I asked for other people to share their stories. Although I won't include those here—as I promised anonymity—the information they provided didn't shock me. I'd undergone most of what they talked about.

Still, it saddened me. It saddened me that people lost friends because friends thought they'd somehow achieved a higher status by getting married. It saddened me that people shunned people who dated men or women outside of their denomination. It saddened me that people didn't see obvious red flags in guys or girls simply because they wanted a couple to stay together because, "Two are better than one."

Singles, I see you. I will advocate for you. This is the book I needed when I was single.

For those who have found someone, please don't be like most of the people in this book. It is sadly so widespread how much these experiences range. And if you think I used any hyperbole in this...I held way back from the stories: experienced and heard.

Let's do better. And let's do differently than we have before.

Acknowledgements

To my Lord and Savior Jesus Christ. You brought my man to me at just the right moment. And made it clear to me that although relationships do take work, there is nothing I could've done on my own to orchestrate that happening. Thank You for reminding me that every relationship is a miracle that comes through You.

To Trey. By my calculations, we will have been married by the time this releases—maybe even a year into the marriage. Thank you for sharing my passion with this subject.

To my family who is ever supportive of my books. I know you had to suffer through quite a bit of my rants about how singles are treated. Hopefully, I can funnel most of that into this book so I can spare you.

To my wonderful friends. I think of Alyssa, Nikki, Carlee, Ellen, Jess, Tyler, David, James, Sonya, and so many others. We're in this fight together, y'all.

To my amazing publisher AJ, and the incredible team at Q&F. And for the poor editors who have to go through this. Sorry for the fragments, y'all. AJ, you were in love with this idea from the beginning. Thank you for giving it a home and for championing this important topic.

To my agent Tessa, and the lovely folks at CYLE.

To the people who sent me their stories about their Christian dating woes. Thank you for sharing, I know it must've taken a lot of courage and strength to do so. I hope I did your stories justice in the themes I explored.

To the fifty-some men who went on dates with me prior to when I met Trey. Thank you to some of you for being kind and sweet. I pray for you and for the women you have found or will find. And to the...others. Umm, thanks for giving me inspiration for several of these chapters.

To the launch team members, cover revealers, reviewers—thank you for giving a voice to this book. I could not have done it without you.

And to the readers. Especially the ones who are "going through it" when it comes to Christian dating and singleness. I hear you, and I will fight for you.